INITIATION IN PARADISE

PARADISE SERIES

BOOK 17

DEBORAH BROWN

INITIATION IN PARADISE
All Rights Reserved
Copyright © 2019 Deborah Brown

ISBN-13: 978-0-9984404-8-4

Cover: Natasha Brown

PRINTED IN THE UNITED STATES OF AMERICA

INITIATION IN PARADISE

Chapter One

Honk! The infuriating woman laid on the horn.

I slid into a pair of flip-flops and hustled out of the house, my annoyance cooling when I laid eyes on my friend's hand, wrapped in something white, resting on the steering wheel.

Fab had called only minutes ago.

"I have an emergency. Will you come with me? I'm sitting out front."

"Are you okay?" I grabbed my bag.

"Just hurry."

"I'll drive," I yelled.

Fab shook her head and motioned me over to the passenger side of the Hummer, which I owned but seldom got to drive.

I hopped in and asked, "What happened?" as Fab sped out of the compound, my new nickname for the street we lived on. After purchasing the block as a wedding gift for his only daughter, Fab's father had had twelve-foot-high fencing installed and added a security gate at the entrance.

"Well…" she started, then paused, tapping her finger on the steering wheel as she waited for the gate to open, and sped out.

Fab's hesitance to answer had me squinting at her and wondering what she was up to. "You missed the turn to the hospital."

"I lied." Fab whipped the pillowcase off.

I stared, first at her, then her uninjured hand, then back at her.

Fab hit the gas as though I'd jump out, hightailed it to the main highway, and turned north.

I turned to the passenger window, oblivious to the scenery passing outside the vehicle, and silently counted, one… two… and snapped my head around. "What the heck are you up to?" I didn't want to know, but since I was trapped in my car, with her in control of our destination, I'd better suck it up and find out. In the back of my mind, I contemplated jumping out at the next signal.

"Really, Madison." Fab rubbed her ear. "It's your fault that I had to resort to such sneakiness to get you out of the house. You need to snap out of your honeymoon hangover. Our husbands are up to something, and we're going to find out what it is."

My husband. I smiled. Creole, aka Luc Baptiste, had kept his undercover name after retiring early from the police force. Getting caught in a shootout and the months of rehab that followed had been the major factor in his decision. However, not being a cop anymore had no effect on his observational skills. At some point, he was going to pick up the tail in his rearview mirror and notice that his wife's car was following him. Although Fab was doing a good job of hanging back, shielding herself by using other cars for cover.

I leaned my head back against the seat. "Whatever you're up to is going to get us in so much trouble."

"Us?" Fab sniffed. "What about them? If Didier had just been upfront, instead of being so evasive, we'd be headed to the office instead." She squealed the tires as soon as the signal turned green.

Didier—also one-named since his days as a highly sought-after model—had since retired and was now on his way to becoming a real estate mogul.

No, I wanted to tell her, I'd be checking on my other business interests. I'd stayed in touch via email since I got back from my honeymoon, but it wasn't the same as visiting in person. It was harder for my employees to cover up their shiftiness when I was standing in front of them.

"I didn't notice any difference in Creole this morning," I said. "Has it occurred to you that your husband could be chasing a real estate deal? Since the two of them are partners, it makes sense for them to check it out together."

We bypassed the cutoff to Highway One, which meant we weren't headed to Homestead or Miami, and veered off on a two-lane highway that boasted mangrove forests on both sides of the road. The shallow waters attracted large flocks of migratory birds and the occasional alligator, if the sign with the snapping jaws was any indication.

"Why can't they be upfront?" Fab countered.

Creole's truck had hit all the lights green and was now so far up the road that the bumper was a faint dot. Reading my mind, Fab kicked the Hummer into high gear and sped after them to close the distance.

"I don't know. And guess what? I'm willing to wait until they get home to ask. I suggest that we turn around," I said, knowing full well that my voice of reason would go unheeded.

There was nothing out on this road except wildlife; a handful of manses hidden by trees, their rooflines barely visible; people living off the grid; and one restaurant. I'd read where most of the off-gridders had been run off by law enforcement due to pesky ownership issues but had just moved back once the headlines from the sweeps died down.

"Damn." Fab pounded her fist on the steering wheel.

She'd lost them shortly after they made a right somewhere in the distance but would never admit it, expecting to find a driveway that never materialized. I predicted that they'd turn up behind us, flagging us down for an explanation.

I'd be leaving that bit of unpleasantness to Fab.

Fab slowed and scoped out the sides of the road. Finding a gravel turn-in, she took it, hitting a pothole and rolling down the dirt track onto a flat piece of land that had been cleared and had an unobstructed view of an inlet of water off Card Sound. A small red box house on wheels was parked to the right, nestled under tall trees and surrounded by a chicken wire fence that set off a pitiful-looking yard. A skinny white-haired woman in her sixties or seventies with a weather-lined face, decked out in jean overalls and rubber boots, leaned against the side of a pickup that had seen better days.

"I'm going to ask her a few questions." Fab parked and got out.

The woman's eyes glittered as she checked out Fab from head to toe. A sinister smile started to take form and disappeared in a blink.

Bad sign—my neck hair suddenly stood on end. I sighed and got out. Fab and I were both armed, with weapons holstered at the middle of our backs. I'd been embarrassed at leaving the house in crop sweats and a long-sleeved t-shirt, but brushed aside the idea of changing in the face of an emergency and was now happy that I had. My knockabout clothes offered protection from the mosquitos and other unidentified flying insects.

"Look, two new friends," the woman said gleefully and waved. "It's been a while since I've had a redhead." Her dark, pin-dot eyes zeroed in on me.

"Would you mind answering a couple of questions so we can get back on the road?" Fab asked, the picture of sweetness, a damsel in distress.

"Come in." The woman motioned to the red house. "I love company. Can never get enough." She cackled.

It was a disturbing sound. I grabbed the back of Fab's top and slowed down her progress in closing the distance between her and the woman, in case she was of the mindset to take the woman up on her invitation.

Crazy alert. I've had plenty of experience and was definitely looking at it on display.

"That's nice of you, but we need to get back on the road," I said.

That didn't set well. The woman scowled, as if to say 'who asked you?'

"It's beautiful back here." I smiled lamely.

In a flash, the woman produced a double-barreled shotgun and pointed it at us. "Get moving. Now." She nodded toward the house.

Fab was in mid-reach for her Walther when the woman pulled the trigger and blew out the windshield of the Hummer, glass flying everywhere.

Fab jerked on my arm, and we hit the ground and rolled into a dense thicket.

"You girls got nowhere to go." The woman's

high-pitch laugh floated in the air. "Except where you'll get eaten by gators." She pulled the trigger again. "Run, sweeties, run."

Fab rose to a half-crouch and motioned me to follow as she crawled deeper into the bushes and straight into murky, ankle-deep water. What lurked in the muck was anyone's guess.

Resigning myself to the fact that I was in over my head when it came to finding a way out, I followed Fab's lead, doing my best to keep up and not let fear get the better of me. She turned slightly, tapping her lips with her finger, and grabbed my hand. If anyone could get us out of this predicament, it was her; she didn't lack in courage or skills.

Another shotgun blast filled the air. Then again. It didn't ruffle the bushes, so what was the woman shooting at? I didn't want to know the answer.

"Come out, come out." The voice, pitched high and hard, echoed behind us. Hopefully, she wasn't as close as she sounded.

Fab picked up speed, forcing her way through the underbrush.

"Answer me." The woman's voice lost volume as it began to fade away.

Tense with fear but not wanting to be the reason we got caught, I pulled my t-shirt up over my cheeks to protect my face from the slapping branches. Our clothing did little to protect us from the dried-out limbs that snagged and tore at the material. I tried to focus, listening for any sound that would mean the woman was advancing on us as we continued our trek through the mangroves.

She'd stopped yelling her "come to mama" commands as we continued to crawl along, hoping we were moving toward civilization. The thought was almost amusing, since we hadn't seen much evidence of it on the drive. Hopefully, the joke wasn't on us, with the woman not bothering to pursue us because she knew all paths led back to her, so she could sit back and be patient.

I trusted Fab's sense of direction—her navigation skills had never let us down. It would be nice to find a sign or, better yet, a stable person to ask and ascertain our location. Thank goodness we weren't alone—we had each other.

The trees curled in on themselves and grew more dense and harder to navigate, forcing us to wade through the shallow water as we stuck close to the crushed underbrush.

I lost all sense of time as we continued our slow hike through the vegetation. Finally we came to a clearing and surveyed the area from our partially hidden vantage point.

"Fab," I whispered.

She shook her head.

Chapter Two

We crawled out of the underbrush and onto another piece of land that had been cleared for use as an oversized campsite. A few trees had been chopped away, but the area wasn't as large as the one the crazy woman lived in. An old silver airstream was parked on one end, next to it an older model Ford pickup, with an aluminum covering serving as a patio, as evidenced by ratty lawn chairs. On the far side, a galvanized steel carport with no sides housed an impressive still setup.

Fab nudged me and pulled her Walther.

Caught off guard once was one time too many. I drew my Glock and held it at my side.

We didn't have long to wait. The door to the trailer flew open, an older man managing to catch it before it banged into the side. He had grey hair, of sorts, a clump here and there. As he stepped gingerly down the steps, he caught sight of the two of us. Startled, he took a step back, checked us out, zeroed in our firearms, and seemed to relax.

"Hey, sisters," he greeted, and continued his trek to the carport, pausing without turning to look back to ask, "How'd you two get out here? Can't be a good story."

"You've got the old-man rapport," I whispered to Fab. "You take it from here."

"Wouldn't have anything to do with the shots coming from Addy Clegg's place, would it?" He reached for a ceramic jug and held it out. "Wanna drink? It's not as good as the last batch, but it'll make the hair on your chest stand up." He laughed low and deep.

We both shook our heads.

If the smoke and nauseating smell coming from the still was any indication, the finished product would be ick! I wasn't the least bit interested in a taste test. I also wasn't sure how I'd explain hair on my chest to Creole. Whatever I came up with, he wouldn't find it funny, and he'd never believe the truth.

Before Fab took a step, she, like me, scanned the place for weapons and, in particular, a shotgun in easy reach. The previous one had been hidden behind the truck, though, where we'd never have seen it unless we were standing on top of it, and to be honest, we weren't looking for one. Who would've thought we would receive that kind of reception when we weren't a threat?

"We took a wrong turn and got out to ask directions." Fab took a couple of steps forward. "Next thing, the old woman started shooting."

"I'd steer clear of her. I've had a couple of

encounters, and she made my man parts shrivel." He shuddered. "You're never going to get your car back. It's most likely gone already, sold for parts. Addy's friendly with a fellow named Deuce. Seen them together a time or two—made sure they didn't see me. Anyway, Deuce has a reputation for being on call for a good deal." He finished checking his gauges and walked over to a lawn chair. Slinging his body down, he stuck his arms out to steady it and keep from falling.

"Your call," I whispered.

"Have a seat," he said. "I haven't shot an unexpected visitor yet and don't plan to start now." He waved at the empty chairs.

Fab closed the distance, me on her heels. She jerked a chair back and, before sitting, tucked her Walther in the waistband of her pants. I stood behind her, acting as a bodyguard.

"So that's what the two back-to-back shots were about," he mused. "Just guessing, but bet it's a signal to one of her mean sonovagun sons to stay clear until she sends another signal. Best bet is to call your insurance company if you're covered. You could call the cops, except I don't have a phone, and even if I did, by the time they got here, your car would be long gone and Addy would be nowhere to be found. And if she were, it would be a 'you said, she said,' and she'd make you out to be liars that prey on old folks."

Phone? I'd really been thrown for a loop not to think of it before. I reached in my pocket. Empty.

It must have fallen out on our crawl through the weeds. I remembered seeing Fab's sitting in the cup holder.

"How far is it back to town?" Fab asked.

"Ten, twelve miles. And since you're on Addy's radar, you wouldn't get far, sticking out like a sore thumb on the two-lane highway."

We could do it, but it would take a couple of hours, and in this humidity, we'd be a wasted, sweaty mess by the time we got back.

Fab sighed. "I'll make you a deal. I'll give you my Walther in exchange for a ride back to town. Once we get there, I'll exchange it for cash."

"I've got a Glock to sweeten the deal," I said.

"Don't need either one of them—got several firearms inside the trailer."

"You name your terms for a ride back, and I give you both our words we'll pay up." I eyed the truck, which looked like the only vehicle on the property. It was the right size to tow the Airstream, but was it capable of getting us to town? Having a beater truck of my own, I knew that looks could be deceiving.

"Doesn't run," he said on an exhale, noticing that I was sizing up his truck. "I've got a skiff. It ain't pretty, but it runs, and I can motor you over to AJ's, a restaurant not far from here. It would still be a hike back to town."

"You do that, and I've got a family member that can fix up your ride. In fact, he can send someone out that can fix it on site. He'll do a good job, and no charge."

"Won't kill me to do a good turn for two pretty girls." He spit on his hand, wiped it on his tattered jeans, and stuck it out with a lopsided grin that showed he was missing at least half his teeth. "Cootie Shine."

Fab shook hands. "Fab Merceau."

I stuck out my knuckles, which he reciprocated, and we bumped knuckles a few times. I managed to keep up. "Madison Westin. I own Jake's on the main highway. Stop in there and drop my name, and you get a discount—free."

Cootie stood and motioned us to follow. He led us through a thicket of trees to a boat tied to a rickety dock that was less than a foot long and had a jagged edge. I'd guess that a hurricane took a nibble out of it. The flat-bottom boat with an outboard was older than Cootie, judging by its looks.

"Is it seaworthy?" Fab questioned skeptically.

"It'll get us through these mangroves." Cootie untied the boat and held out his hand to help Fab on board. She, in turn, held out a hand to me.

Fab and I sat on the front bench while Cootie settled in the back and started the engine, which was loud in the still air. He steered us out on the water and into a narrow waterway of the sound that was hedged in by thick growth on each side.

I put my head on Fab's shoulder. "I'm not sure how we explain today, because frankly, it would sound made-up, even to me."

The slight breeze whipped our hair around, and the sun beat down on the short ride to the only restaurant around. In fact, the only commercial business in the entire area. Cootie pulled up alongside the dock at the restaurant and tied off, helping us out.

"How do I get in touch?" I asked.

"It's not necessary."

"But if…"

"My turn-in is two miles from the junction of the roadway." Cootie grunted. "You two be careful."

Fab thanked him and kissed his cheek, which left the man blushing. We both waved, climbed the stairs to the restaurant, and stepped into the open-air bar. All of the waterfront tables were filled, and interestingly enough, not a single customer paid attention to our arrival.

Chapter Three

It was surprising that a restaurant in such an isolated location was half-full on a weekday. That said something for either the food or the lack of competition.

"You think you can turn on the charm and get the bartender to let us use the phone?" I elbowed Fab and, out of options, we wound our way around the tables to the bar.

Fab slowed, turned, and asked, "Why are we stranded out here?"

"Car trouble. We… uh… decided to walk, and when we realized our error and turned around, our ride had been stolen."

"Don't leave my side." Fab grabbed my arm, and we ended up standing in front of a middle-aged bartender who'd been eyeing us. "Can I use your phone?" She gave the story I'd come up with, sticking to it almost word for word.

"That's bull," he sneered. "I saw you two dock that piece of crap and come up the steps. You need to get out of here unless you're offering something sexual, and then I'll think about your request."

"Could you be a bigger pig?" I asked,

forgetting that we needed a favor.

"I could call the cops." He pointed to the main entrance. "Get moving."

We turned away. I said, "I could make a scene until he did call the cops."

Fab shook her head, grabbed my arm, and led me slowly in the direction he pointed. "Let's make that the last resort. You're the one with the plans. Now what? We're still in the middle of nowhere, and the only business out here is no help."

"Remind me to send Toady back here to kick the holy snot out of that man," I said.

"Madison. That's not appropriate talk," Fab scolded, morphing into Mother, which made us both laugh.

Toady was an associate of Fab's and did any butt-kicking necessary, and when it came to his favorite girl, heaven help anyone who disrespected her.

"We can't walk," I whined. "Addy Clegg is still on the loose. That's not a name I'm apt to forget. I'm going to get my baby back. Or have someone come out and snatch her house out from under her." Another job for Toady.

"Calm down." Fab looped her arm through mine. "You need to come up with another plan, since that's your area of expertise."

We stood on the road in front of the building and surveyed the parking spaces, delineated by chipped, faint lines that ran the length of the property. I spotted a pickup parked at the far end, a grizzled, bearded man lifting a large metal basket out of the truck bed and disappearing into the back entrance.

"Come on." I ran to make sure that we didn't miss the man on his way back out. We didn't have long to wait before he reappeared. He noticed us standing at his front bumper right off and shot us a questioning look.

"We're in desperate need of a ride back to town." I stepped forward. "We can't pay you now, but will be able to once we get back."

The man tugged on the end of a black beard riddled with grey and gave us a once-over. "I can drop you at the turnoff to Highway One, if you don't mind riding in the back. Payback's not necessary."

"Thank you so much."

Fab and I climbed into the bed.

"It smells back here," Fab grouched.

I looked down at my clothing and then at hers. "It might be us that smell. I don't know about you, but I don't think I've ever been so sticky, dirty, or grimy in my life."

"We're alive."

"There's that."

We fist-bumped and leaned back against the cab, using our hands to provide limited coverage for our faces from the sizzling sun. I watched as we passed mile after mile of nothing but jungle and was happy that we'd scored a ride, no matter how uncomfortable it was being jostled around back there. True to his word, once back in civilization, the man pulled to the side of the road and let us out.

We waved and shouted our thanks as he roared off, waving back.

"You do realize we're still a damn long walk from home." Fab pointed to the Overseas that ran south, ending in Key West.

"We can do this. The Cottages are only a couple of miles from here, and then we can bum a ride from Mac."

I owned a ten-unit property of individual cottages on the beach, and Mac Lane was my manager. Her main job was to keep the circus from spilling into the street. On occasion, one of the tenants would get loose, but Mac would round them up and, in her forceful way, tell them to, "Knock it off."

"We could hitch a ride," Fab suggested.

"How many times can we tempt fate? We've done it twice now, and the third time might be a disaster." I didn't wait for an answer and started walking.

"There's that. New rule: we don't get out of the car without our phones, no matter how tame we think the situation."

"Agreed." I didn't tell her that I'd had mine and lost it in the weeds. We walked mostly in silence. "I just realized that without my keys, I can't get in the house. So you get to finally update our home security system. I want a keyless entry pad."

Fab took her lockpick out of her pocket and handed it to me. "Your husband will have a flipping fit. He'll think that I'll use it to come and go as I please."

"Because you will. So I'll spring it on him as a surprise. How sneaky is that?" We giggled, which was a first that day and an enjoyable, lighthearted moment.

We hiked down the highway, past businesses and landmarks that we passed every day. Fab, in shortcut mode, directed us across a trash-filled lot to a side street that dumped us into a residential neighborhood, then shot down an alley and around a corner. Fab knew every way to shorten the route, though it did surprise me that we hadn't trespassed through people's yards. A half-block from our destination, I saw that Mac's truck wasn't sitting in the driveway and grumbled, "No way."

"Now what?" Fab demanded, staring down the street. "So much for Mac driving us. Thankfully, your drunk tenants don't drive, and I wouldn't get in a vehicle with one of them anyway."

"The professor doesn't drink; we'll bang on his door." I led the way.

It surprised me that the property was quiet; not a single person slumped over drunk on their porch or peering through the blinds. The art deco units were situated around the driveway in a u-shape. I rented half the units to regulars and the other half to tourists and, to the shock of the community, ran a waiting list for your next vacation adventure. The guests came for the antics, and we aimed to please.

We turned the corner. I slowed passing the pool area, making sure that no one was passed out and in need of relocation before they took a tumble into the water. Fab, ahead of me, beat on Crum's door, giving the impression that at least six cops were waiting for him to answer.

Professor Crum was, in two words, a hot mess. If I hadn't been the one to call to verify his references, then call back to double-check them, I'd never have believed that he retired from a top-rated college with impeccable references.

His white head poked out the bathroom window as if no one would notice, even though it was less than a foot from the front door. He made eye contact and slammed it down. Seconds later, he threw open the door. "You know how to scare an old man," he said snootily, ramrod stiff in vulgar-fitting tighty-whities a size too small.

I'd long ago trained my eyes to stay on his face. Done with her antics, Fab stepped over behind me, her way of saying, *You deal with him.*

"You break the window; you pay." I motioned. "Cut the histrionics about being old; there's nothing wrong with you. Ask any woman in the neighborhood." The professor had a reputation with the women. "We need a ride…" Fab poked me in the back. The last thing we wanted was him knowing where we lived. "To Jake's."

"Sold my truck," he said with a big smile. "Made a killing. I'm hitting the auction tomorrow to see what kind of deal I can get on another one." His expression turned to disgust as he eyed us. "I'd invite you in, but I don't want you getting my furniture dirty." Still standing on the porch, he jerked the door closed behind him, as though we'd attempt to rush him.

I didn't bother to remind him that he rented the cottage furnished, and therefore, "his" furniture belonged to me. "Didn't know you were still in the car-thieving business." He bought ridiculously cheap, and when he didn't sell outright, he'd take payments from some unsuspecting schlubs who couldn't afford bus fare, let alone a car, hoping to get it back and restart the cycle. Once or twice, it'd almost ended his life, but he was a slow learner for a man who made jokes about others' IQs, or lack thereof.

He straightened and sputtered. "Can't help you." He cracked open the door, preparing to slip inside.

"Can I use your phone?" I asked.

"I use Mac's when I need to make a call."

I reached around him and grabbed the knob to stop him from slithering inside and shutting the door in our faces. "I'll borrow your Barbie bike then. Do you happen to have another good deal hanging in your shed?"

When he did have a car, he parked it on the street, and I'd let him install a shed in his parking space to house his "finds" from garbage bins.

"What do I get out of it?"

"The satisfaction of doing something nice for someone, namely your landlord. Which you can use as a reminder to her of your benevolence, so the next time she wants to kick your butt to the curb, she'll give you a reprieve."

Fab laughed in my ear. So she approved of my arm-twisting.

"Let me get my key." He disappeared inside and was back out before Fab could put her foot to the door.

On the way to the shed, I said, "You never said whether you've got two bikes or not." I wasn't certain it was possible to fit two grown women on a kid's bike. He nodded before I could ask for a skateboard and a piece of rope. "Here's the deal. We're going to park the bikes in the kitchen at Jake's. Corral Mac and ask her nicely to go get them and bring them back in her truck." Crum grumbled. "Free meal," I added. Then, after he opened the door, "I get the pink bike."

Fab rolled her eyes.

Crum rolled out a turquoise twin and handed it to Fab. "Be careful. These are my money-makers." He grouched and held onto the handlebars until she acknowledged that.

Just great, screwing people on the price of a used kid's bike. I kept the sentiment to myself. "Your assistance is appreciated," I said, having weaseled inside the shed when he was otherwise occupied and pushed my bike choice back out.

"The seats are hard, not to mention small," Fab grumbled as we peddled out of the driveway. She turned away from the highway and started down a side street.

"Oh no you don't," I yelled after her. "The direct route, please. I'd like to get there before closing and not have to sleep in the parking lot."

"Exaggeration much?" Fab snarked back. "We could walk it and still get there hours before closing."

Chapter Four

Fab and I curved back to the main highway, staying on the bike path, and from there, it was a straight shot to the bar. It was a quick trip, and we soon cruised into the parking lot and around the back of Jake's — a tiki bar that I owned on the main drag. The rest of the businesses that shared the block were closed — in truth, they were rarely, if ever, open. Fab rented her lighthouse to Gunz, an old business associate, for a pittance, along with his assurance that he was going legit. Twinkie Princesses, the roach coach, never opened — they were a favorite, as they sent their rent checks on time and never caused any trouble. A rumor was floating about that the women were entertaining the idea of selling, but that hadn't materialized. Junker's, the antique garden store, was the only place with regular-ish hours — usually mornings, as he closed to ferret out more finds to sell at a six-hundred-percent markup.

The two of us rode single file through the kitchen door and parked the bikes in the corner, garnering a double take and a grin from one of Cook's kin, who was on grill duty. The big boss was gone for the day, his door locked.

"I win." Fab got off her bike and shot her fist in the air.

I shook my head, refusing to think about my various aches and pains, and exited the kitchen. Kelpie was behind the bar, putting on a bump-and-grind show for her regulars. She looked up, noticed me headed in her direction, and waved. I motioned to her, and she tagged the other bartender and ran to meet me, her multi-colored pink hair swinging around her shoulders.

She looked us over from head to toe. "You two look like—"

"I'm your boss," I cut her off.

"But your inner beauty still shines through." She smiled cheekily.

"Good save," Fab grumped.

I stared past Kelpie's shoulder. "Who's behind the bar?"

"That's the new hire." Kelpie's eyes turned to Fab, communicating, *You tell her.*

"Can you get me the key to the office? I'll only be here long enough to make a few calls."

"Your husbands are out on the deck with some shifty fellow," Kelpie said. "His eyes are too close together."

"You sound like my grandmother spouting off words of wisdom," I said.

The three of us turned and headed toward the bar, and I tugged on Fab's arm, pausing in front of the door to the game room, the perfect shortcut to the deck. It was used by the regular poker group, which had grown so much in membership that the members had split up and now used it on different days. I had advertised it as a venue for your next shindig and gotten no takers, but as it turned out, the room was a moneymaker anyway. Cutting through the game room was a good idea, since we looked like we'd been dragged through a swamp and I didn't want any customers to see me and ask questions I didn't want to answer.

"Why is the door locked?" I asked.

"Boss' orders." Once again, Kelpie's eyes shot to Fab. "It slows the cops down, and the players like the 'secret' entrance off the deck."

Some secret, since the entrance was a double set of doors that were clearly visible, inside and out.

"New employees. Cops. Locked doors," I said. "Have Doodad schedule an employee meeting. And make sure that Fab gets the memo. Can't wait to hear everything that went on while I was out of town."

"None of it's bad." Kelpie winked at Fab, who growled back at her. "It's all about perception. Everything can have a happy ending."

I turned to Kelpie. "I need a drink, and make it a pitcher."

"I'll also take a pitcher and, on the side, a glass full of olives."

I looped my arm through Fab's, and we stuck

to the sides of the room as we maneuvered across the packed bar and around the arcade machines, not attracting even a nod. It surprised me to see the 'Keep Out' sign on the door to the deck, but I didn't even pause or knock before opening the door.

Three sets of eyes stared, as if to say, *Can't you read?*

Creole jumped up, kicking his chair back. "What the heck happened to you?" He checked me over, which I should have been getting used to, he lowered his eyebrows in annoyance while he did it.

I stepped back from his outstretched arms. "I smell bad."

He twirled me around. "You okay?"

"A very long story that requires refreshments."

Didier stood, murmuring, "Cherie…" and drew Fab into his arms despite her protests.

The shifty fellow turned out to be Help, an undercover friend of Creole's. He'd kicked back in the corner, doing his best to blend into the woodwork, a smirk on his face. He once told us his name was Stephan and didn't bother to disguise the lie. Since he'd never ponied up his real name, Fab and I gave him an apt moniker, since he responded to every one of our calls by showing up and offering assistance.

I chose a chair that was close to the door and could be hosed off, and Creole moved next to me.

Fab took Creole's old chair and sat next to Didier.

"What the heck happened?" Creole demanded. "Why didn't you call?"

"Carjacked," I announced. "No phones." I held up my hands.

A knock at the door cut off a response that I knew would match the outrage on Creole's face, which also matched Didier's expression. Kelpie stepped outside and set down a margarita in front of me, a martini for Fab, then turned around, and the busboy handed her the pitchers, which she also set down.

I licked my lips. "Be on standby in case we need a refill."

Kelpie grinned. "Gotcha, Bossaroo." She closed the door behind her.

I tipped my glass at Fab. "To being alive." Over the rim, I winked at Help. "What brings you out of your hut? Murder? Another felony?"

"I'm socializing with my two friends here." Help squinted back.

"Good one." I downed my drink, doing my best not to lick my lips again, and reached for the pitcher. One step ahead of me, Creole already had it in hand and refilled my glass.

Fab downed hers and held her glass out to Didier, who filled it and added a spear of olives.

"My patience is running thin here," Creole announced. "I'd like to hear how it was that when I left this morning, you were on the couch with your feet up, and here you are, hours later, looking like you went one-on-one with a wild animal and it was a draw. Same outfit, although it was cleaner then."

"Can I have a two-minute reprieve? And I'll need to use your phone."

He fished his phone out of his pocket, putting it in my open hand.

"Let me make this call regarding my SUV. The window of opportunity for getting it back is closing, if it hasn't slammed shut already." I scrolled through his phone, found the number I was looking for, and hit connect. "This is your favorite step-daughter," I said when Spoon answered.

"You okay?" I heard him say away from the phone, "It's Madison." Mother must be standing nearby. She'd married her boy toy—Jimmy Spoon, younger by ten years—and was living happily ever after.

"I got carjacked."

"You and Fab okay?" Said with a note of tenderness that one didn't often hear out of the big man unless it was directed at Mother.

"We're good." I flashed Fab a small smile. "It's a real possibility that my SUV is in the felonious hands of a cretin by the name of Deuce." I saw a flash of recognition on Help's face. So he knew the man, or of him anyway. "I want it back, and I'm willing to pay the ransom."

Spoon whistled. "I'll get on it. You'll be needing an interim ride, so stop by the shop in the morning and I'll hook you up."

"Keep in mind that it has to be large enough for me to haul my posse around." That got a laugh. "Mostly Fab, since I highly doubt she'll relinquish her role as driver."

We hung up. I gulped a breath of air and exhaled slowly to steady my nerves. "You and Deuce old friends?" I asked Help.

"Never heard of him." He shrugged.

"I'd like to hear what the hell happened." Didier said, out of patience. "And now."

"I second that," Creole fired back.

"You want to flip to see who goes first?" I asked Fab.

"You go ahead while I continue to dream about being up to my neck in a bubble bath."

"We took a wrong turn and stopped to ask for directions." That should've been a red flag, but not one of the men said anything. "That's when a woman stepped in front of my SUV, aimed her shotgun, and pulled the trigger. Blew out the windshield of the Hummer."

The men shared shocked expressions.

"Fab grabbed my arm and dragged me into the brush. Thank goodness for best friends." I locked eyes with Fab. "We crawled along." I held up scratched hands. "Slogged through filthy water. A sweet old man gave us a boat ride. I'm repaying the favor, big time." My voice choked.

Creole pulled me into his arms and kissed me hard.

Didier smooshed Fab's hands to his lips, whispering in her ear, and pulled her to his side.

The door opened on a knock, and Kelpie stuck her head out. "Refills?"

Help pointed his finger around the table. "Three beers."

Kelpie turned and waved in sign language across the bar.

"Please tell the kitchen that I'll need a sampler times two. To go." I raised an eyebrow at Fab, and she nodded. "What about you?" I asked Help.

"He's staying the night at our house," Didier said.

That shocked Fab.

"Not in my bedroom," I said. When the couple took occupancy of the house, Fab had given me and Creole a room, all ready for us to take them up on their offer to move in.

"We got a guest bedroom ready. Just in time," Didier said.

The new guy handed Kelpie a tray and disappeared, and she served the guys. "I'll get the order taken care of and make sure there's plenty of food."

A customer pushed past her and stormed out onto the deck. "Why can't we sit out here? There's plenty of room. You people can't hog it all to yourselves."

"I'm the owner and can do what I want," I snapped back crabbily.

"Oh hey." She flashed a two-handed dance wave. "So cool about the shootout the other night. Sorry I missed it."

Kelpie pointed at Fab, wide-eyed. I wanted to ask Fab if she could feel the tire marks from the bus that just rolled over her.

Didier grinned and tugged her harder to his side.

"That's too bad." I smiled weakly, noting my sarcasm was lost on the woman. "Maybe next time."

Kelpie grabbed the woman by the arm and hauled her out the door. "This is a business meeting," she explained, and with a glance back over her shoulder as she followed the woman, she said, "No one died," and closed the door.

"I can explain," Fab said.

"No doubt. It will be another topic on the agenda of the meeting you're required to attend."

"I'd like to be there." Didier continued to grin.

"What did you do today?" Fab asked. "You three hang out together all day?"

"Actually, Creole and Didier were doing me a favor," Help answered. "I bought some property, and they came out to inspect it and give me their opinion on the options I'd have for development."

"Where is it located?" I asked.

"North of town," Help said vaguely.

"Card Sound?" If I hadn't been staring at him,

I'd have missed the flicker of surprise.

"We agreed not to discuss the details until Help decides how he wants to proceed," Creole said.

"You never did say how you two ended up at Jake's," Help said, effectively changing the subject.

"We walked, then availed ourselves of the opportunity to boost a couple of bicycles and rode the rest of the way." At his look of surprise, I added, "They're cheap, so it's only a misdemeanor. The children left them lying in the street. Good lesson to pick up your stuff." In truth, they were a find on trash day or a markdown from a garage sale, something last-minute that hadn't sold that day.

"So no one got hurt?" Creole asked with a shake of his head.

"Most people would think that was a true story," Didier admonished.

"We don't care about most people," I said to Fab with a flick of my mop of red hair, which was bushed out from the humidity and full of enough sweat that it was pasted to my neck. I pulled out a strand and sniffed, making a face.

Fab mimicked me and stared at her long brown hair in disgust.

"I realize that we've been interrupted a few times, but we have yet to get all the details about what happened today," Creole snapped. "We'll save it for when we get home." He pulled me to my feet.

"On our way through the kitchen, we should grab garbage bags to spread across the seats," I said.

"Let's cut back through the poker room." Fab nodded at the doors. "Lessens the chance that we'll be tomorrow's hot gossip."

Creole and I stopped in the kitchen while the rest went out to the parking lot. He helped pack the orders after I asked him to make sure that they were bagged separately. I found the spare bags and pulled off several, then went outside, handing some to Didier.

I tugged Fab out of earshot of the two men. "We're not coming over. After a long, disinfecting shower, I'm going to give Creole the details, and I'll be putting the blame on him and Didier for sneaking around. I won't even have to fake a few tears because I'm ready for a good cry."

"Good one." Fab hugged me. "Thanks for that. I knew I wouldn't get away with trying to put off that conversation until morning."

Chapter Five

I'd meant to fill Creole in on the details of our adventurous day but didn't factor in tequila on an empty stomach and the added effect of the longest shower under the jets I'd ever taken, washing my hair twice in case any critters made it past my searching fingers. I'd gotten out and pulled one of Creole's t-shirts over my head because it smelled like him and comforted me, then laid down on the bed with the intention of only closing my eyes for a second.

When I opened them again, the sun was streaming through the windows. I looked around, disoriented at first, then breathed a sigh of relief at being home in my own bed.

"Good morning," Creole whispered in my ear. "I'll be right back with coffee."

"You're the best husband."

He rumbled out a chuckle.

I watched as he disappeared into the kitchen, our two spoiled housecats, Jazz and Snow, jumping down from the bed and filing out behind him. It was long past their breakfast time, as they like to be served at dawn and were kept waiting for a more decent hour most mornings.

Creole had remodeled the house into one wide-open space, and the only thing separating the bedroom from the living space was a screen. I got up and went into the bathroom, splashing water on my face, then looking in the mirror and wincing at my sunburned face. I took out a special lotion that I kept on hand and dabbed it on. Getting back in bed, I arranged the pillows and leaned back against the headboard, ready to drink down a whole pot of coffee.

Creole came back, handed me my mug, and crawled in beside me.

I savored the first sip and smiled at him over the rim. "I know you've been waiting; probably somewhat impatiently."

He flipped over one of my hands, running his fingertip lightly over the scratches. "I want to know who to beat the hell out of besides this Deuce character."

"He's just some guy making a buck off his illegal trade. But I'm happy I didn't have to go face to face with him."

"I'd like to hear what the heck happened and prefer that you not skimp on the details. I made some calls, and imagine my surprise when I found out no police reports were filed."

"Yesterday, I got a frantic phone call from my best friend, who was worried by her husband's unusual, evasive behavior and said she was waiting out front with the engine running…" I grimaced. "I should have told her emphatically no and to deal with her own problems. There is a point in this drama where I'd choose to change tack and possibly alter events…maybe for the worse. One never knows." I proceeded to relay the events of the previous morning up to where we got out of the SUV to talk to the old woman. "If I had a do-over, hindsight and all, I would've insisted that Fab take her phone — surely we wouldn't have both lost them. And I'd have moved my Glock to my front waistband, for whatever good that would've done. Had we had time to draw our weapons, I have no doubt the woman would've enjoyed a shootout."

"I'd prefer that you avoid all possible shootout situations. Granted there was no way to anticipate her reaction, but in the future, when you need directions or help of any kind, choose a more public venue." Creole took my mug out of my hands, set it on the bedside table, and wrapped his arms around me, kissing my head. "Smells better than last night."

I giggled. "There's more." I continued with the rest of the details, including meeting Cootie, without whom we'd still be stuck in the weeds, or worse.

"'Cootie'…sounds like someone you'd befriend."

"It does, doesn't it? I've never had a moonshine connection before."

"Heard it's worse than rotgut tequila, and years back, I barfed for days on a bottle of that swill. I ate the worm," he boasted.

I flinched. "There's a tradition I'm happy to say I passed on."

"Cootie doesn't know it yet, but he's made some good friends. Didier and I may be able to upgrade his off-grid living standards. He helped you; we'll return the favor."

"I'm going to get Spoon to send someone out there to get his truck running. It's crazy to live out there without transportation, and his boat doesn't fit the bill."

"Do you remember the name of the bartender at that hole?"

"You are not going to go break his face." I kissed his knuckles. "But it's hot that you'd think of doing it." I resumed my storytelling, and when I got to the part about the bicycles belonging to Crum, he burst out laughing.

"He didn't steal them off some unsuspecting kid, did he?"

"Nooo… He's not a thief in the criminal sense. He digs in the trash, frequents garage sales at closing, offers next to nothing on things he thinks he can flip for a few bucks, and charges outrageous prices. It's a big game to him, and he does pretty well."

"You and Fab are amazing, not that I didn't already know that." Creole hugged me. "Let's face it, you two, in some pretty adverse conditions, kept moving until you got back to civilization."

"It's only because I focused on putting one foot in front of the other, not in some croc's mouth, and not letting Fab out of my sight."

Creole leaned his head back and was quiet for a long moment. "Wife, swear that what I'm about to tell you stays between us." He held out his pinkie. "No one, and that includes Fab. You're going to have to keep this secret from her. Didier might have told her already, but we haven't talked, so I don't know that for a fact."

I linked my finger with his and leaned in to seal my secrecy with a kiss.

"Help will have to understand," Creole said. "I'm not going to lie to you by omission."

"If this has to do with an ongoing police investigation, I understand you not being able to tell me."

"Of sorts, but not in the way you think. Help bought a parcel of land years back for when he retired. That day is approaching, and so, to jumpstart his new life, he packed his old Winnebago and parked it out in Card Sound to begin an amenity-free life."

I scrunched up my nose.

"In his pursuit of the lazy good life, he discovered three bodies. He called it in to his boss, who sent out an investigation team. Everything was done by the book, no shortcuts, and they came to the conclusion that the individuals, all men, were murdered somewhere else and dumped on his land."

"There's a multiple-murderer running free amongst us?" I blew out a breath. "You're not on the force anymore, so why get you involved? Can't your involvement get you in trouble? And Didier?"

"Didier's involvement was a fluke. When Help called, wanting to talk, he made it sound benign and not about multiple felonies, so when Didier offered to ride along, I took him up on the offer."

"Why not just tell Fab?"

"You'll have to ask him. He should have known that Fab would do whatever it took to solve the mystery, even if there was none. Yesterday could've ended up much worse, and all because of some sort of game-playing between the two of them." Creole shook his head in disgust. "There's more."

I grimaced.

"The Feds are now involved, and they've set their sights on Help as one of their prime suspects. Hence him calling me and the reason he didn't want to talk about it over the phone. He wants help proving that he's not a murderer."

"I don't suppose he has a suspect list?" I asked. "Let me guess: he didn't know any of the victims?"

"Nope."

"If you want backgrounds run, you can use Xander," I offered.

"I don't want you involved," Creole said adamantly.

"Same goes for you." I shook my finger at him, and he bit the tip. "I suggest Help keep a diary, or some way of keeping a record of where he is at any given moment, in case another body turns up and he needs an alibi."

"He's afraid if that happens, he'll get locked up just to see if the carnage stops."

"That's a dumb idea. If whoever is doing it gets wind, which is a certainty since such salacious news will make headlines, they'll find another dumping ground." I winced at the thought of yesterday's outing and how many more ways the day could've gone wrong. "We must've been close to Help's property yesterday. You need to give him a heads up about his neighbor, Addy, and that he needs to steer clear. He's got enough trouble."

"You also need to be careful. Be aware of your surroundings until the murderer is behind bars."

"No need to worry about me going back out to Card Sound anytime ever. In fact, I plan to send Toady to make contact with Cootie to make sure he's okay."

"I'd like to think that you're going to kick back and stay home today, regardless of whatever emergency your friend comes up with. You're going to be feeling your aches and pains."

"My plan for the day is to go to Spoon's and pick up a car, stop at the phone store, then take your advice—come home, and kick my feet up." I smiled at him. "I may curl up under the umbrella on the patio and catch up on paperwork."

"In the meantime, I've got some time before I have to leave." He pulled me on top of him and kissed me.

Chapter Six

Before Creole left the house, I called Fab on Didier's phone. I'd have sent a text, but didn't want her saying she didn't see it.

"Come over and get me. I need a ride to Spoon's," I said in a whiney tone, really laying it on. "If not… I'll have to hike to the highway and walk because I've imposed a rule for myself—no more hitchhiking. It's hot, and I'll get sweaty."

"Are you finished?" Fab asked in exasperation. "You sound like a six-year-old."

Creole stood across from me at the island, grinning at my antics.

"Is that a yes?"

"One hour."

* * *

As usual, the woman was early, and I was ready for her. I grabbed my bag and raced out of the house to knock on the driver's side window of her Porsche. Fab cracked it open. "Can I drive?"

She shook her head as though she hadn't heard me correctly. "No." She squinted and powered the window back up.

I walked around and got in the passenger side, biting back a complaint that it felt like I was sitting in the road.

"What kind of car are you getting?" Fab asked as she put her sports car in gear and roared over to the highway.

"I'll take what I'm offered and try not to gripe about it." I leveled a stare at her, which she ignored.

Fab knew every shortcut in town and utilized all of them often. She pulled into JS Auto Body five minutes faster than her usual time. Jimmy Spoon ran an appointment-only auto repair shop for luxe autos and the restoration of older models. To anyone driving by, if it weren't for the sign, it wouldn't be apparent by looking that there was a business behind the twelve-foot-high fence.

"Did you know your mother was going to be here?" Fab asked, pointing to the Mercedes SUV parked in the driveway.

I sighed and got out. "Maybe she's worried about me."

Just as we got to the front door, it buzzed. Nothing happened on this property that security cameras didn't pick up.

"Hi." I smiled at Mother and Spoon, both sitting behind his desk, making a formidable pair. Before Fab could go sit on the couch, her favorite place, I nudged her to a chair in front of the desk. She could sit beside me for moral support, since Mother's scowl telegraphed irritation.

We'd barely sat down when Mother said, "Why don't you tell us what happened?" *Really happened* was implied, but not said.

I gave her the G-rated version of events—that we stopped to ask directions and got a rifle pointed at us.

"When was the last carjacking we had around here?" Mother asked.

"You think I'm making it up? For what reason?"

"I didn't say that," Mother snapped. "I'm just thinking you left out the part where you two went looking for trouble and found it."

I nudged Fab's foot.

"Not guilty." Fab held up her hand.

Spoon stared at the two of us as though trying to read our thoughts. *Good luck, big guy, you've been blocked from mind-reading. I've had plenty of training from the master sitting at your side.*

"We're both happy that you're okay," Spoon said.

"Thanks." I smiled lamely, not adding that it didn't sound like it. More was coming; I just needed to be patient.

"Did you call the police and report your car stolen?" Mother asked.

I ignored her question. "Were you able to contact Deuce?" I asked Spoon. "If not, I'll head over to the sheriff's office and file a report now."

Spoon picked up his phone and made a call. "I've got the owner of the SUV sitting in front of me. They're wanting to know if a police report should be filed."

Fab growled softly at the fact that he didn't put it on speaker the way she preferred. We were in complete agreement at that moment, but neither of us had the nerve to suggest it.

Spoon chuckled into the phone.

Both Fab and I bristled, but managed to stay quiet.

"It's parked at AJ's, ready for pickup," Spoon relayed.

I nodded.

"Thanks." He hung up.

"You have to stop involving my husband in things that are dangerous; I'm talking about the types of situations that could get him killed," Mother said. "It's my understanding that this Deuce character is a criminal."

"I tend to forget that we're not invincible. I won't do it again." I understood her anger and would feel the same in her shoes.

"I love Spoon and don't care to be a widow again." Mother sighed. "There's an easy fix to this problem without anyone getting hurt. File a police report, let them investigate, collect the insurance, and go buy another car."

Spoon put his arm across Mother's shoulders, hugging her to his side. "I don't mind helping, but your mother worries over it. None of us wants to live looking over our shoulder."

"Another thing," Mother said. "Doesn't your insurance cover a rental car? If not, fine. Just know that it's another favor my husband has to call in."

Apparently she didn't hear the part where Spoon offered. "I was about to tell him that I've got it covered and thank him for his offer."

"I don't want to be mean…" Mother said, taken aback.

"I get it," I said. "I wouldn't want my husband putting himself in harm's way." I didn't see how a loaner would be that big a deal, since he'd offered in the past, but didn't want to start an argument.

"In our defense," Fab said. "I thought a simple hand-off of the Hummer was better than involving the police. And Spoon, you should get in the habit of saying no."

"On that, we're agreed," Mother said. "I'll be calling with the date of our next family dinner."

"I'd like to schedule a playdate with Mila." I held Mother's stare.

"Do you think that's wise, considering the trouble you attract?"

I didn't bother to defend myself and assure her that it would be a day spent on the beach picking up shells. Next, I'd hear about sunburn. "We're going to have a day of fun, no matter what I have to do to make it happen." I'd kidnapped my niece once before, and the threat hung in the air that I'd do it again.

Her eyebrows shot up. "What would be fun is if you came to my house."

Fab snorted. Mother's eyes shot to her, her lips pursed. I wished I'd been the one to do that.

"We've got a meeting at the office." I stood.

Fab shot to her feet. She'd been ready to bolt five minutes ago when her foot started tapping.

We all hugged, a deafening silence hanging over the room.

"This is my number until I get my phone replaced." I scribbled the number for a burner I'd found in the kitchen drawer on a sticky note and handed it to Mother.

"I can have a flatbed pick up your SUV," Spoon offered.

"I'm going to take Mother's suggestion and file a report with my insurance company; they can have it picked up." I smiled. If anybody had thought about it, they'd know that the opportunity had passed to report said theft, since I'd dragged my feet this long and now couldn't do it without lying, which insurance companies frowned on and prosecuted people over.

I wanted to run back to the car, but somehow managed to walk at a normal pace.

Fab backed out of the driveway. "Who's picking up your car?"

"You're going to drive me to AJ's. I'll get behind the wheel and drive off."

"Is it ever that simple for the two of us?"

"It will be today," I said, with an assurance that was wavering. "Was I wrong to think that asking nicely and offering cash to get the car back was better than giving the name of a man running a criminal operation to the police?"

"Lesson learned—we need a few new connections we can count on when unexpected issues come up."

"I love your ability to problem-solve."

"Speaking of new connections… I've got a surprise for you."

I groaned. "You always forget that I don't like surprises. Not to mention, there's a bunch of them waiting in the wings for me to open from my time away on my honeymoon. Please reassure me that no one died."

Fab had volunteered to morph into me while I was gone and promised there wouldn't be a high body count.

"I thought about shooting a couple of your tenants, but managed to restrain myself." She laughed as she pulled up to the security gate at her business. She waited for it to roll back and drove into the underground parking, where a car I didn't recognize was parked in one of the spaces.

The property housed two warehouse buildings; one converted to office space, the other unused. We got out and trudged up the stairs to the offices of Fab, Didier, and myself. Two businesses housed under one roof—Fab's

Investigation firm and Didier's real estate/design space. I'd just needed a place to spread out since Creole and I were short on space.

Fab opened the door, and the man sitting in front of her desk stood and smiled at her. "Tank," she said, introducing the several hundred pounds of bald, over-six-foot muscle. "Our new lawyer," she added smugly, proud of herself.

Tank and I checked each other out, head to toe.

"Lawyer?" I looked askance at his flowery Hawaiian shorts, button-down short-sleeve shirt, and cowboy boots. What was it with wearing boots in a tropical zone? He wasn't the first person I'd seen who made that choice. "I have a few questions."

"It's my day off. Wasn't about to suit up."

"I need coffee." I turned, and Xander waved at me from where he was sitting at the kitchen table with his laptop. "Didn't see you sitting there." I rounded the corner and set my bag on my desk.

The twenty-year-old was a new hire. He sucked at pickpocketing, and I'd thought, why not hire him to work in the office? He'd turned out to be wicked smart, down on his luck, and primed for a job that kept him out of jail.

"Do you have a notepad handy?" I asked, heading straight to the microwave to whip up another cup of my morning concoction.

Xander whipped out his phone.

"I want you to research crime in Card Sound. In particular, murder. Flag any mentions of body-dumping and any other weird goings on, no matter how insignificant. If any articles mention a Stephan, see what more you can find out." When Help finally came out with the name Stephan, he'd offered up a couple of different last names, so I couldn't be more specific than that. "I don't suppose you have access to police reports? Nothing illegal, mind you."

Xander snorted. "It would all be illegal. The cops frown on unauthorized individuals accessing their files."

"I'll call my other information guy," I said. "I don't want you taking any risks."

"Let me see what I can work out. I've talked to GC a couple of times since you stopped taking his calls; maybe I can work it out to be your go-between."

GC had been our previous information specialist. "In case you've forgotten, that relationship soured when his brother turned Fab's and my names over to a drug dealer."

"I remember. I was there. First time I ever had a gun pointed at me." Xander grimaced. "Back to GC. Somehow, we went from talking about murder to computer programming; he stopped with the dumb twit kid attitude, and we've had some good conversations. In case you run into him and he asks, my name is VP."

I laughed. "You're working that Vice

President title of yours." I finished stirring my coffee and crossed the room to sit in my old spot from before I got my own designated space, dragging a chair into the corner behind Fab's desk. Since I'd opted for a skirt that morning, I wouldn't be putting my feet on the corner of her desk.

"So, Tank, is that the name you use in the courtroom?" I asked. "What's your specialty?"

His brown eyes bored into mine. "Got it covered. If you need more specialization than I can deliver, I'll find the man/woman for the job."

"Do you have a resume?"

"Not on me."

Fab leaned back in her chair, enjoying the byplay, judging by the smirk on her face.

"How about you hit the high points," I said over the rim of my cup.

"I'm already hired."

I sniffed. "If you and I don't have rapport, this working relationship isn't going to work out, since I'm always the one chasing down someone of your ilk. We'll need to get along."

Tank laughed. "In a previous life, I lived in Dallas and practiced criminal law. Not all wins, but no client got the chair. Needing a change of pace, I moved to the Sunshine State, parked my boots, and put out a shingle at one of those pay-by-the-hour office places. Got to look legit. Just so you know, I'll only be taking cases that interest me, and I'm not so full of myself that if a case is totally out of my wheelhouse I won't speak up. I draw the line at faking it."

I squinted at him, a memory tugging at the back of my brain. He returned the look with his massive arms crossed, covering his equally massive chest. "Tank? Your name seems familiar. Why is that?"

Fab laughed. "We met at the jail. Told him to look me up when he got out, and here he is." Ta-da in her tone.

"How is it you weren't disbarred? Doing time and all?"

"It was a case of mistaken identity, and once it was straightened out, I was released to mingle in society." Tank's look dared me to disagree and was meant to make me squirm.

"How fortunate for us."

"There's something we agree on."

I cleared my throat. "Do you mind if we run a background check? I'll need a name."

"You're an unusual bunch. Patrick Cannon. I prefer Tank, unless we're standing in front of a judge, and then it's Mr. Cannon, sir."

"You single? As in no girlfriend and no pending divorce?" The skin above his eyes twitched, which I assume was a surprised look since he had no eyebrows. "My mother likes to meddle in folks' love lives, and I thought it would give her something to do besides be annoyed with me."

"Gee, thanks. But I've got my love life covered."

"You change your mind, bring it up at the next staff meeting. Be prepared. The dictator over there—" I nodded at Fab. "—likes to snap her fingers and watch us come running. I'm not sure if Fab told you, but we're a full-service boutique agency and we're here for all your investigation needs. Our new policy is that everything has to be legal, not even close to the grey line. Any reports you need, VP over there—" I pointed to Xander, who was laughing at me. "—can work his magic and get them delivered. All for the easy payment plan of swapping services."

"Works for me."

Fab ended the meeting by pointing at her watch, a reminder that it was time to go get my Hummer.

Chapter Seven

It seemed odd to be blowing up the Overseas in Fab's Porsche, since we always rode in the Hummer. We headed north, bypassing the turn for Highway One and veering onto the road that cut through the jungle.

"In all the time I've lived here, I've only driven this way once, and that was the other day. I'd hoped not to come back."

"Do you know the latest?" Fab asked breathlessly, staring at the road.

"Probably not. So tell me."

"Help lives out here," she said in a half-whisper, as though we weren't the only two in the car. "If you call it living… No running water would bug me the most. And I think I'd get over my love of candles real quick."

"Focus." I snapped my fingers. "Get back on point."

"His property is being used as a dumping ground for dead bodies." Her tone was filled with excitement. "It's what the guys were doing out here the other day."

"I think Help should find someplace else to live until they catch the killer." I stared out the window, the roadside thick with mangroves.

"What if it turns out to be a serial killer? He can't let the killings continue to go unsolved."

She better not be thinking about getting involved. "Even better reason to move."

"I'm going to offer to set up surveillance cameras. That way, if it happens again, he'll have it on tape who dumped the body. He doesn't want to get charged just because he's convenient."

"That's so sweet of you," I said, not meaning a word. "Have you forgotten he's a cop and has probably had the same thought? Besides, your husband, Didier—" In case she'd forgotten. "—is going to say hell no—all Frenchy and sexy—like he usually does." I cocked my head with a slight smile. "I won't be able to enlist as backup, as Creole will have me locked away somewhere if he gets wind of this idea. So you'd be coming out here by yourself."

"Stop with the dramatics."

I pointed to myself and scrunched up my nose.

"It's not like I'm offering to sit out here and be a target or go tent to tent and question the neighbors. I'd just be coming back with my contractor and overseeing the installation."

"It's actually beautiful and peaceful and green back here, but the more I hear since… yesterday—but it seems longer than that—the more I just want to avoid the area altogether." I leaned my head back against the seat. "It's irksome that Addy's going to skate on stealing my car, but after talking it over with Creole, I'm letting it go and not obsessing on revenge that could go horribly wrong."

"So Creole took it okay? Didier said it was the last time he'd turn the tables and get all sneaky, like I do most of the time. We both ended up apologizing."

"Creole would've preferred that it be handled differently. Addy isn't in the clear yet, as Help will be sharing the information with his boss, and then there's this Deuce character. Help knows the man, no matter how noncommittal he tried to stay."

"I briefly entertained coming back out here and setting fire to her house on a dolly."

I laughed. "You know, those small houses are all the rage, but most people secure them to the ground unless they're moving. In her case, she could pull out in a hot second, but then she'd stick out because I don't think I've seen one on the road before."

"That would make her easy to find."

The drive seemed longer than before. We didn't have the excitement of following the guys and had only the trees for scenery. Between turning off the Overseas and reaching AJ's, we didn't pass more than a handful of cars.

"Here's the plan: drop me off, and I'll get in my SUV and follow you back. I'd appreciate it if you'd keep me in your rearview mirror and stick to the speed limit so I can keep up. Once we hit town, you can leave me in your exhaust fumes."

Fab slowed and pulled to the side of road. Once again, the parking lot was full of cars — they must do stellar marketing to do such good business despite the remoteness of the location. The Hummer was parked in the last space next to the trash area.

I got out and grabbed my purse. "I'll see you back at the office." I walked over to my car, and the first thing that caught my attention was the mismatched set of tires, not a one of them the same size. *An accident waiting to happen.* My heart rate rose as I thought that maybe, if I drove slowly, I could make it home in one piece.

Fab had u-turned and was now hugging the opposite side of the road. She powered down her window. "What's going on?" she yelled.

I waved her off and grabbed the spare set of keys out of my pocket.

Apparently my non-answer wasn't satisfactory. Fab u-turned again and coasted to a stop just ahead of the Hummer.

I opened the door and unleashed a string of filthy words under my breath. The interior had been stripped. Since the dash was missing, along with the steering wheel and ignition lock, it was unclear to me how it got here. Had to be a tow truck, but I bet if I went inside and asked, no one saw a thing.

This was a slap in the face for not turning that criminal, Deuce, in to the police, along with Addy, assuming I could locate the property so she could be found again. Cootie would know, but it probably wouldn't bode well for him if word got out that he'd helped in locating the twosome.

The sound of the kitchen door hitting the wall less than two feet away grabbed my attention. A tall, weasel-faced man squeezed by the car next to mine, headed to a truck that had just pulled up and double-parked. As I stood there, caught in his stare, he tipped a nonexistent hat and put his hands behind his back, coming back with a handgun, which he aimed right at me, taking a shot that tore through the skin on my left biceps.

He needs to spend more time at the range. Without a second's hesitation, I drew and shot back. He dropped to the ground, dead.

His waiting ride squealed off down the road, back towards town.

I fingered my arm. It was a clean shot, straight through, and blood covered my fingertips. I bent over, resting my head on the side of the Hummer and gulping for air.

Fab cut her engine and leaped out, running over and hooking her arm around me. "You better be okay." I nodded. "What the hell was that?" She walked me over to her car and pushed me up against the passenger door.

Over her shoulder, I noticed a few heads

poking out of the entrance, no one thus far willing to venture any farther. "Wild guess— insurance that I'd never mention Deuce's name. He couldn't be sure I'd show; he just got lucky…and then it ran out; if that's him leaking blood on the pavement."

"Cops are on the way," an unfamiliar voice yelled.

A couple of good-sized men, figuring the coast was clear, walked out to where the body lay and bent down for a closer inspection, neither touching him. One fished his camera out of his pocket and got a couple of shots.

"What am I going to tell the cops?" I asked in a small voice. "I need help getting my top off to wrap my arm." The right side was easy, not so much the other side, which burned like the devil.

Fab tied it under my armpit, and I held it in place. "The truth," Fab said in a no-nonsense tone. "Sort of, anyway. He shot first, and you returned fire in self-defense. If it's who we think it is, once they ID him, there won't be much of a sympathy level. Thankfully, he can't hit his target and you can."

I groaned. *Why is it never a clear-cut answer for the two of us?*

"Leave out the part about retrieving the Hummer, unless asked, which I highly doubt that they will."

"More bad news there besides the tires."

Fab turned and checked the car over, her eyes

sparking with anger. "That's an accident waiting to happen."

"It needs to be towed; the inside was stripped. Do not call Spoon. In fact, the only person that needs to know I was shot is Creole, and you can make that call." I leaned into her side.

The first cop car roared up, a second one right behind, and the flashing lights of an ambulance bringing up the rear.

I'd find out later that there were several eyewitnesses. It would have been interesting to know where they all disappeared to until the cops arrived, but at least they stuck around. They all lined up to tell the same story. The dead man—Deuce, as it turned out, who should have sent a thug to do his dirty work—pulled a gun without any provocation that witnesses saw and shot the red-haired woman, who shot back, and he dropped like a sack.

I'd had no clue that getting shot sapped one's strength like that and didn't offer any resistance to being laid out on a stretcher and rolled into the back of the ambulance. On the way to the hospital, I passed out.

I struggled to open my eyes and finally woke up in a hospital bed, my arm stitched and bandaged, Creole's blue eyes staring into mine from where he was sitting by my side. "I'm happy to see your face," I said sleepily.

"Love you," Creole said, brushing my hair back and kissing my cheek. "As soon as the doctor gives the okay, I'm taking you home."

"Are you going to nurse me back to health?" I smiled and traced his cheek. "I feel pretty good right now, no pain anyway, but I imagine that's the drugs talking."

"I have visions of you being the worst patient ever." He kissed me again. "I've informed Fab that she can help keep you entertained and off your feet until you recover."

"Where is Fab?" I asked.

"She's busy organizing your life. It's getting to be a habit with her."

"Did she tell you…?"

"She called Didier and had him tell me. We met the ambulance here at the hospital—she never let it out of her sight—and she gave us a rundown on the day. That Deuce bastard is lucky I can't yank him back from the beyond and kill him again."

I reached up and tugged on his t-shirt, bringing his lips down to mine and kissing him.

The door opened, and a smiling nurse entered. "Ready to go?"

Chapter Eight

A week later, Nurse Creole gave me the okay to socialize and invited Fab, Didier, and Help to dinner. He placed the order for the pizzas and had Didier pick them up.

"I should've let Didier decide what to eat; we could be sipping kale-and-tofu shakes," Creole said, amusement in his eyes.

I bent slightly and made a barfing noise.

Creole shook his finger at me and grinned.

The doorbell rang, which was a rarity. Creole walked outside and opened the gate for our three guests.

Fab was the first across the threshold. "Didier insisted that we announce ourselves like normal people." She rolled her eyes.

Behind her, Didier reached out and pinched her butt. "I saw that." He set the pizza boxes on the counter. "Don't argue. I'm well-versed in your antics."

Fab gave him a moony smile.

I was about to make a retching sound when I caught Creole's frown. "You're no fun," I whined and flicked the lids open, making sure my shrimp topping got ordered.

Creole slapped my fingers and slid the boxes out from under my hand. He took them outside and set them on the table, which he'd set earlier with my supervision. Didier followed with an oval bucket of iced beer and water, and I tossed Help a roll of paper towels. Nothing but the best china and linen for guests.

A knock—actually, more like someone pounding on the back door with their fist—had me stopping in the middle of the kitchen. Fab, who stood on the opposite side of the island, shrugged. It wasn't her for once, but someone was emulating her trick.

"Open up," a male voice shouted.

I recognized the voice and opened the door to my brother, Brad, and his daughter, Mila, who he held in his arms. Mila yelled, "Bonesy,"—her version of bonjour, taught to her by Fab's father—and leaned forward for a kiss.

"How did you get in?" Fab demanded.

"Thanks for the welcome, sister from a different mother." Brad sniffed. "I have a key and codes. And a damn good thing." He started to hand me Mila, who was wiggling for the handoff.

Fab stepped in front of me and took Mila, and they traded Eskimo kisses. At Brad's scowl, she said, "Madison hurt her arm."

"What the hell happened?" Brad eyed the large gauze pad secured with an ace bandage. Good thing he hadn't come yesterday before the dressing wrapped around my arm was removed.

Since we were having guests, I'd traded Creole's shirt for a full skirt that I could pull on and a sleeveless top. Brad's reaction was a reminder to wear sleeves until the wound healed so no one would be the wiser.

Fab entertained Mila with an unrecognizable animal sound, eliciting a laugh from the little girl.

Brad ignored Fab. "Good thing I know how to follow the pizza boxes, since I never get invited to my own sister's house, like ever, for dinner. Wouldn't know a damn thing if I didn't." He whispered the last bit. "I happened to drive by the pizza place as Didier was headed to his car, arms loaded."

I one-arm-hugged him.

He wiped his cheek, where I'd left multiple kisses, on his sleeve. "Mila is the only one allowed to leave spit on my face. And Emerson." He winked.

For once, my brother had a girlfriend that everyone in the family loved. Smart, funny, and not crazy.

"Well…" I hooked my arm through his and led him out to the patio. "As you know, you're just in time for dinner. I hope you're hungry; we'd love for you to stay." We stopped in the doorway, and the guys stopped talking and shifted their attention to Brad. "Look who's here."

"My favorite." Brad eyed the bucket sitting on the side table. He reached out and grabbed a bottle of beer, inspected the label, then popped the top with the opener sitting nearby and sat down.

Fab shimmied around me and sat between Didier and Help. Mila climbed on Didier's lap, and he ripped off paper towels and shoved them in the top of her t-shirt, fashioning a makeshift bib, then put a piece of pizza on a plate for her.

I claimed my seat in the opposite side of the table, between Brad and Creole.

"I'm not going to take it personally that you get an invite and I don't." Brad had zeroed in on Help, and to his credit, his expression remained neutral. "Let me guess, you're the reason my partners have been whispering around the office, leaving me out of discussions. Based on the last time I saw you, I suppose you have another dead-body update of some kind."

Help snorted, conveying, *Not funny.*

Dead silence around the table.

"Just great." Brad sighed. "I suppose all this furtive sneaking about has something to do with the bandage on my sister's arm. Mother must not know, or I'd have gotten a frantic phone call."

"No, she does not, and you're not going to tell her," I said.

"Cool. Bargaining chip." Brad sipped his beer. "Can't wait to hear the details." He helped himself to pizza. "Just know that when Mother does find out, she's going to flip out all over you. Trust me, she *will* hear about it, but not from me."

I gave him the abbreviated version of events.

"After years of being your partner in mischief, I can see through the plot holes." Brad sighed and half-stood, reaching for another beer. "Any reason I'm not to be trusted?" he asked, sitting down.

"You hate drama," I reminded him.

"There's something to be said for ignorance." Didier chuckled. "Don't say you weren't warned."

"Emerson says I need to get over that or I'm going to miss out on all the good stuff where the two of you are concerned. Appears she's right."

Help broke the silence. "I'm having a few issues with a property I own."

Brad perked up, since he was knee-deep in the real estate business, partnering with the rest of the family. The hands-on day-to-day duties fell to him, Creole, and Didier. "Where's it located?"

"Card Sound."

"I'm seeing a pattern here." Brad glanced at me. "Not to be rude, but what's out there?"

"Nothing. One of the reasons for buying. Got a great deal," Help said, conveying that that might not have been a good thing.

Mila laughed, and all eyes cut to her. Didier was teaching her how to cut her pizza with a knife and fork, her hands resting on top of his.

"French boy." I sighed. "Pick it up with your fingers and chow down." I demonstrated.

The guys laughed. Didier ignored me and whispered in French to Mila, who responded with a giggle. I expected her to be multi-lingual before she went to kindergarten.

"You'd have thought this would've been my first question when you walked through the door," I said to Fab, "but what's the update on my SUV?"

"Good news and good news." Fab beamed, a fist-pump implied. "Called Gunz, and he had it picked it up on a flatbed and taken to his auto body guy. Super secret fellow, no name and touted as an artist. He gave it his professional once-over and said it would be a while getting it back." She let an "and" hang in the air before adding, "In the meantime, Gunz set you up with a loaner ride for as long as you need. In return, we track and return cars whose owners are delinquent on payments."

Gunz was a longtime friend of Fab's who would pretty much do anything she asked and she the same for him.

The men growled, which had Help laughing, and Fab ignored them all.

"You make it sound like retrieving an overdue library book," I said. "People aren't generally happy when their cars are repossessed. Not to be the downer at the table, but I've got experience with the role, and I'm not interested in such jobs.

The next person to shoot at me might not be a poor shot."

"You know…" Fab said, breezy smirk firmly in place, "I've got those jobs assigned already."

"Thank goodness for Toady," I sighed. Another associate of Fab's, who would do anything his Frenchie asked. He once saved my life, so I was rather fond of him. "His biggest responsibility is turning out to be keeping us out of trouble with our husbands."

"Both Gunz and Toady sent their regards, along with offers to kill Deuce if he weren't already dead." Fab grinned. "Toady gets extra points for being creative in how he'd dispose of the body."

Toady had once mentioned human snacks for alligators, but I'd never delved into the details.

"I bet if I forego the eat-and-run trick and hang out for the evening, I'll hear all kinds of things. I'm waiting on the dead-body update," Brad reminded us.

Creole and Help exchanged silent communication. Help shrugged. "You trust him. It's fine with me. Since he's got a kid, though, he might not want to get too involved."

Fab lifted Mila off Didier's lap and disappeared inside to wash her hands and face.

I stood and followed them into the house, grabbing some kids' books, a pillow, and a blanket, then went back outside. I threw the blanket over one of the double chaises, which the cats saw as an invitation and jumped up. Fab came back and set Mila down between the cats, and she turned her attention to them, stroking their fur.

Fab sat on the end of the chaise.

"So, you want to be in the know?" Creole picked up a knife. "Put your hand over here." He motioned to Brad. "You have to swear by all that's sacred to keep your mouth shut and seal it with blood."

I grabbed Brad's arm. "No blood at the table."

"You take all the fun out of stuff," Creole said, amusement in his tone. "Any update on the Deuce case?" he asked Help.

"It's officially closed." Help swiped his hands together. "The witnesses' stories were all basically the same. Madison was cooperative and answered all the questions put to her. There's nothing to suggest that they need to dig any deeper." He finished off his beer and held the bottle out to Creole, who exchanged it for another. "By the time the cops ran down an address for Deuce, who'd done his best to remain elusive, the warehouse he'd been using had been cleaned out. No interesting finds."

"Addy Clegg?" I asked.

"Not a trace of her and no sightings. The consensus is that she hightailed it out of the area," Help said.

"I'd like to know how she managed to hit the road hauling a house and not get noticed,"

Didier mused.

"My guess is that she's got it tucked away somewhere nearby, and when she thinks the coast is clear, she'll come out of hiding," Creole said.

I raised my hand. "I've got news—or information anyway—to share. It won't come as a surprise to anyone except Help…unless, of course, someone already told him." I looked around the table at the blank faces.

Creole twirled his finger with a shake of his head.

"Got it—get to the point." I quirked my head. "I had an associate run various reports on Card Sound, unsolved murders, and crime stats in general, and it turns out there's more unsavory activity than one would expect. Before you moved out there," I said to Help, "two other bodies were found near your property. You know what's irksome? No follow-up articles."

"What kinds of reports?" Help demanded.

"Informative ones. One even included photos with nice large X's indicating where the bodies were found. To my untrained eye, they appear spray painted in the dirt. I'd think they'd wash away or get buried under muck, but then, maybe the authorities didn't need them to be permanent." I smiled at his scowl. "I had a copy made for you."

"I don't have any news," Fab spoke up. "But I do have a really great idea." She went on to pitch her security camera plan to Help.

He perked up at that suggestion. "We should talk. If you're agreeable, you'd have to go out and have a look around."

I shuddered at the thought of going back.

"We'll take a team to cover us," Help reassured us.

"That reminds me," Brad said. "A couple of the new businesses at the Boardwalk approached me about adding additional security measures in their storefronts, and I told them you'd be in touch. I'll send you an email tonight with the contact information. I talked you up as being the best."

"Thanks," Fab said. "They're easy jobs, and thus far, not a one of them has ended with me in cuffs."

Didier didn't share the others' smirks.

The guys stood and cleared the table. I settled in the chaise next to Fab, who scooted the sleeping Mila over and rearranged the cats, which garnered a meow, but neither jumped down. She waited until the men were all in the kitchen and out of hearing range to say, "I've got a job tomorrow, and I'd like company for the drive to Miami."

Since I hadn't been anywhere except the sheriff's department in the last couple of days, I didn't moan about the long drive. "Is this a tennis shoe job?" Code for trouble, for which we needed to be prepared to run. "I'm going to need details because it will be impossible to sneak past Creole. He's been working from home, as you know."

"Hmm...this job could be classified as a welfare check on my client's house. He's out of town and wants to make sure that the staff isn't partying it up."

"There must be a catch," I said to her annoyance.

"Didier said the same thing." Fab pouted. "Do I need to remind you that the uber-rich are particular in their needs?"

"Good one." I half-laughed. "I'm in. You tell Creole."

"Tell me what?" Creole demanded from the doorway.

"It's probably about Fab's latest job," Didier said, moving around him and sitting beside her.

Brad handed out beers and water and sat back down at the table with Help.

Fab repeated her story.

"How do I get that kind of cushy gig?" Help asked, downing his beer.

"I should do a ride-along," Brad offered. "Give you tips for where you're going wrong."

I did a double take to make sure that Brad's hair hadn't caught fire from the look Fab sent his way. She continued to glare at him.

Creole and Didier entertained Help and Brad with a few stories about gigs that had ended up with us in cuffs, which my brother was beyond annoyed to be hearing for the first time. I needed to remind him that some of those stories dated back to the days when he was a commercial fisherman and wasn't always in port.

Help wanted to know if we'd ever been hauled off to jail. Creole was the one to tell the story of the time Chief Harder had picked me up from an out-of-the-way jail and given me a ride home after I was falsely accused of kidnapping by a kid who thought he was a comedian. They had a good laugh over that one.

"I want to thank you for the invite," Help said, standing. He fished his phone out of his pocket and handed it to Fab. "Put in your number, and we'll discuss your idea."

I stood and walked inside with him, where I pulled out a drawer in the coffee table and extracted a large manila envelope, handing it to him. "These are the reports I talked about."

"Word has it that you discovered my true identity," Help said.

"I did, and your secret is safe with me." I locked my lips. "Georgia boy, born and bred. Good family. Did well in school, excelled in sports. Soon to be a retired, decorated law enforcement officer. It's a pleasure to know you."

"And you." He kissed my cheek.

Chapter Nine

Fab arrived bright and early the next morning and, to her annoyance, had to park, come inside, and present herself to Creole for a grilling. He'd already informed me that I wouldn't be setting my toes outside the house until he knew what Fab's case entailed.

Creole had questioned her like a perp with a long rap sheet he had under his personal microscope, wanting details of this new job. He hung over her shoulder as she checked her phone and wrote down the client's name and address. Out of patience, Fab had flounced out of the house.

"A gangster-mobile," I said, my voice full of awe, as I followed Fab out to the driveway and circled the black Escalade with limo-tinted windows. I didn't touch, not wanting to leave fingerprints. Fab would flip, and we'd have to stop and have it re-detailed.

Creole held the door while I slid into the passenger seat, then leaned in and kissed me.

"Stay out of trouble," I said, and winked at him.

"Same to you." He narrowed his eyes. "Any problems, deviation in plans, anything, you call. Got it?" He crossed his arms and glared at Fab.

I nodded, and he closed the door. Fab hit the locks and gunned the engine, roaring down the block and out to the main highway.

"Your husband is lucky I didn't shoot him for being annoying," Fab grumbled as she flew down the highway, hopping on the turnpike going north.

Lifting the coffee cup from the holder, I was pleased to find it was still hot and smelled delicious. "Thank you. This is a nice surprise." I took a sip and leaned back with a satisfied sigh.

"I knew you'd want something to drink."

Not wanting her to go back to complaining about Creole's high-handedness, I derailed her, changing the tenor of the conversation by oohing over my new ride. "Maybe I should drive."

Fat chance, she communicated without voicing the words.

I sniffed the air and leaned over, looking at the odometer. "It smells new, but it isn't. I wasn't expecting anything so nice."

"I didn't have a specific request. Gunz made the choice. If you think I'm particular about my rides, he's even worse."

"So where are we going?" I asked as we flew up the Overseas. "When you were questioned by Creole, I noticed you were a bit vague on the details. He noticed too, but got tired of grilling you, so he relented when you forked over the address."

"Star Island."

"You're reaping the rewards of me being cooped up. I'm not going to complain, but you'll need to feed me and keep me in drink." I slurped the last of my coffee. Fab had ordered the extra-large caramel, whipped but no cherries. I didn't ask because I knew they didn't stock them, and she didn't think I was the least bit funny. ("No one puts cherries in their coffee.") I knew that but liked to prank her. "Reassure me that you have codes and keys and there will be no breaking and entering."

"I promise. No crimes. At least, not today. I've got the code and will get the key when we get there. Apparently, this job is a little more involved than Mr. Bostwick originally let on, and he went into more detail when he called this morning. The housekeeper will be there, but she won't be staying, as she has a family emergency or something. Don't let me forget—Mr. Bostwick wants a call while I'm still at the property."

Fab flew up the Interstate to the Causeway, making record time thanks to light traffic, then over to Star Island. She pulled up to a security gate and, true to her word, entered a code, and the gates opened.

I looked in the side mirror and didn't see any flashing lights. So far so good.

Fab drove up the long brick driveway, circled

the fountain, and pulled up opposite a yellow Mediterranean two-story mansion, complete with a six-car garage with living quarters on the second level.

If I had to guess, I'd say it was a paltry twenty thousand square feet, give or take a few feet. "How much do you suppose this is worth?" I peered up at the arched windows and counted. Fourteen, to be exact.

"I'd guesstimate forty-five million."

"Is this one of the cheaper casas on the island?" I asked, and stared out at the tropical landscaping; not a weed or dead flower in sight.

"If you're looking for a bargain, this wouldn't be the area," Fab said in her snooty tone, then laughed at herself. "Out." She pointed. "Be on your best behavior and don't touch anything."

"Like I'd leave my fingerprints behind." I got out and looked down at my tennis shoe-clad feet. Knowing Fab's jobs, I'd come prepared and now wished I had on the cute sandals I'd stuffed in my bag. But the job wasn't over yet, so maybe I'd made the right choice after all.

I followed Fab up the four steps to the front door. She rang the bell. Another surprise. I'd been certain that a lockpick would be involved, even though she'd promised Didier and Creole that wouldn't be the case.

The door flew open and a harried middle-aged woman stood on the threshold, one hand gripping a leash, from the end of which a rodent masquerading as a German Shepard stared with squinty eyes at the two of us. It resembled a guinea pig on steroids.

Already behind Fab, I stepped back, ready to make a run for it and also to ensure I didn't take a tumble down the steps.

"Mrs. Merceau? I'm Marlin, the head housekeeper." Fab nodded, engaged in a stare-down with the rodent. The woman didn't bother with a handshake and instead, thrust the leash at her. "King needs to go for a walk." Her tone of authority matched anything Fab could dish out. She produced plastic bags from the pocket of her black A-line tent-style dress and shoved them at Fab.

Fab side-stepped her, shaking off the leash. "What's going on?" she demanded.

Marlin appeared confused. "Your responsibilities include walking King. It's quite the mess if it gets on the floor, and *you* have to clean it up."

The rodent squatted.

"For heaven's sake," Marlin screeched and dragged the animal over to the planter that wrapped around the fountain. "Mr. Bostwick doesn't like King using this area. He insists that King be walked and do his business where it can be bagged and thrown in the trash."

Fab and I exchanged looks, both in the same state of, *what's going on here?*

"What exactly is that animal?" I asked.

"It's a capybara. I was rather shocked at first, and I'll admit it took some getting used to, since I figured that when the Bostwicks mentioned getting a pet, it would be a cat or dog. But then it was explained to me that wealthy people enjoy more exotic animals."

Fab followed Marlin halfway to the planter. "I'm here to check on the house and leave."

"You can't leave King by himself—ever," the maid said, horrified. "Mr. Bostwick left written instructions for you in the kitchen, and they detail everything that you'll need to do, hourly and daily."

"This is a house-sitting gig?" I asked. "Mr. Bostwick expects Mrs. Merceau to stay here with King until he returns?"

"Uh, yes." Marlin shook her head slightly, conveying we were both dimwits. "Knowing Mr. Bostwick and how exacting he can be, I'm certain he expressed his wishes in precise terms."

I looked at the horror on Fab's face, the housekeeper sizing her up as not up to Mr. Bostwick's usual standards, and King uprooting a couple of plants to cover his business, and burst out laughing. Fab's glare only made me laugh harder. The only rational thought I had was getting pictures.

It wasn't until Fab grabbed the back of my shirt and gave me a hard shake that I knew she'd come up behind me. "You are the worst friend," she hissed. "What. Am I. Going to do?" Steam rolling out of her ears, she hadn't seen the humor yet. If ever.

I took a couple of deep breaths to get ahold of myself and approached Marlin. "I'm Madison," I introduced myself. "We seem to have a slight problem in that Mr. Bostwick wasn't forthcoming on the details of the job."

"Are you saying he lied?"

"I'm suggesting more of a miscommunication. So maybe you could explain what the job entails." I smiled at her.

"Have you never house-sat before?" Marlin's tone of snootiness rivaled Fab's. "I cannot give up my vacation time. My niece is getting married in New York, and I requested the time off months ago. It's not like I can reschedule."

"We're going to work this out so that everyone's happy," I reassured her. How I wasn't sure. "Just show me what's expected." I motioned for Fab to follow. She pulled her phone out of her pocket and followed, slow as a snail, as I scurried to catch up to Marlin, who'd hightailed it into the kitchen, which was the size of my house. I paused briefly to admire not only the square footage but the high-end finishes, stainless appliances, and view of the pool. There was an island in the middle of the room that seated no one, since it contained a cooktop, grill, and double sinks. On it lay a two-page single-spaced checklist. The first column itemized the tasks—which included feeding, walking, and cleaning up after the dog rodent—in order of importance. In addition, there was a fish tank somewhere in the house, along with the responsibility of keeping the indoor plants alive, plus supervision of the gardeners and pool crew, and at the bottom, "Clean up after yourself." The other columns gave the time for expected completion of each task and room for notes, each item to be checked off and initialed.

Marlin laid a set of keys down in front of me. "Do you have any questions? I can't be late for my flight." Without waiting for an answer, she ran to the corner, grabbed her suitcase, and rolled it out the side door.

"Get back here," Fab roared and started after her.

I grabbed her shirt and brought her to a stop before she could get out the door, then walked her back to the island. "What are you going to do? Shoot her? You'd still have to take care of the rodent."

"I was going to bribe her." She whined at the sound of the engine roaring out of the driveway. "You've seen one family wedding, you've seen them all."

"Did you call Mr. Bostwick?" I wanted to laugh, but had to stay calm in the face of Fab's agitation.

"Bostwick had the effrontery to admit to tricking me," Fab sputtered. "He blathered on about not being able to find anyone suitable to care for King and then he thought of me. Me? Why the heck me?" The utter seriousness of the situation hardened her eyes. "He has faith I'll do a good job."

What rubbish!

"Then the… man… said I could use him as a reference if I wanted to expand my services. I refrained from asking him if he was senile and instead tried to impress upon him that I only had cat rapport. He didn't need to know that it was only with your cats, since he doesn't know you."

"How did you leave it?"

She glared at the weasel lying on the kitchen floor eyeing us suspiciously. "He didn't listen to a word and overrode me, saying that with the fees I charge, I could get off my high horse and do a damn good job. And he had the nerve to say he expected a reduced rate."

"Did you mention that you have a husband and you're newlyweds?" Of sorts. I wasn't certain how long one could classify one's self as such, but the two were deep in wedded bliss, and Didier wasn't going to stand for even one night away from his wife.

"Oh yeah. He gave permission for Didier to spend the night. But we're to stay clear of the master." Fab banged her head on my shoulder. "What do I do?"

"First, let's poke around in the refrigerator and find something cold to drink. I'd prefer alcohol, but I think we need to keep a clear head."

We opted for bottled water, since that was our only choice, took it into the adjoining dining room, and sat at a glass table that could easily seat twelve. It only had four chairs—where the rest were was a mystery.

Chapter Ten

Before leaving the kitchen, I had grabbed the list and shoved it across the table for Fab to peruse. "The way I see it, the biggest obstacle is that." I pointed to King, who had followed us and now lay in the doorway, blocking the entry and eyeing us in a way that suggested neither of us lived up to his expectations as caregivers. "Most of this list is manageable." Fab shoved it back at me with barely a glance. "The other hurdle is that of Mr. Bostwick expecting you to spend the night for…how long?"

"Ten days."

"I shook my head. "There are also fish on this list, which will need to be fed. I'm thinking that's nothing more than sprinkling food in the tank. It's not like they need to be walked or anything."

"My first inclination is to run out the door, just like the housekeeper, except that…" Fab flicked her finger at King. "…would die and so would the fish and plants. I wouldn't do that to the animals. Heaven forbid, anything were to happen to the rodent. Bostwick would come after me. Of that I'm certain, and he has the resources to do it."

"A real animal lover doesn't leave town without knowing said animals are going to be taken care of. This job pay your usual fee?" I ask.

Fab's faced flushed with anger. "Thinking this was just a trip over and back, I let him pay in advance. Which he did willingly, knowing full well he was screwing me. He must have had a good laugh at my stupidity. That occurred to me halfway through the call, and I brought up the increase in my fees and said that if the additional payment didn't arrive by messenger in the morning, I'd walk away." She whooshed out a sigh. "I reiterated the total because, frankly, I don't trust him, but I stopped short of saying that to him."

"Take a deep breath. I've got an idea…maybe." I retrieved my new phone out of the pocket of my skirt. Fab had purchased twins while I was at home recuperating. Thankfully, it was almost identical to my old one and the learning curve was minimal. I scrolled through a pet care website, looking for information on what we were dealing with. "The capybara is classified as a rodent and pretty much gets the same care as a dog. They make for good house pets and a great way for one rich person to impress another. Since they're socializers, they shouldn't be raised as only pets."

Fab groaned. "Almost forgot, or I just wanted to. Since Bostwick already had me by the shorts, he added to the misery by throwing in that a playmate/new friend is being delivered this week."

"Bostwick is a gigantic turd."

"Madison, really."

"Yes, Mother, I'll behave. Why doesn't Bostwick want to be here to welcome the new addition? I would if it were my new pet. What's so important, something life or death?"

"R&R in Bali, resting up from his harried life as a billionaire on one of those hammocks over the water." Fab snorted. "We're to give rodent number two a special welcome."

"Any more surprises?" I rested my forehead against the table and laughed.

"I hate you."

"I would too." I worked to choke back the laughter. "Someday…you'll look back on this and laugh."

"If you're done amusing yourself at my expense, we need to come up with a plan that doesn't involve me *pet-sitting*." She spat out the last two words.

"Who do we know that has animal rapport?" I mused.

"You. I know you." She slapped the table. "Toady." She picked up her phone.

I slapped her hand down. "Hold on. Let's think this through. Toady is a good choice, except he won't show well should the neighbors see him. Plus, Bostwick will be shocked if he comes home early, but I'm thinking you'll never take another call from him anyway."

"The heck with Bostwick."

"Then walk. Leave the animal to fend for itself and tell Bostwick to get his behind back here."

"Even if I was willing to do that, you wouldn't let me. King doesn't deserve to starve to death because of his selfish owner. So what's Plan B?" Fab laid her head on the table.

I picked up my phone and, although surprised, was pleased to see that Fab had gotten Xander to enter my contacts. He'd run a trace on my old phone and didn't get a signal—probably died in the wilderness. "Interested in a side job that pays *really* well?" I asked our assistant when he answered, then put him on speaker.

"Oh heck yeah," Xander said excitedly. "What's the catch?"

"There's a raft-load of them, but I'll start with the good one first. Mansion-sitting in Miami for ten days."

"Sounds like I need to ask for hardship pay," Xander joked.

"The most important question is do you have animal rapport?"

"I don't know jack about animals. I wasn't allowed to have any growing up."

"How about learning on the job?" I asked hopefully.

"Okay…" he said hesitantly.

I gave him the details and had him look up capybara while I waited so he could see what the job would entail.

"It says here, these cap-things eat their own poop. So no cleanup there."

I lowered my head and laughed.

Fab cuffed me. "Grow up, you two."

"You could open the door and let him back into the wild," Xander suggested.

"That's not helpful," Fab snapped. "You think you can do the job or not?"

"If you two show me what to do, I'm sure I can handle it."

Fab and I exchanged *us?* looks.

"Toady's here, waiting on Frenchie," Xander informed us.

Fab held out her hand, which I pushed away.

"Toady, huh?" My mind was spinning with thoughts of Plan C. "I was wondering how I was going to get you out here, and he might be the answer to that problem. Plus, he's got wild animal rapport. He'd be perfect to coach you in the care of King." I raised an eyebrow at Fab, who nodded. At this point, she'd do anything to keep from being stuck here. "Put him on." I handed the phone to Fab.

Fab explained her predicament.

"What a hole and a half," Toady said angrily. "Don't you worry, Frenchie. Give me a couple of hours to get VP out there. He'll need to stop by his place, get some clothes, and tell his roommate he'll be out of town for a few days and that he didn't flake and skip."

I knew there was never a chance Toady would refuse Fab help. She ended the call and handed me the phone. I texted the address to Xander and Toady.

King stood, stretched, and headed to the back door. I craned my neck and watched him go, then got up and chased after him, opening the door to the backyard. "Is the front gate closed?" I yelled over my shoulder. The last thing I wanted was for King to go on the run and the two of us have to chase him down.

"Yes," Fab called back.

I leaned against the doorframe and waited on King, who wasn't in a hurry to come back inside. After scratching around, he laid down on the lawn and rolled around.

Fab rested her head on her arms and kept her eyes closed. I knew she wasn't asleep. It was only an attempt at avoidance and hoping that nothing else would go wrong.

I went in search of the fish and found a tank built into the wall of a game room. More instructions taped to the front. I left them there, flinching as I read that when it came to feeding time, it would be with the smaller fish from the tank below. I balked when it came to feeding big fish with smaller ones. Good thing it wasn't my job, or I'd go to the pet store and get the flakes in a can I remembered from my goldfish-owning days as a kid.

Fab had moved into the living room and

stretched out on one of the sofas, clutching a pillow to her middle. I followed suit and took out my phone, texting Creole that it would be a while.

Both of us jumped when the house phone rang. The caller ID said, "gatehouse."

Fab sat up. "I have no clue how to open the gate," she said, looking out the window. She slid her shoes back on and went out the front to meet Toady at the gate. True to his word, it'd taken the man two hours to arrive at the house.

I opened the back door and spotted King asleep where I'd last seen him. "Hey King. Want to come in?"

He jumped up and beelined for the door. I stood back until he passed me. He prowled around the room, sniffing the furniture, before heading into the front entry, where Toady and Xander were standing.

Both men waved, but the focus was on King, who skidded to a halt and checked out the newest visitors, then made his way slowly over to Toady, who held out his hand. The rodent sniffed him and rubbed his furry face on his jeans. Toady gave Xander a quick lesson in how to befriend the animal, and it wasn't long before King snorted his approval.

"Let's take King out back," Toady suggested. Once back on the lawn, King ran around in circles.

I pulled Xander aside and motioned for him to

follow me back inside, where I showed him the checklists in the kitchen and game room. After we were done, Fab and Toady came back inside, and Fab went over her own list of instructions.

"Don't worry about Xander," Toady said. "I'm not leaving until he's comfortable being left alone here. I can also check on him every day."

"Just make sure King doesn't croak." Fab thanked them both and told them to make themselves at home, and if they needed anything to call, no matter what time.

"He's got a playmate arriving in the next day or two," I said, a note of apology in my tone.

"I only learned that tidbit after we got here," Fab said in exasperation and told them what she knew about the new rodent, which was very little.

I made the call-me sign to Xander, and he nodded.

"Don't worry about Xander; he'll do fine. No need to worry about King either," Toady reassured us.

We walked out the front, and Fab breathed in a lungful of fresh air. "Could Bostwick have hired someone more ill-equipped to handle an animal than me? He didn't so much size me up as being good with animals as being able to handle this crisis, and in that, I guess he was right. But how I'd like to fill his backside with bullets."

"Not until after you get paid," I said.

"If Bostwick thinks he's going to stiff me, he'd better think again. I'll send Toady to collect."

Chapter Eleven

It took a couple of days to set up the employee meeting at Jake's and accommodate everyone's schedule so no one could complain about other commitments. I was anxious to meet the new hires. It took grit to work at the bar, what with the divergent personalities that came through the door, and the patrons were quick to exploit anyone who couldn't hold their ground. As it turned out, both new bartenders quit before the meet and greet. However, the vacancies were quickly filled by members of Cook's family, which is where I'd have started in the first place.

Fab had dumped the Bostwick drama in my lap, shuddering at the mere mention of his name. When I told Creole about it, he'd laughed his head off. Toady turned out to be the saving grace, assuring me that he wouldn't let the kid get in over his head. In return, I assured him that his usual fees would be paid and brushed aside his offer to take a pay cut for the job, reminding him that Bostwick would be paying.

At my direction, the front door of the bar was locked and the usual suspects gathered out on the deck. I ordered a bucket of cold drinks and turned on the ceiling fans and lights in the outside space.

"Grab a chair," I directed.

To my surprise, Cook had decided to attend. He came out with a tray in hand, followed by three of his relations in their thirties, and set a draft beer and a side of bacon in front of me. I stared at it, not sure what to say. "Yum." I looked at Fab, who sat opposite me. She shrugged.

"It's a hot seller. Who doesn't like bacon?" Kelpie harrumphed, not happy with my lackluster response.

Yeah, who?

"A better idea would've been to wrap it around the outside of the glass. But…" Kelpie engaged in a stare-down with Cook. "We don't have the right kind of glasses, and it's too much work."

Cook mumbled under his breath—something about crazy—and she mimicked him.

Welcome back!

I was afraid to ask if they'd come up with any more bright ideas while I was gone, and had to remind myself what this meeting was about. I went down a short list of issues and barely got any feedback. "Anything else I should know about?"

"Live music starts this weekend," Doodad announced. "Got to compete with the other bars in town. We've got the next two weeks booked, so be on the lookout."

Doodad—aka Charles Wingate III, a veteran of the Civil War…the history of it, anyway—had been a great find. I'd found him spouting facts to tourists for a few bucks and hired him to bartend. Not long after, he'd pitched himself for the manager job.

"Maybe we just need a better jukebox; one that sounds like live music." No one laughed; they thought I'd lost my mind. "Who did you hire?"

All eyes shot to Fab.

That caught me by surprise. It was her idea and she hadn't shared?

"I hired *The Cloggers*," Fab said, a dare-you-to-disagree look on her face.

I shook my head. "As in Dutch shoes dancing around the floor?" No response. "Not a one of you remembered that this is a tropical bar?"

"They demonstrated it for us, and it can be done to Jimmy Buffet," Fab said.

Kelpie hummed Margaritaville off-key and stomped her feet.

"For the following week, we booked *Rednecks*," Doodad said with a smirk. "Both groups put on a floor show in addition to the music."

"There must have been tequila in my morning coffee and I didn't notice it." I rubbed the back of my neck. "We have two weeks of questionable entertainment, and if we still have customers afterwards, then what?"

"Hold your water, Bossaroo," Kelpie said.

"Once word gets out, the entertainers will come to us."

"I'm going to go out on a limb and assume you've checked these groups out and the police haven't been called to their prior gigs," I said.

Once again, all eyes shot to Fab.

"They can't be held responsible for what other people do," Fab snapped. I groaned. "We all agreed that a gunfight would bring in the crowds." At my look of horror, she added, "But I reluctantly squashed that idea and went with the next best thing." She pointed inside and up at the ceiling.

"I almost forgot." I craned my head for a better look at the brightly painted red spots where, presumably, bullets had entered. "Did it occur to anyone that people might come in wanting to shoot up the ceiling, just so they could get their mark of infamy? What if someone dies?"

"Don't borrow trouble, as my granny says," Kelpie said with an eyeroll.

"The ceiling is getting re-painted." I continued, despite Kelpie's groan, "Last chance for any updates."

"We now have daily specials," Cook said. "Hence the chalkboard." He pointed over his shoulder. "That was Prissy's idea." He glared at Kelpie. "She 'didn't want to repeat them every ten seconds' were her words."

"Another idea of yours?" I asked Fab. "You

were busy being me."

"How do you expect to raise revenue without the occasional gimmick?" Fab asked, "duh" in her tone.

"I've done my part," Cook said with a sneaky smile that suggested he'd been hanging around Fab too long. "We now serve fried iguana with fresh vegetables."

Lizard? That took a moment to sink in, and then I made a barfing noise.

Disapproving eyes turned on me.

"It tastes like chicken," Cook defended.

"That's a tired excuse, and one that people use when they don't know what the heck else to say," I said. "You have a purveyor for lizard?"

"Got a trapper that sells them direct. I buy frozen."

"It's the hottest delicacy right now," Fab said, as though I should know.

"That's swell." *Note to self: make sure I know what I'm ordering.*

Doodad cleared his throat. "There is one last item. I don't want you hearing it from Kevin after he's put his 'sky is falling' slant on it. We had a male customer slump over in his chair and fall to the floor."

"Good thing he wasn't sitting on a barstool," Kelpie said.

Doodad poked her in the back. "He had to be rushed to the hospital and have his stomach pumped. Wife put some concoction in his drink that was supposed to kill him, which it didn't. Heard she confessed and they're getting a divorce."

"Don't forget the happy ending," Kelpie said.

"Yeah, hum, we put it out that the guy died, which he didn't," he assured me.

"That's happy how?" I asked.

"Cha-ching." Kelpie shook her torso.

"As you know," I said, "I got married, and the husband hates these kinds of antics, although he might try the beer. Anyway… I'm not going to forbid these activities outright, just keep them toned down and stop short of the cops being called in." I banged my glass of beer on the table, almost spilling it. "Meeting adjourned."

Kelpie was the only who didn't go back to work. "Do you have a minute?" she asked. "Can we talk in private? It's not about me." She eyed Fab, who was staring back at her.

"Ignore her." I nodded towards Fab. "She'll find out anyway; she'll skulk around until she ferrets it out."

Kelpie got up, closed the door, and reclaimed her seat. "As you know, Doodad's house was blown down by a hurricane and he's been living in what amounts to a storage shed. I was thinking you could help him."

"That was a long time ago," I said, thinking back to the last major one that blew through, leaving a lot of damage in its wake. "I'd have thought the insurance company would've paid off by now. I know he had insurance because I asked."

"Insurance danced him around, insisting that the claim didn't match their description of the property, and eventually told him to flip off and they'd see him in court."

"I'm supposed to pretend I got this information how? Since I'm making the leap that you don't want to be outed?"

"You'll think of something," Kelpie said with assurance.

Fab laughed.

"I suppose I will. Give me a couple of days."

Chapter Twelve

It took several days of back-and-forth phone calls between Help, Fab, and her security guy — who, as it turned out, had a name: Monty Round — to get the job in Card Sound green-lighted. Now Monty was ready to check out the area and make his recommendations.

I wanted to beg off but didn't. When I'd announced our plans to Creole the previous night, he'd flipped, grabbed his phone, and stomped outside, growling, "Oh hell no."

I'd hoped that, by the end of the conversation, Fab and I would have bodyguards that had orders not to leave our side.

The next morning, Fab didn't endear herself to Creole by sitting outside the house, honking frantically. Creole grumbled under his breath as he stomped across the room. Hand on the knob, he turned and grouched, "You need to confiscate the car keys from her, and in the future, you determine who drives. Have you even driven it yet?"

I flashed him an *are you crazy?* look.

He started outside, then stopped and turned around, closing the distance between us. "You ready?" At my nod, he picked up my bag and slid it over my shoulder, then led me out.

"You draw the short card and get guard duty?" I asked.

"I volunteered." He rewarded me with a sinister grin.

Fab was designated driver, no matter who was in the car. Occasionally, Fab and Creole argued over the point, but most times, like Didier, he didn't care. He did reserve the right to annoy her on occasion.

Creole twirled his finger for her to roll down the window, and when she did, he said, "Stick to the speed limit." He opened the back door, helped me in, and slid in after me.

"Good morning," I said cheerfully to Fab and Didier.

Whatever Fab said, Didier looked at her and laughed. Once she cleared the security gate, she squealed the tires all the way to the main highway.

"Keep it up," Creole yelled, "and I'll be the one driving."

Fab actually eased off the gas.

Didier's eyes shone with amusement; he was enjoying the show. "We're meeting Monty at the Bakery Café. He's swinging by after he finishes up another job. I suggest we grab some breakfast."

"Sounds good," Creole said.

The rest of the drive was uneventful. Fab

pulled into the parking lot, looped around, and exited to the street, parking in front.

"You checking faces against wanted posters?" Creole asked, getting out. He reached in and scooped me up, kissing me before setting me on my feet. He felt up my back, finding my gun. "I told Didier not to forget his firearm. I didn't tell you, figuring you wouldn't leave it behind."

Fab waved to our favorite waiter and pointed to the end table…as though he didn't know.

"Too bad there isn't some nice couple occupying our spot so Fab can demand they move or risk a bullet in the backside," I said, which got laughs from the guys and earned me a glare from Fab.

The waiter took our order and started back down the sidewalk, where Brad intercepted him, adding his own order. "Put it on their check." He pointed with a cheeky grin, then closed the distance and jerked a chair across the concrete. "Look what we have here, and once again, no invite."

"Where's Mila?" I asked.

"Enrolled her in preschool three days a week." Brad leaned sideways and kissed my cheek.

"Bet Mother flipped over that one." I grimaced. "Trying to get on Mila's social calendar is already difficult, and now school."

Mother was the real culprit. She'd groaned and complained about having no grandchildren; then, starting with Liam and now Mila, she hogged their time. Liam was Brad's ex's son, who the family had adopted. He'd opted to go to the University of Miami to stay close.

"My daughter needs to have friends that are under the age of twenty," Brad said, taking a drink of the coffee that'd just arrived. "Speaking of Mother, expect a call. She's planning a family dinner."

"You eat here often?" I asked.

"On occasion. I usually hit the drive-thru, but I saw you pull up and thought, why not crash the party?"

"You're getting good at that," Creole said with amusement.

"Thanks," Brad said without shame. "Where's your dead-body updater?"

"We're on our way to pay him a visit," Didier said.

Fab gave him the evil eye.

"What?" Didier asked, surprised. "I was supposed to lie? Why?"

Brad blew it off. "No need to explain. Just so happens I've got plenty of free time today, since the other partners will be late getting to the office, so I'll ride along. Thanks for inviting me."

"You're getting worse than Mother," I said.

"Or it could be said I learned from the best. And that bit of pushiness doesn't come close to some of Mother's antics."

The waiter arrived with our breakfast and some much-needed coffee refills.

After he left, Brad looked around the table, asking, "Anyone want to fill me in on today's adventure?"

Fab spoke up and gave the briefest account possible of what we'd be doing on our little trip out of town.

"You have a firearm?" Creole asked Brad.

"Locked in the car."

"I suggest that you accessorize, since you're planning to come with us," I said.

Fab tapped her watch. "Eat up. Monty's going to be here any minute, and he doesn't like to be kept waiting."

A few minutes later, a service truck pulled up parallel to the curb, and the man behind the wheel leaned over and rolled down the passenger window. Lifting a bullhorn, he shouted, "Time's a-wasting."

"He has a bullhorn, and we don't." All eyes shot to me. I held up my hands in defense. "They come in handy." We used to have one, but it had disappeared when the Hummer was stolen.

We piled into the Escalade, and Fab pulled around the truck and led the way out of town.

Granted, there was nothing to look at save for trees and marshes, but it was beautiful and peaceful. Occasionally, a car passed us.

Creole scooted up and hung his head between the seats. "Slow down," he said to Fab. "The turn-in is up ahead. There's a slight dip, and then gravel up to his trailer. You can gauge it by the large house sitting behind the trees on the opposite side of the road."

"Coming up on the right is the restaurant where I got shot," I said.

"*Nobody* goes wandering off on their own," Creole said sternly. "Got it?"

We all murmured our agreement.

Fab slowed to a crawl and found the turn-in with the help of Creole tapping her shoulder. Monty's truck turned behind her and followed us into the clearing, where Help stood outside his Winnebago, waving us forward.

Everyone got out and exchanged hellos. Fab, Monty, and Help poked around and conferred on security plans and what would go where in the area. Fab had brought along photos of where the previous bodies had been found, in hopes that Help might recognize that particular area.

The guys split up and roamed the property on their own while I leaned against the Escalade, moving my Glock to the front of my waistband.

Fab and Monty conferred over plans, Monty scribbling on his notepad, and quickly made decisions, Help agreeing to what they decided. Monty waved and left.

"He'll be back at the end of the week," Fab said as she and Help walked over to where I was standing.

Help motioned for the guys to come over. "I've got an update on the Addy woman. Figured out where she was living and checked out the spot, then went and introduced myself to Cootie, who was taken off guard by my sudden appearance. I dropped your name and he loosened up, figuring I wasn't an accomplice of Addy's. He verified that she'd hotfooted it out of here within hours of the shooting. A truck showed up, hooked up her house, and hit the highway in the direction of the bridge. There's plenty of wilderness out that way."

I raised my hand in front of my face.

"Yes, Ms. Madison?" Help acknowledged in an amused tone.

"Would you show us the way to Addy's? A look around might yield some information. And afterwards, I'd like to stop and see Cootie. Give him one of my cards."

Eyebrows shot up at that.

"This isn't news," I defended myself. "You know I promised to do something nice as payback. If it weren't for Cootie, who knows how the day would've ended. We could still be out here, slogging through the bushes, trying to get home. I have no doubt that Addy would've tracked us down. She had the advantage of knowing the terrain."

"Is it too early for a little swig of moonshine?" Brad asked.

"You first." Didier laughed. "You survive, and I *still* won't try it."

Heads nodded in agreement.

"Do you want to go the scenic way, through

the underbrush?" Help flourished his hand. "Or the pussy route and drive?"

"I'll go scenic." I brushed my hands over my jeans, which I'd paired with a long-sleeved top. I came prepared for bush-crawling.

"No," Creole said emphatically. "Have you forgotten your arm's still sore? You'll get hurt, scratched up or bit—"

"I want to do this." He knew that I still had the occasional bad dream about that day.

Brad put his arm around me, looking down at me. "You did it. I want to do it."

"Sometimes we're still kids." I half-laughed.

Brad hugged me hard.

"It won't be so bad," Help said. "You won't be getting on your hands and knees. Once I found out the old broad had skipped, I used a machete to chop a crude path so I could keep an eye on comings and goings without being spotted."

"I'm driving," Fab declared.

"Pull in at the curve sign," Help directed. "I got a friend who works road crew to let me have one. It's a great marker without being obvious."

Fab and Didier got in the Escalade and headed out.

The rest of us hit the bushes, Help in the lead, then Creole, me, and Brad. I felt safe surrounded by several hundred pounds of muscle. We skinnied along the path, brushing limbs out of the way, but it wasn't as dense as before. Soon, we stepped out into the clearing where the small house on wheels had been parked and found it empty, just like Help had said. Fab parked in the same place as before, and she and Didier walked around as she pointed and gave a mini-tour of what had gone down that day.

Brad was poking around on his own. After a minute, he called, "Hold on a second. You two cops get over here."

That left me out, so I hung back. "Fab's going to be mad she missed something."

"No, I'm not," Fab grouched from behind me, phone in hand, always ready to take pictures.

Brad pointed to an oversized, stained burlap bag. In fact, it was two that had been pulled together to meet in the middle and tied with rope. It was tucked in the underbrush and crawling with bugs.

Help snapped off a branch and poked it gently. "This doesn't look good. Let's hope I don't need to get the coroner out here again." He pulled a knife from his back pocket, bent down, and sliced the bag open. He jumped back and covered his nose. "The coroner." He stepped away. "It's, uh…badly decomposed."

I backed up to the far side of the car, the farther away the better.

Help pulled his phone out and called in the discovery.

It was a half-hour before a cop car arrived. Help stood out on the road and flagged him down. The officer got out and shook hands with

Help, who proceeded to fill him in and lead him to where the surprise had been found.

"What's going on?" Cootie had snuck up behind me and was standing there, partially concealed by the bushes.

I squealed, which caught Brad's attention, and he hurried over. I made the introductions and told Cootie about the find.

The man grimaced. "Don't want the Sound to get a reputation as a dumping ground." He inched back towards the mangroves. "Don't tell anyone about me. Authorities will send someone to roust me out. Homesteading's banned; you've got to produce a deed. Good luck getting one of those. Cha-ching."

I opened the car door and reached in my tote, pulling out a business card and handing it to the man. "Stay in touch. Anytime you come to town, free meal at Jake's. Password is Madison."

"Once I get my ride fixed, I'll do that," Cootie said.

"That reminds me. I set it up for three days from now. Noon at AJ's. Be there. A friend, Toady, is coming out with a mechanic to see what it'll take to get your truck fixed. He's easy to identify: he's only got one tooth. It's gold, front and center."

"I don't—" Cootie sputtered.

"I've got this all taken care of." I'd mentioned it to Toady a couple of days ago, and he'd been agreeable. I'd have to call again and firm up the plans before my self-imposed deadline. "You can lead Toady and his friend back to your place, and if necessary, they can hook up your truck and tow it. If that's the case, it might take a while to get it back, but you can contact me for updates anytime."

"You know, sister, you don't have to do this," Cootie said.

"I want to. You shouldn't be living out here without a ride."

Cootie laughed. "Aren't you something?"

"That's been said about her before," Brad said.

"I'm going to sneak out of here now." Cootie stepped back into the mangroves.

"Cootie," I whispered loudly. When he turned, I added, "Watch your back." He nodded and disappeared.

"Don't introduce him to Mila; she'll want to take him home." Brad grimaced.

Another cop had shown up. He asked us a couple of questions, took our contact information, and said we could leave. Didn't have to tell us twice; we piled into the SUV and got the heck out of there.

"That was fun," I groaned from the backseat.

"I want my application and password to join the secret group," Brad said. "I'm not going to be odd man out anymore."

Chapter Thirteen

Fab dropped Brad at his car, which he'd left at the Bakery Café, and headed home. I begged off from any more excitement, claiming I had calls to make. The first call was to Toady to make sure that he hadn't forgotten his offer to go out and supervise the repair and possible pickup of Cootie's truck.

"I've got it taken care of," Toady assured me. "A friend of mine had a towing business back in the day. He's retired now, but he didn't sell the truck and still runs side jobs on occasion. I started to warn him about the area, but he knew all about it. A couple of friends camped out there until they were run off for trespassing."

"I want to thank you for helping out. Cootie could've just said beat it instead of helping us."

Toady let out a throaty laugh. "No thanks needed. One thing about you guys' jobs: they're never dull. Speaking of…"

I groaned, afraid I was about to be served some bad news.

"The Bostwick job is a good example. Xander's a great kid, and you don't have to tell him twice, but he's basically in over his head being a house manager. Bostwick called, expecting to talk to Fab, and proceeded to run over the kid until I took the phone away. Lied about my credentials as an animal specialist and said the young man was my assistant. Only the best for Ms. Merceau's clients."

"You're the best."

"Bostwick hung up happy as a clambake."

Hmm…okay.

"I'm staying at the manse," Toady announced. "It's a paid vacation, and we're taking advantage of all the fancy stuff. Don't worry, we're cleaning up after ourselves. Besides, a second rodent is going to be delivered tomorrow, and I gotta be there to make sure all goes smoothly."

"I'm tacking a bonus for the two of you on Bostwick's bill."

"Now you're talking, girlie."

I hung up, thinking they were having a good time and that boded well for Fab not having to go back out there and pet-sit, which had me laughing again. I hoped none of the neighbors spotted Toady and reported back to Bostwick.

Then I called Jake's and got Kelpie, who said Doodad was in the office.

"Don't tell him I'm on my way unless he bolts for the door. Then stop him."

Fab would be annoyed that I hadn't called to tell her about my trip to Jake's, but it was about Doodad's personal business, and if he wanted to share, he could do it.

Lucky for me that Didier had been right behind us when we pulled in the gate the day before. Fab had parked at my house, got into his Mercedes, and they pulled back out to the highway. I slid behind the wheel of the Escalade and sank back into the leather seat. There were plenty of tempting buttons on the dash to push, but I refrained and made my way uneventfully to Jake's. I parked in the front for a change, got out, and scanned the lot. All was quiet. I turned an eagle eye in the direction of Junker's to see if he'd brought in a new shipment I hadn't seen yet, particularly new garden items. Then had to remind myself that I had little room for planting at the house.

Kelpie had regulars lined up at the bar, ready for entertainment as she shook her large assets and danced to the music blaring from the jukebox while serving drinks.

"I'll have a Shirley Temple, load up on the cherries. And one of whatever Doodad drinks." I headed down the hall towards the office.

"He's in the kitchen," Kelpie yelled.

I nodded and stopped in the doorway of the kitchen. "Hey you," I yelled. Both Cook and Doodad turned to glare. I laughed and pointed to Doodad, motioning for him to follow me. I stopped back at the bar, put the drinks on a tray, and carried them out to the deck.

"Am I getting fired?" Doodad slid into a chair

across from me after kicking the door closed.

"Who would I hire to replace you?" I tipped my soda against his.

He appeared to give it some thought. "That would be a tough one."

"Why is it that you're still living in a storage shed?" I asked, having made the decision that being direct topped beating around the bush, which would annoy the man.

He was taken aback and looked at me with surprise, then sighed out a frustrated breath. "The insurance company decided to play hardball and leave me out in the cold. Barring some kind of miracle, I'm on my own to rebuild at my expense or sell for land value."

"Those are limited options. What about a lawyer?"

Doodad brushed off the idea. "That takes cash and a lot of it."

"Maybe not. Are you willing to fork over a percentage of what you get from insurance to pay a lawyer? The exact amount could be agreed on in advance."

"Already tried that and couldn't get any takers. One snottily said, 'Nothing from nothing…'"

I pulled my phone out of my pocket and scrolled for a number. "Do you take cases on contingency?" I asked when Tank answered.

"Who is this?" he snapped.

"You're telling me my name and lovely face

didn't come up on your screen?" I scrunched up my nose at Doodad, who laughed.

"I charge by the hour."

"A friend is in need of a good lawyer, and I thought of you." I ignored his snort and ran down the details of the case.

"Hate to hear that story," Tank said. "It's happened too many times. Folks get taken advantage of, and if you ask me, there's no reason except for greed. You make your payments on time, you expect coverage, and then can't collect? That's theft, in my humble opinion."

"That mean you'd be interested in speaking to the potential client?" When he didn't answer right away, I said, "He's the manager at Jake's and can be found there most anytime. Don't dawdle. If you're not interested, say so."

"I can't do it today, but I'll be by tomorrow."

We hung up.

"I don't know how you found out about my housing problem and don't care, but I'm thankful."

"Tomorrow, you'll be interviewing your potential lawyer, Patrick Cannon, aka Tank. He's easily recognizable, as he's built like his moniker would suggest." I gobbled down a stick of cherries. "Don't forget to put on your sparkle."

Doodad watched me with amusement. "I'm looking into going organic on the bar fruit."

"Not my cherries you're not. Organic ones

taste like…excrement."

Doodad laughed. "Got it."

"Be sure you taste test before making any changes."

He nodded. "So…" he started and stopped.

"Somebody died? What? Am I going to need another drink?"

Doodad opened the door and yelled, "Refill for the boss."

It didn't take long for the door to open. One of Kelpie's regulars set my order in front of me and curtsied before backing out.

"Isn't it unprofessional having a customer serve the drinks?"

"I wouldn't worry about it. Garter's a regular and probably got a free beer out of it." Doodad hesitated, then said, "Feel free to say 'not interested.' Won't hurt my feelings any."

I took a deep breath. "I'm ready for your pitch."

"I don't know what you're doing with your house, now that construction is completed or almost. What about renting it to me? I don't need to tell you that it's not good to leave it empty. As you know, it'll attract squatters. And when you kick them off the property, they'll do damage on the way out."

A crazy man had burned down my house, but thankfully, no one had been seriously hurt. "The interior is finished. The exterior and landscaping needs work. I hadn't given any thought to the squatter problem and should have."

"I could also oversee any outside contractors, make sure they're not sitting around drinking beer instead of working, milking the bottom line."

"I've got experience with that. Let me talk it over with my husband." I laughed. It was the first time I'd said that. "It doesn't have any furniture, but it does have appliances."

"I got me a bed and a television."

"In the meantime—"

He cut me off. "Don't go all soft on me. I made it this long, and look at me." He pointed to himself. "A fine specimen."

"Anything else I need to know about?"

The door flew open and Kelpie stuck her head in. "The pole's here," she said, excitement in her voice.

I tapped her leg, and she moved to one side. I craned my head and looked inside. Crum stood off in one corner, a huge metal pole leaned up against the wall behind him. To my relief, the man had donned overalls. No shirt, but it was a vast improvement over going out in just underwear.

"What the devil?" I asked in shock.

"I got to get back to work." Kelpie ran off.

Doodad rubbed his eyes and huffed out a breath. "This was your friend's idea. Fab approved it, anyway. You know, the one you left in charge while you were honeymooning it up."

"I didn't think Fab would actually show up. Thought you'd all run wild, like you do when I'm in town."

"I figured. Fab's a force. Kelpie had her ear for every dumb f—ing idea she could come up with." Doodad grimaced. "Sorry. There would've been more changes if it hadn't been for Didier showing up and reining in his wife. He thought it was funny that she wanted to steamroll me until I told him I'd roll him under the bus, backwards and forwards, when you got back. That wiped the smirk off his face and he jumped in, carrying a squeaking Fab out of the bar to the clapping and catcalls of the customers."

"I don't suppose you got pictures?"

"If only… I'd totally blackmail Fab."

Before I could ask more questions, Crum stormed through the deck door. "I delivered on time. You need me to get my crew to install?"

"I've got my guy coming tomorrow," Doodad said. "In the meantime, haul it out here and put it in the corner. Don't want it falling on anyone."

Crum nodded and turned around.

"Hello to you too," I yelled at his back.

He waved over his shoulder without turning.

I stood and put the glasses back on the tray. "I can't wait to hear this story."

"If you ixnay the idea, I'll get rid of the pole; it can be like it never happened. Digger Dudes will probably go for a second one. They like their new nickname, so you can stop with the horrified look."

"Why would Dickie and Raul buy one?"

"Branching out is all I'll say. They can tell you."

Fab and I had become good friends with Dickie and Raul, the duo that owned the local funeral home, who were always on the lookout for new and innovative ideas for funeral send-offs. I couldn't imagine how a stripper pole would factor in.

Doodad held the door open as Crum came in on one end of the ten-foot pole; on the other end, Joseph, who I hadn't seen earlier, grunted as he passed. They put it in the corner where Doodad directed.

"They came out good, don't you think?" Crum beamed. "Used recycled materials from the last few storms. Had me some help, but it was my idea."

Doodad took a check out of his pocket and handed it to Crum, who scowled at it and sniffed it, as though smelling it would tell him anything. "I prefer cash."

"I need proof of the business expense, so take it or leave it," Doodad shot back.

"Come on." Crum jerked on Joseph's shirt. "I'll treat you to a burger."

Joseph waved as he stumbled alongside the big man.

"Crum's got a friend that makes the stripper

poles, and he pimps them out," Doodad said. "He got Kelpie all excited, and Fab agreed to the purchase. I did warn her that I'd expect reimbursement if you flipped out."

"It's going to go where? What happens when a drunk falls off and hits their head?" I winced at the thought.

"It's going in the middle of the dance floor, next to the jukebox."

We didn't have a dance floor, just an empty space that didn't have a table and chairs. The only dancers swayed and gyrated when they were excessively drunk.

"This is on you," I said.

"Since we've got Jimbo most nights, I'm going to have him lifeguard the pole when he's not driving drunks home." Jimbo was our designated driver.

"Reassure me that this is going to be a water-free attraction," I joked.

Doodad burst out laughing. "Sure. If it wasn't, you know someone would drown."

"I want a warning sign posted, and any pole twirlers need to sign an indemnity agreement."

"Maybe I can suggest to the bands that they incorporate it into their act."

"I'm going home now." I turned and laughed my way out to the car.

Chapter Fourteen

Mother called everyone in the family and gave a few days' notice that we were invited to dinner and attendance was mandatory. She'd said it with a laugh, but was serious, adding that no excuses would be acceptable.

"What do you suppose your mother is up to?" Creole joked on the drive over.

I sighed. "It's really her own fault that when she plans a get-together, everyone thinks she's up to something and wonders if they're the one in her sights."

"Because she usually is."

"And you married into the family anyway."

Creole laughed as he pulled up in front of Fab and Didier's house and laid on the horn. Gave it a rest, then didn't let up the second time until the door opened. Didier was laughing and Fab had her arms crossed and a grouched-out look on her face.

Didier put his arm around Fab and appeared to have to tug on her to get her to move, which she did begrudgingly. When Didier reached for the handle, Creole hit the door locks in rapid succession.

"Stop." I laughed.

"Fab's about to find out she's not the only one who can be annoying." Creole unlocked the doors.

Didier opened the door and helped Fab inside and slid in next to her.

"You need to grow up," Fab snapped.

Creole turned and poked his head between the seats. "I'm hurt. I'm channeling my inner Fab and thought you, of all people, would like her." He squealed out of the driveway.

"You leave marks, and you'll be getting a bill," Fab said.

I turned toward the window and laughed. The wild and silent ride over to the wharf where Spoon parked his boat had just begun.

The guys laughed it up while they walked down the dock, Fab and I behind them.

"Caspian called to let me know he was invited, and I asked if he knew what your mother was up to. He just laughed and said, 'I hope it's something good.'"

"Your father's a good fit in this family."

It had been a long time since we'd had any kind of gathering on Spoon's boat. In fact, since we'd used it at all. Mother and Spoon occasionally took it out on the water and stayed away for days at a time.

The family was seated around an oblong table that Spoon had had custom made. We managed to make it through dinner without a scene, wolfing down the grilled seafood and vegetables that Spoon had prepared and the guys offered their help with. Afterwards, Fab, Emerson, and I cleaned up and had everything put back in its place in record time.

Spoon had set up a mini-bar on the rear deck and was filling drink orders. We filled the cushioned seating that wrapped around the sides and back.

Mila, who'd fought off sleep during dinner, was now fast asleep on the couch inside. She was exhausted after a day of learning to swim and then romping around the room with big men willing to entertain any request she made. Tonight, being flown around the room like an airplane by Didier had prompted the most laughter out of her. The guys always vied to see which of them could be the most entertaining.

"A toast: to family." Mother held up her glass.

"Hold on, folks," Brad said, teasingly. "The real reason we're here is about to be revealed." He hooked his arm around Emerson and pulled her close. "I'll protect you."

"Family." Caspian held up his glass in a show of support.

The rest of us followed suit.

"Any family news we haven't heard?" Spoon asked as his eyes scanned each face, lingering on me longer than I felt comfortable with.

Creole, who noticed, leaned in and whispered, "What have you done now?"

"That's so unsupportive." I made a face, which made him chuckle.

"I've got news," Fab said. "I'm here—just barely—to tell you that Creole is the worst driver, having endured the ride over with him behind the wheel."

Everyone laughed, but no one believed her.

I shot her a thumbs up, which Creole pushed down.

"Join me in a toast to Madison," Mother said.

Creole nudged me.

"That she's alive and well and able to attend after being involved in a shoot-out. Did she call her mother? No."

"That's not exactly what happened," I sputtered. "The man shot first, and lucky me, he wasn't a good shot."

"Why you?" Mother demanded.

"Mistaken identity, I guess. I'd never met him before." Which was the truth. "The cops investigated and closed the case."

Mother stared with *hmm* pursed on her lips, but didn't ask any more questions. "I don't want you getting hurt or worse."

"I suppose my daughter was involved?" Caspian roared.

"No, she was not," I told the man emphatically. Sort of, anyway.

"Well, not according to the headline that originally caught my attention or the rest of the articles that I read," Mother countered. "Imagine my surprise at seeing my daughter's name, and not as innocent bystander but as one of the shooters. The article said that the man involved didn't fare well. It was reported he died."

I could have pointed out that if she hadn't laid down the law about asking Spoon for help, that day would've gone differently, but finger-pointing wouldn't change anything.

"I hope he's enjoying hell," Creole said.

Mother frowned. "Show of hands, how many knew before right now?" She looked around at the rest of the guests. No one raised their hand.

"Now who would admit to that?" Caspian joked. "No one?" He winked at Mother, which garnered a low feral growl from Spoon.

Fab muttered something in French to her father, who preferred Papa, and he grinned, not the least bit repentant.

"Did you need legal representation?" Emerson asked. "Just know that you can call me anytime. Just because I practice family law doesn't mean I can't hook you up with someone good if I can't handle it."

"Fab and I hired Tank," I told her. "Actually, Fab did, but she did allow me to interview him, and after talking to him, I approved. The big test came when I called with a case and he didn't turn prissy on me."

"I was introduced to Tank by a colleague. Seemed nice enough," Emerson said. "Still, don't lose my number."

"I'm happy you took my suggestion and got a new car." Mother once again had me in her sights.

"It's nice," I said, hoping that would be the end of the conversation.

Fab smirked.

Spoon zeroed in on me. I squinted in return, letting him know he wasn't going to hex me. "It would be nice to have a do-over on that day." His expression softened. "Next car, call me first. That way, you don't owe any favors to anyone, unlike the last guy you bought from."

He had me mixed up with Fab, but I wasn't going to start that discussion. A change of subject was called for. "Fab needs to tell everyone about her rodent-on-a-leash job." I flourished my hand at her.

Fab, not the least bit annoyed that I'd used her to steer the conversation in a different direction, jumped into the retelling, embellishing here and there to make the story more entertaining. After recovering from being horrified, Caspian laughed along with everyone else.

I caught Liam's eye. "I'd like to introduce you to Xander. He's the new kid on the block and could use a friend his own age."

"That's a terrible idea," Mother interjected. "That young man is a criminal. I'm sure you haven't forgotten, since Fab was his victim."

"Not anymore. He's turned his life around and admits he didn't enjoy his short career on the wrong side of the law," I said. "Besides, how can you not like the idea since I got it from Brad?"

"Thanks, sis." Brad mimicked the sound of tires squealing. "But we were talking about Mila having friends her own age, not the pickpocket."

Liam grinned.

"It's unclear why you hired him," Mother grouched.

We'd met Xander when he attempted to snatch Fab's purse, which didn't work out the way he'd expected, in that he didn't get the wallet he desired, but instead got a chance to turn his life around. He'd taken it and didn't disappoint.

"Apparently, a reminder is called for. Xander's wicked smart and knows his way around a computer. If you need a reference, look no further than the big man himself." I pointed to Spoon. "What was it you said, he brought your records out of the dark ages? And Didier gave him high marks for not only knowing what he was doing but being easy to work with. I wholeheartedly agree on the latter."

"I'll give him a call and get myself an invite to the mansion for a beer," Liam said.

Caspian changed the tenor of the conversation to a more business-like one. "Since we're all here, how about an update on the dock project?"

Brad took over and told everyone that a price had been agreed on and contracts signed for the parcel we wanted to acquire to continue the expansion of The Boardwalk. It was now full steam ahead for the fun spot for adults and families to eat, enjoy the rides, and hang out.

"What's up with the haunted motel?" Spoon asked Creole.

"Tell us you abandoned that idea," Mother said with an exasperated shake of her head.

"Got a call today that the sale's on hold or cancelled. Which one was unclear, as I was speaking to a loan officer not familiar with the file. I'll have to follow up and figure it out."

Creole had made an offer on an abandoned motel as a wedding gift. Rumors of a ghost residing there had dogged the old place and made it an interesting piece of the town's history.

I looked over at him, *What happened?* written on my face.

"As most of you know, real estate closings get put on hold when there's a named storm out in the Gulf. Insurance companies don't write policies until it's moved on out. To further complicate the matter, the person who had the file at the bank quit, and it's in the process of being assigned to someone else. It's my hope that they'll honor the offer that was already accepted and not force us to start over."

"I've got contacts at the bank. I can put in a good word for you," Caspian offered.

"That's sweet of you," I said. Creole nodded in agreement.

Spoon clasped Mother's hand. "We've got an

announcement. We decided to sell the boat and already got an offer, which we accepted."

"Tell them the best part." Mother smiled at him.

"We're looking for something new with more room for fun and entertainment."

While Caspian listed off a few things they should be on the lookout for, Liam walked towards the galley. Once out of sight, he beckoned me to join him.

Creole noticed and whispered, "If he wants anything illegal, the answer is no."

I got up and did my best to remain unobtrusive as I joined him while he refilled his soda.

Liam faced the group, his back resting against the counter. "I don't want anyone sneaking up on us. Grandmother watched as you left and is now staring along with the rest of them, but at least they're making an attempt to pretend they didn't notice."

"Sneaky family." Like him, I stood to one side to keep a clear view of the area.

"Need your help. A friend does, anyway, and ASAP. She doesn't have a lot of money but could swap favors."

"The answer is yes, and I know the favor I want in return."

"My friend, Glacier—"

I half-laughed. "Where do parents get these names?"

"Some vague story about where they were doing it when…you get the picture."

"Brr…"

"Glacier recently met Mr. Wonderful. He hit all the points on her checklist except for the one about not being an a-hole. They went out on a date, and not only did he stick her with the check, he stole her SUV. Drove off and left her stranded at the restaurant."

I shook my head in disbelief. "The reason she didn't call the police?"

"She doesn't want her father to find out. She enjoys her status as the perfect daughter and doesn't want him to be disgusted that she was duped."

"No judgement, but if this had happened to me or Brad, we'd have told Mother and she would've tracked his butt down and kicked it hard."

"Dude's name is Robert, and he's apparently been joyriding around in the SUV, because he hasn't been back to the apartment he shares with a couple of other guys. Or they're covering for him, but I didn't get that vibe when I talked to them. Spent the last two nights driving up and down nearby side streets, and the car's nowhere to be found."

"Me and my backup will get on it tomorrow." I nodded toward Fab. "I'll need info."

Liam pulled a folded sheet of paper out of his pocket. "Everything I got on the guy is here. I also included Glacier's information."

"I'll text this info to Xander. Maybe he can turn up another address for this Robert. If nothing else, he can send a picture so Fab knows she's beating the heck out of the right kid. You know, if he's not cooperative."

"Your favor?"

"Talk to Xander and tell me what you think of him. I think I'm a decent judge of character, but it would be nice to know that he's not jerking me around and I just haven't caught on yet."

"Your radar for that is pretty good, so I doubt that's happening. But I'll let you know." Liam peered around me. "Grandmother's getting antsy. She's not going to be able resist crashing the conversation much longer; we should go back. Then we don't have to make up a story."

As we walked back to rejoin the others, I asked, "You staying overnight?"

"I'm staying at Brad's. I promised Mila I'd cook her breakfast. Probably going to run a con on her: throw cereal in a bowl and boast about my culinary skills."

"Sweet. Brad fixed me many a breakfast before we hiked the five miles to school, up and over the mountains."

Liam laughed. "Mila's going to enjoy the family stories as much as I do when she gets older."

I shoved his notes in my pocket. "We'll get on this, and I'll call you tomorrow with an update.

Tell Glacier not to worry. This kid doesn't stand a chance once I sic Fab on him." I stopped and bent over to whisper in Fab's ear, "We've got a job tomorrow. So no excuses."

Her father wasn't the least bit bashful about leaning over and listening in. "It better not be dangerous." He shook his finger at me.

I shushed him. "I'll have the prodigal daughter call with the details, but we're not talking about it here. *Capiche*?"

"Yeah, I get it. I'm going to hold you to that phone call," he said sternly to his daughter.

I sat between Creole and Didier.

"How much trouble are you in now?" Didier asked.

Creole laughed.

"No more than usual." I looked up at Creole. "How do we get out of here? There's no dessert. Who does that? And in this family."

"Stand up, take a couple of steps, and pretend to faint," Creole coached. "I'll catch you and carry you out."

"That trick is not part of my repertoire and would need practice. Falling on the floor doesn't appeal to me, and it would get my dress dirty." I smoothed my hands over my black dress.

"Too much drama, you two," Fab leaned across Didier and whispered. She stood up. "We're leaving because the guys have an early business meeting."

Brad winked at me. "Almost forgot," he said.

He held out a hand to Emerson, and they went inside to get his daughter.

We hugged and kissed and said good-byes all around, then walked down the dock to the parking lot.

Chapter Fifteen

Fab picked me up early and didn't utter a word until we'd cleared the coffee drive-thru, where she placed the order without asking what I wanted. Good thing she didn't double her own choice, or I'd be stuck with the latest mushroom blend and no whipped cream, which I'd throw out the window.

"Where are we going?" Fab demanded.

"Miami-ish," I said, enjoying being deliberately vague.

"'Ish' would be where, exactly?"

"Now you know what it's like going places with you." I smiled, guaranteed to annoy her further. "Just keep driving. I'll wave at you when it's time turn." I leaned down, pulled the sheet of paper that Liam gave me out my bag, and entered the car thief's address into the GPS. Sensing that Fab was about to pull over and push me out on the side of the road, I related my conversation with Liam.

"What did Creole say when you told him?"

"He left early and the 'what are you doing today?' inquisition got tabled. Before you continue with your grilling, I'm going to ask this

Robert character *nicely* for the whereabouts of the SUV and hope he didn't pass it off to a fence."

"Thief boy—since that's easier to remember— is going to cooperate because…?" Fab tapped her chin. "You're so scary?"

"If he doesn't cooperate when confronted, then he's never going to, and I'll tell Glacier that her only option is to report the theft to the cops."

Fab sped up the highway, easily finding the address and coasting to a stop in front of a four-plex on a quiet, tree-lined street.

I fished my phone out of my pocket and pulled up a picture of the Jeep Cherokee in question, with a nice clear shot of the plate for verification. "Let's cruise the block. Maybe Robert has it parked close by, although Liam said he and Glacier did a block-to-block search."

"Doesn't thief boy know that he can be charged with a felony?" Fab asked while we took a completely fruitless spin around the block.

"I'll ask him."

"Since it appears that I've been relegated to the role of backup, what will I be doing?" Fab sniffed.

"You're going to stand back, paste on a busy face, and make sure nothing goes south." I demonstrated. "There's no plan B, so don't ask. I'm not going to threaten him, since he's young and I don't want anyone getting hurt."

"Are you carrying?"

"I am, but I'm leaving it in the car." I took my

Glock out of my holster and put it in the glove box.

A car pulled away from the curb, and Fab took the spot, giving her a diagonal view of the property and the doorstep.

I got out and smoothed down my jean skirt, then looked up and down the street. All was quiet. I walked across the walkway to the unit on the left. As I extended my hand to knock, the door opened. The girl with partially purple hair and a backpack over her shoulder was just as surprised to see me as I was to see her. She let out a muffled squeal as she'd stuffed her mouth with smooshed bananas on bread.

"I'm here to see Robert."

She motioned me inside and pointed to the hallway. "Second door," came out garbled. She then left, closing the door and leaving me standing in the mess of a living room. Clothes, dishes, and books were lying around, the sports channel muted on the television.

I took a deep breath, headed down the hallway to the second door, and knocked. "Robert," I called out in a calm voice.

I didn't have to wonder what I'd do if he didn't answer. Another door at the end of the hall opened, clearly the bathroom, and a college-age boxer-clad boy, complete with morning scruff, stood in the doorway staring. "Who the hell are you?"

"Robert?" I asked, sounding hopeful.

He eyed me up and down. "He moved."

"I'm here to locate a missing Jeep. If I can get the location, I'll leave and that'll be the end of it."

The remnants of sleep vanished from his face, replaced with anger. "Get out, bitch." His hand disappeared behind the door and came back into view holding a broom above the bristles. He took a swing directly at my head.

I blocked the blow with my arm, managing to protect my face, stumbled back into the wall, and screamed.

He jabbed the handle like a poker at my midsection, and I reached out, grabbed hold, and jerked, but he was stronger and wrestled it back.

A male face popped out of the other bedroom.

"Call the cops," Robert ordered.

The door slammed shut, the lock clicked, and I suspected he was doing just that.

I wanted to relieve Robert of the broom and shove it up…but he had a hundred pounds on me, and I figured in hand-to-broom combat, I'd be the loser. I shifted to retreat mode, sliding along the wall without taking my eyes off him, and made it to the front door. I wrenched it open and hustled outside. "I just came here to talk calmly about the situation with Glacier."

"I don't know what you're talking about. I do know you're going to jail," he snapped with confidence.

I took a few steps backward along the walkway, not wanting to take my eyes off the kid. A cop car screeched to a halt at the curb, getting my attention. Fab, who was leaning against the passenger door, straightened and started forward. I shook my head at her. One of us would need to arrange bail. I put my hands up and walked toward the cop as he got out.

"Stop right there," he shouted, which I did, leaving my hands in the air. "You the one that called?"

"It was him." I inclined my head over my shoulder to where the guy I figured was Robert, who'd put on a pair of jeans, was bolting down the walkway, pitching the broom into a hedge under one of the windows.

"She broke into my house," he accused. "Arrest her. I'm pressing charges."

Another cop car rolled up.

I sighed. "I didn't. A girl with purple hair invited me in."

"You're a liar," he shouted, having come close enough to hear what I said.

"You need to stand back and put your hands in the air," the officer directed Robert. To me, he said, "Do you have identification?"

"In the car," I said. "I need to disclose that I have a permit to carry. My Glock is in the car, but I have a waist holster on—empty." I slowly lifted my shirt with one hand and did a slow turn.

The other officer had gotten out of his car and joined his partner. They exchanged a few words before the first one turned back to me. "I'll take that ID and your version of events."

Fab had moved away from the SUV and was on her phone, talking or shooting video, it was hard to tell. Both, if she could manage it.

I opened the car door and grabbed my purse off the floor, taking out my wallet and handing him my license and carry card. I told him why I'd come and what had happened since I arrived at the door. He examined my arm and the colorful bruise that was already forming. "Do you need a paramedic?"

"I'm good. It hurts, but better that than my face."

He half-laughed. "You're right there."

"One more thing. He's lying about purple girl. When I got here, she was on her way out eating a banana sandwich." I made a face. "To prove that I'm telling the truth, there have to be banana skins in the trash or lying on the counter—the residents appear to be short on housekeeping skills."

"This Glacier woman will confirm your story about the car?" the officer asked.

"I've got a picture of the car in question." I held out one hand and reached in my pocket with the other to retrieve my phone.

He chuckled. "This isn't your first arrest?"

"I'm married to a retired cop, so I know the drill." I kept all the times I'd been questioned for one thing or another to myself.

"You wait here. Don't make a run for it."

Appearing amused with himself, he walked over to the other cop, who was on the phone, laughing with someone after ordering Robert to have a seat on the empty planter on the porch.

Fab, now half a block away, was still on the phone. I gave brief thought to the idea that she might be talking to the second cop and dismissed it as absurd. I cleared my mind, refusing to focus on possible outcomes, and leaned back against the car door. I noticed that Robert was glaring, which I ignored, refusing to look in his direction again.

The second cop, who had thus far done all the talking on the phone, now handed it to the one who'd questioned me, and he appeared to be answering questions himself, chuckling a few times.

The cop finished up his side of the call, handing the phone back and walking over to me. "This Glacier woman doesn't want to press charges; she's only interested in getting her car back?"

I nodded. "She doesn't want her father to find out about her poor dating choice."

"He should have been her first call," the officer grumbled. "I'm going to have that talk with my daughters when I get home."

"Lucky girls." I smiled at him.

"Don't go anywhere." He crossed over to his partner, who was beckoning to him.

After a brief conference, they both came over

to me. The second officer said, "Robert is dropping the charges against you." *Stupid ass* hung in the air. "The Jeep is in the parking lot of the Target on Dixie, keys in the cup holder."

"Thank you. I'll head over there now," I said.

"Is that your friend?" He nodded in Fab's direction. "Heard you guys travel in pairs."

"You have friends in high places," the original officer said, clearly having more questions that he didn't ask.

"The chief," I squeaked. I couldn't imagine how he got involved, but I'd bet big money Fab didn't call him. "I'm going to owe him."

"He said big time." The second officer laughed.

"Follow me to the Target," the first officer said.

"Can we do it with lights and sirens and screaming through the streets?" I joked.

He squinted one-eyed at me. "No!"

I waved to Fab, got in the car, and slumped back against the seat. The adrenaline rush having worn off, my arm hurt like the devil.

Fab slid behind the wheel and handed me the phone. To her, I said, "Follow the cop car; we're headed to Target." I checked the screen. "I love you," I said as I put it to my ear.

"You better not be hurt," Creole barked.

"My arm hurts."

"The bastard told the cops he had to defend himself. He's lucky I don't have his address."

"So you were the one that called in the big guns?" I asked.

"You're lucky you're one of the chief's favorite people. He doesn't hold me in the same regard, and I worked for him for years."

"That's not true or he wouldn't take your calls. We should have him to dinner. At Fab's house." That garnered a humph from Fab.

"We need to include Help. The chief has heard rumblings about the bodies that were recovered and isn't happy that one of his men was involved and he didn't hear the details from Help firsthand."

"I'm surprised he didn't know that Help was on the suspect list."

"He just got back from vacation and has some catching up to do. He was grumbling about the stack of paperwork sitting on his desk," Creole said, his tone conveying that he didn't miss that part of the job. "Tell me that you're headed home and today's drama is over."

"I'm recovering the Jeep. If it's drivable, I'll be returning it to Glacier, and then we're headed home. Fab just nodded, so we're in agreement." I sent a kiss through the phone. Fab gagged. After hanging up, I put the phone on the console.

"Details." Fab snapped her fingers.

I hit the facts from when purple hair opened the door. "I don't know if Glacier ever got a taste of Robert's anger, but it's fast and red-hot. She's lucky to be done with him. It's a good thing she wasn't able to confront him herself."

"I should've gone with you to the door."

"You saved me from going to jail," I said emphatically. "Which is probably where I'd be headed while they got everything sorted out. For a guy who committed a felony, he didn't have any hesitation about calling the cops on me for something I didn't do."

It was a short drive down the busy highway, the traffic signals in our favor. The officer spotted the Jeep at the end of one of the aisles and drove straight to it.

"It's got tires; that's a good sign," I said.

Fab pulled into a space a row away from the car, and we got out. The cop already had the door open and was searching the inside. We stood back and watched.

He finished and got behind the wheel, and it started right up. Fab and I exchanged a grateful smile. He got out and walked over to us.

"I know it's none of my business, but did Robert have an explanation as to why he left it here?" I asked.

"Robert's story is pretty much the same as Glacier's, except he claims that she ditched him and he didn't know what to do when she wouldn't take his calls. So he got scared and left it parked here."

"Who knows what the truth is," I said diplomatically. I knew what I thought, having experienced his temper personally. A guy like that doesn't get scared. "Glacier is a friend of my nephew's, and I'm going to forbid him to date her. If he had that in mind, he can get over it."

The cop laughed. "If only it were that easy. I'd forbid my daughters to date until they're fifty."

"Thank you for all your help deescalating the situation and keeping me out of jail," I said with a smile.

"Old Robert backed off when we told him he'd also be transported to the precinct. We also suggested to him, and strongly, that he not level BS charges that could come back to land him in cuffs."

"If you're ever get down to Tarpon Cove, stop at Jake's. We have a cop discount—free. Voted best dive bar in Tarpon several times, and we serve the best Mexican food around," I said.

His phone rang. He pulled it from his pocket and waved to us as he walked away.

"I'm going to put the address in the GPS and follow you, so don't lose me," I said. I leaned into the Escalade and entered the information, replaced the GPS on the dash, then got into the Jeep and u-turned to follow Fab out to the highway.

It took less than ten minutes to get to the address that Liam had given me, which was a parking lot associated with the University. I parked the Jeep under a tree in the closest spot to the entrance and left the keys under the mat, sending a text to Liam to retrieve them ASAP.

"I'm in need of a margarita, preferable a pitcher, and a tray of mini tacos," I said, sliding into the passenger seat.

"We can't get sauced and drive. Our options are takeout or going to Jake's and calling a car service."

"Is that what we're calling our husbands now?" I laughed. "I say we take the party to your house and picnic on the beach."

"Another great idea."

I leaned back against the seat and closed my eyes.

Chapter Sixteen

Fab flew back down the Interstate towards home, making it in record time due in part to relatively light traffic.

We were on the Overseas just north of Little Blackwater Sound, a beautiful stretch of the highway with glimpses of water on both sides, when Fab shrieked, "You're not going to believe this," one eye on the rearview mirror.

"What?" I flipped down the visor, not sure what I was supposed to be looking for. "Hint, please."

"Coming up beside us…that sedan trying to shake somebody off the hood."

A car swerving back and forth in its lane caught my attention. Sure enough, there was someone stretched across the hood, hanging onto… I'd guess the groove where the windshield wipers fit. Fab braked suddenly and swerved to get out of the way, two cars from behind us driving erratically around us with horns blasting.

The driver of the sedan edged closer to our driver's side door and jerked hard on the wheel. The partially clad man went airborne and rolled across the hood of the Escalade, then across the road. I powered down the window and hung my head out as he plummeted down a short embankment and out of sight.

"You need to pull over," I said.

"But I didn't…" Fab said, as freaked out as I'd ever seen her.

"I know, but you need to anyway. We don't want anyone pointing fingers, saying anything different," I reasoned.

It was several miles to the next turn lane before we could double back, then double back again. The only way we were able to identify the exact location was because two other cars had stopped and three people had climbed down the embankment and were scanning the water. A chain-link fence with a small section missing ran along the water. Fab parked behind the rest of the cars and stayed in the car.

"If that guy wasn't dead when he hit the water, he probably drowned." I hung my head out the window.

"I want to go home," Fab whined.

"You might be the only witness. You can at least give the cops a description of the other car." The woman knew makes and models at a glance.

To my surprise, Fab wanted no part of getting out and snapping pictures. We waited in silence until the cops showed up, eyes pasted to the spot, hoping the man would come crawling out of the water.

Fab answered the officer's questions directly and gave them a description of the car and the missing man. Her description of the driver was sketchy, but other than that, the only thing she wasn't able to supply was the license plate number.

My only contribution was, "I saw a body fly across the hood, land in the road, then disappear out of sight."

The cops took our contact information. Soon we'd be in the notepad of every cop in South Florida.

As soon as we were back on the road, my phone rang. I answered but didn't say anything.

"That's not funny," Creole grouched.

"Hi honey."

"You're not home, and do you know how I know that?"

"Hmm…you're there and I'm not."

"Exactly. I'm afraid to ask why not."

"We were involved in a traffic… hmm… incident." I hemmed and hawed, still finding it hard to believe what we'd witnessed.

"You okay?"

We're fine." I looked at Fab, who seemed less freaked out now. "Can't say as much for the other guy." I gave him a bare-bones version of events.

"I'll see what I can find out." He let out a long sigh.

"Fab and I are placing an order for a pitcher of

margaritas, one of martinis, and tacos. We originally decided the location should be the beach at Fab's, but I'm thinking we should loll about on her new living room furniture, which would be more comfortable and less hot, thanks to the air conditioning."

"How long do I have to make this happen?" Creole asked, not the least bit annoyed by the specific request.

"We'll be there in fifteen minutes, depending. Assuming the rest of the ride is uneventful."

Chapter Seventeen

I opened my eyes to light coming through the window, signaling morning. It was a grey and overcast day, with rain predicted, but that didn't mean we'd get any. As it turned out, neither Fab nor I had been in the mood to drink very much the previous night. After we ate very little and related the events of the day once again, I asked Creole to take me home. I reached out and patted the empty space next to me, disappointed to find I was by myself in the big bed. Rolling over, I spotted Creole sitting at the island and his eyes locked on mine.

He held up his mug. "Coming right up." He brought over two mugs and crawled onto the bed beside me.

I lifted my mug and toasted him. The scent floating in the air had me wishing I could gulp it down.

"Got an update for you," Creole said. "The fellow from yesterday was found, deceased, caught in a fishing net. They also arrested the driver of the car. Apparently, after tipping a few back at a local bar, the two men got into a fight that spilled out into the parking lot. Instead of walking away, the one guy thought it would be a great idea to jump on the hood and was apparently unwilling to let go. It didn't occur to the driver to pull over or, better yet, not leave the parking lot."

I sighed, having already figured that the situation wouldn't end with both men being able to walk away. "I'm going to have to call the body shop guy and tell him the loaner has a dent. I'm turning out to be good for business."

"I'm relieved that it didn't end with that guy coming through your windshield."

"Freaked Fab out, but there was nothing she could've done differently. She was having a difficult time yesterday; I hope she's feeling better."

"Fab, Didier, and Brad left for Card Sound earlier to oversee the installation of the security system. Knowing you wouldn't want to go, I bailed for both of us, and Brad stepped up and volunteered to ride along."

"I can't say I'm sorry that I'm missing out on that trip."

He lifted my arm and lightly fingered the bruise. "How's it feeling?"

"I rubbed some pain lotion on it before going to bed, and it looks worse than it feels."

"I had a talk with Liam."

"Now he's never going to call again."

"I told him to warn Glacier that the guy had a hair trigger and suggested that if he was planning to date her, he should get to know her better as a friend first so he has a good idea of the type of person he's getting involved with. That way, she'll know as well. I ended it by saying that if a similar situation should arise, he could call anytime."

"Thank you for that." I leaned my head against Creole's chest.

"I've made plans for the two of us for the rest of the day. You eager to hear what they are?"

He tickled me until I screeched, "Yes."

"We're going to do absolutely nothing. Together."

* * *

Creole careened around the corner to The Cottages. Our do-nothing day had been interrupted by a phone call. Creole had grabbed the phone out of my hand and held it out of my reach until it stopped ringing. He was about to relinquish it when it beeped with an incoming message. He groaned and thrust it at me.

I waved it off, knowing if a text came in that fast, it would need my immediate attention. "I insist that you read the good news."

He stared down at the screen. "Get changed."

"Do I get a hint about what kind of wardrobe choice I should be making?" I looked down at my t-shirt dress, which had rapidly become a favorite for its comfort.

"Dead body at The Cottages."

"Which tenant?" I screeched, flying into the closet and coming out in a jean skirt, t-shirt, and tennis shoes—my uniform for when I didn't know what to expect.

"Doesn't say." He pulled on a shirt and also shoved his feet into tennis shoes. Holding the door open, he said as I scooted through, "Mac's not answering."

Creole helped me into his oversized truck and sped down the highway, traffic cooperating. We arrived, only to have a cop wave us off from turning down the street. Creole drove around the block and parked at the opposite end, and we ran down the sidewalk.

"Where's your damn phone?" I yelled to Mac, who stood in the middle of the driveway, waving her fist at… I wasn't sure.

Mac patted the sides of her skirt. "Left it on the desk again." She took off at a run.

Waiting for Mac's breasts to fly up out of the towel thing she had wrapped around her neck and hit her in the face made me forget why we were there.

Mac skidded to a stop at the office door, yelling over her shoulder, "They're out by the trash."

Kevin came around the corner from that direction, laughing his head off.

"What's going on?" Creole demanded.

Kevin caught his breath and said, "I was told

to mind my own business. Besides, it's my day off." He squinted down at his cargo shorts and tropical shirt—his day-off clothing, which replaced his usual deputy's uniform. He started laughing again and walked in the direction of the office.

"You wait right here." Creole kissed my cheek.

"I'm coming. It won't be my first dead body. Besides, I'm going to need pictures for Fab."

"You look so normal."

"I warned you before the I do's," I said with a lifted brow. "Too late now."

"Don't be expecting me to change my mind— not happening." Creole grabbed my hand and tugged me away from the pool area, back out to the front and around the side of the property to where we'd have a good view of the dumpster and not get in the middle of any investigation. Two patrol cars had pulled up and were parked, blocking off the area from the street.

Creole pulled me to a stop at the sight of the body that had been dumped outside the fenced trash area. It had been wrapped in a garbage bag and secured with duct tape. "You can take pictures from here." He walked over to the officer in charge.

Mac ran up behind me. "Anything happen?"

"Nothing good. So far."

Mac lowered her voice, turning to one side. "Kevin says it's a joke. He doesn't know what was put in the trash bags to fill them out, but it's not a body. He tried to tell the new officer, the one on the right, but he didn't want to hear it."

"It's not funny," I hissed. "If it turns out that this was the bright idea of one of the tenants, they're evicted."

"I don't think so. Kevin says there's a gift tag on the outside of the bag with Crum's name written on it. Probably from one of his disgruntled girlfriends." Mac looked around and continued, "Kevin's going to double-check to make sure he's not running any scams."

"Creole," I called out. He turned and frowned. I turned to Mac, "You get any close-ups?"

"Of course, I did." Mac snorted, hands on hips, chest thrust out.

I stepped back, not wanting to get hit in the face, and crooked my finger at Creole, who walked over. "You're going to want to hear this. That is not a dead body. At least, according to Kevin. No clue how he knows, but he seems certain."

Creole looked over his shoulder at the crime scene.

"A prank of some sort directed at Crum, it would appear," I said.

Creole grumbled, "Dumbass," under his breath, to which I half-laughed. He frowned and stalked back over to the two officers. The one on his phone hung up, and Creole had a short conversation with the two. The three men stared at the supposed body.

One officer walked over and nudged the bagged form. The other got out a knife, which he used to slit the bottom half open. Trash fell out.

"Did Kevin say how he knew?" I asked Mac, who hadn't moved from her vantage point, her phone out as she clicked away.

"This exact same thing happened up in Homestead. Kevin says the 'body' resembles a picture that someone posted online. I'd never have called the cops and wasted their time if I'd known it was a prank."

"How were you supposed to know? You did the right thing. I'm not happy, but it beats the real thing," I said. "I wish Crum would get a steady girlfriend and stop all this prowling around. Not sure what he does to inspire revenge in his women, but it's happened more than a few times. He's lucky one of them hasn't totally flipped and offed him."

"I'm going to try scaring him with that scenario. But he's one of those people that doesn't listen to good advice, so I'm not holding out hope for this time."

Creole joined us. "The new guy, Piner—" He pointed to the first officer. "—thinks Kevin pranked him."

I shook my head. "That's not Kevin's style. Besides, according to Kevin, somewhere on the bag is a tag with Crum's name on it. My guess is that it's someone trying to scare the man or send a warning."

"I agree," said Mac. "I'll get Crum to clean up the trash; it's the least he can do. And if he balks, I'll tell him I'm sending him the bill for cleanup. That will get his butt moving." Mac cut through the palm trees and back to the other side of the property.

Creole grabbed my hand. "Let's go."

Chapter Eighteen

"Let me check on the inmates first." I tugged on Creole's hand, pausing at the end of the driveway. "Since we're here, it would be good to make sure there won't be any more frantic calls. Today anyway. You ready to be sidekick?"

Creole pulled me into a hug. "Seriously?" I nodded. "I'll be wanting a dozen IOUs."

"You don't need them. You ask, I do."

"I'm going to remind you of that later."

Kevin dribbled a basketball in our direction, stopping a foot away. "Just wanted to report that someone stole the hoop." He motioned toward the barbecue area where the hoop had been moved to from its original spot in the middle of the driveway. There was plenty of room in the seldom-used space and no chance of getting hit by a car pulling in too fast.

"That's not possible," I snapped. "It had to weigh a ton."

"This is one of the few times that we're in agreement." Kevin shrugged.

Creole glared at him but bit back what he'd

been about to say.

"What are *you* going to do about it?" I asked.

"Did you file a report?"

"Since this is the first I'm hearing about it…"

"I'll keep an eye out. But unless you painted your name on it, bye-bye hoop." Kevin waved and dribbled a few steps away, then stopped and turned. "Almost forgot. I drew the short straw last night and got the disturbance call for Jake's."

"No wonder you're in a good mood. How many of my customers did you haul off to the pokey?"

Creole chuckled.

"That would be jail, and no one. Noise complaint, and it must have been a disgruntled customer. When I arrived, I couldn't hear a thing in the parking lot, and only music when the door opened. Inside, everyone was dancing, beer in hand, slinging it everywhere. The dance contest was a big hit, and not a single fight over who was going to win the free beer. Didn't stick around for the winner." He made a sad face and grinned. "For once, no one ran out the back, and I got my soda to-go."

Creole gave me a questioning look.

"Fab and Kelpie put their heads together and came up with a plan to have live bands and dancing contests," I told him. "It wasn't the Clogger band, was it?" Judging by Kevin's *who?* look, I took the answer to be no.

"Now that we're married, I suppose I should

keep up on the latest happenings at Jake's," Creole said.

"Trust me, it'll give you a headache." Kevin turned at the sound of voices. "I'm surprised Crum's not getting questioned about the dead-body gift. It's my day off, so I'll get the replay from Mac later." He dribbled back to his cottage.

Crum rounded the corner, shirtless, but with pants on for once. A disheveled man stumbled along next to him in shorts and a dress shirt, looking as though he'd woken up from a night of drinking and was still drunk, judging by the sway to his walk.

"New tenant?" Creole asked.

"Better not be."

Crum made eye contact with me, then grabbed the man's arm and attempted to get him to turn back in the direction of his cottage.

"Hold on," I bellowed before they reached it.

Creole sped up, and we closed the distance quickly, not giving Crum time to get his door shut and force me to resort to threats to get him to open it.

"Hi, we haven't met." I eyed the stranger, who was clearly hungover and not quite focused. I didn't get a response from either man. Crum had a deer-in-the-headlights look. "Who is this?" I asked both men in hopes of getting a coherent answer.

"Brother," the drunk said at the same time Crum said, "Cousin."

Creole snorted. "I'd think you'd be keeping a low profile with a murderer on the loose and *you* a target of interest," he directed at Crum.

"Told Mac I'd get right out there and clean up the mess." He didn't make eye contact, fidgeting from one foot to the other. "I don't know why I have to be held responsible for what some crazy woman does."

"You could start by being honest with these women you hook up with," I said. "Let them know you're only good for a one-night stand and that's it. Or get yourself a pay-by-the-hour girlfriend."

Creole laughed.

Crum straightened to his full height and glared at Creole, who laughed harder.

Crum's brother/cousin clutched his midsection and groaned. Crum slung an arm around his shoulder and led him away from the door. "You can't barf in my house. Do it out here where it can be washed away."

"Whatever the two of you are up to, he can't stay here," I called after the two men. Out of the corner of my eye, I caught sight of Joseph waving frantically from the pool area. "Crum... I'm holding you one-hundred-percent responsible." I grabbed Creole's hand and led him to the pool gate, entering the code to go put water on whatever fire Joseph had burning. At least, the pool water was right there.

"If you're tired of this already, you can grab a

cold drink in the office," I said to Creole.

"No way. I'm going to stay within hearing distance. That way, you don't have to repeat anything and I don't have to wonder if you're telling the truth. There are times when the events that play out here are hard to believe."

Joseph had ducked out of sight, and I found him — in stained jeans and a t-shirt, greasy, disheveled hair sticking on end — tucked in the corner on a chaise that he'd dragged partially behind the tiki bar.

"The cousin/bro story is a flat-out lie." Joseph said as we approached.

"You've got big ears, and you're hanging out with the professor too much."

Joseph snorted, and it sounded more like a honk and painful. "There are no secrets around this place. They've shopped that same story around for the last hour or so and only went inside when the cops showed up. I heard Crum yelling at him, but couldn't make out the words. A couple of the bad ones came through clear." He grinned, scratching the several-day scruff on his face.

I held my breath, waiting for a bug to drop onto his shirt. Mac swore that it'd happened in the past and she couldn't wait to share. "A big black one." She'd held her fingers apart, indicating cockroach-size.

"If he's not related, then who is he?" Creole snapped.

"Patience, babe." I patted his arm and laughed at his eyeroll, then turned back to Joseph. "Just tell us what you do know."

"Two nights ago, sometime after midnight, that guy wandered in off the street and went from cottage to cottage, turning the knobs, not hitting pay dirt until he got to Crum's door."

"How do you know all this?" I asked.

"Do you want to hear the rest or what?"

I crossed my arms and glared at him.

"Where was I? Oh yeah. He went inside, made himself a sandwich, and sacked out on the couch. All that, and he didn't even eat the sandwich."

"Where was Crum?" Creole asked.

"This is the good part. The whole time, he was in his bedroom, sawing logs, which is why he's been ordered to keep his window closed so the sober guests won't complain. I suggested to the old lady who complained when she checked out that if she had a stiff one, she'd sleep better." He grinned.

"The end?" I asked.

"Oh heck no. Crum got up in the morning and found him. Asked the guy, 'What the hey hell?' Now, this is the good part: dude said, 'I live here.'"

"Great," I mumbled.

"It took a while, but Crum finally dragged it out of him that he's been living in a car parked down the street since the wife kicked him out and kept the dog."

"The dog was a good choice," Creole said, straight-faced.

I nudged him. "I don't understand why the man's not gone by now. Unless there's cash in it for Crum?"

"Crum's got a soft heart." Joseph wheezed. "He's got a lot on his plate right now and thinking about involving the man in a couple of the schemes...businesses he has going. We'll be staying busy and out of trouble. That should make you happy." He wheezed again, and it took a minute for him to catch his breath. "So far, everything's legal, so don't go worrying none."

"I've got a new lawyer, in case you need one. But I'd appreciate you giving thought ahead of time to whether one of your schemes will get you arrested." Sooner or later, he'd need the lawyer, because that would definitely happen.

"Don't tell Crum I blabbed. Although, with a kick in the behind from you, maybe he'll stop being a do-gooder and focus." Joseph closed his eyes; all the gossiping had worn him out.

"Make sure you stay hydrated. Don't want you feeling woozy and falling in the pool and drowning."

Joseph gave me a thumbs up. "I want me a theme funeral, just so you know." He fake-snored, a new habit he'd picked up as his way of ending a conversation.

I looped my arm in Creole's and headed for the gate.

"I'm afraid to ask, but I'll brave it. We headed to Crum's?" Creole asked.

"Oh heck no. That's what Mac's for." I nodded to the woman prancing in our direction.

"What the heck is that get-up she has on? If she puts someone's eye out with one of her… hmm…"

"Breasts," I whispered.

"You could be held liable."

"Get rid of cousin/bro," I said when she got closer. "I'd prefer right this second, but do the best you can, as long as it's no later than tomorrow."

"You're a thief," Miss January shrieked, running up. She skidded to a stop and teetered to an upright position, smoothing down her housedress and brushing her stringy hair away from her face. "She won't give me back Kitty." Half in her cups, the woman stuck her finger in Mac's face.

"If you hadn't left her out on the porch all night, I wouldn't have had to send her to the veterinarian again," Mac snapped.

"That's sweet of you." Miss January calmed considerably and appeared to be trying to recall if she'd known that tidbit of information. She turned and eyed Creole up and down like a tasty morsel. "Aren't you a cute one?" She winked.

"I haven't changed all that much since I was your neighbor, except I'm married now." Creole stepped away from her and hugged me to his side. In his undercover days, he'd rented a cottage and used it to sneak about and have a place to sleep. He was the ideal tenant: paid on time, was rarely around, and never stirred up trouble.

"Keep your hands to yourself," I said, "or we'll have us a smackdown."

Miss January cackled and slapped her knee through the thin cotton of her dress. "When I was younger, it would have been on." The reality was that she wasn't that old; she just looked twice her age thanks to a fifth of vodka a day. Health issues didn't help, but she and Joseph were of the same mindset: ignore them.

"When will Kitty be back?" I asked.

"A week or so," Mac said evasively. "Since Kitty hasn't been well, she requires more attention. When you get her back, she'll look a little different but will require less care."

"Woman," Miss January's latest live-in hollered from the porch, "what are you doing out here? It's hot." The Captain stomped down the stairs, ignoring the rest of us.

Miss January scurried over to him, hung on his arm, and they went back inside.

"Friendly guy." Creole snorted.

"He's shy," Mac said with a wink at me.

"Let's hope he's not wanted," Creole said.

"Is Kitty at the taxidermist again?" I asked.

"Kitty's perched on the top shelf in the office. That boyfriend of Miss January's is the one that threw her outside. He's lucky it wasn't in the trash, and I told him so. He'd planned to dispose of it the next day. He confessed that he found having a dead cat staring at him downright creepy, but he didn't want to hurt Miss January's feelings by telling her that it'd croaked. Probably afraid he'd have to pony up for a funeral."

"Your plan is to hope Miss January forgets, and if she remembers, tell her the same story?"

"Nooo." Mac put her hands on her hips and thrust out her chest.

Creole watched in amusement.

"I took pictures of Kitty and sent them to a stuffed animal artist in Lauderdale. She's making a stuffed look-alike. It won't be exact, but I'm hoping close enough. I did upgrade to battery-operated, so it'll shake a little."

"You should be paying me with all the talents you've been able to add to your resume," I said.

Mac snorted. "Like anyone else would ever hire me for some of this stuff. You're just saying that so I won't ask for a raise again." Mac cut me off. "We're pretty much out of excitement for the day. Maybe a little more when I boot cousin/bro. I called Crum back and cancelled the body clean-up. I fetched it myself, restuffed and taped it up, and dragged it to storage. Tomorrow, when the tour bus arrives to load up the guests for a day of sightseeing, I'll drag it back out, scare 'em a little. I'm thinking I could make a couple more. Multiple bodies would be far more shocking."

"Once word gets out that they're not real, you'll have disappointed guests on your hands," I warned. "Forward me the pics you took of the crime scene so I can take credit and impress Fab."

"She'll know," Mac cautioned. "Hard to put one over on that woman."

I looked up at Creole. "Are you ready?"

"Pretty much."

We waved and walked back to the truck.

Creole got behind the wheel and looked over at me. "I can't believe the stuff you deal with, and you never once reached for your Glock."

"You lived here back when; you know how it can be. Today was tame."

"The only interest I had in this place was you, and it's still that way."

Chapter Nineteen

Creole rounded the last curve before our house and slowed. "What the heck is going on?"

A white pickup truck was parked in front of the house, Fab standing not far away.

"Surprise!" I said.

He came to a sudden stop. "What?"

"Our security system is getting an update, which includes a keyless entry. I thought it was a good idea after losing my keys. I joked that I was going to surprise you, but I actually planned to tell you and forgot."

"Good idea." Creole pulled up and parked next to Didier's Mercedes. "Except Fab will have the code."

"It comes with directions on to how to change it." I'd known that would be a concern and questioned Fab about it in advance, getting her reassurance before agreeing.

Didier leaned against the bumper of his car. "He's almost done. What have you guys been doing?"

"After the discovery of a dead body, stuff got weirder from there, if you can believe that," Creole said, and told him what'd happened.

"Fab's got an update of her own. She made me promise to let her tell you."

I took my ringing phone out of my pocket, checked the screen, and answered. "You're not in trouble, are you?" The guys' eyes shot to me. *Liam*, I mouthed.

"Not this time."

I smiled at the phone, and the guys went back to their conversation.

"Went out to Star Island and hung out with Xander and Toady today. Spent the day floating in that gigantic pool and using the water slide. In case you forgot, the Bostwicks are going to be back in two days. They might not take kindly to the idea that they've had houseguests in their luxury party house, enjoying the amenities more than they ever have. I got that from the maid, who's back from her vacation."

"They're not tearing it up, are they?" I closed my eyes, trying not to anticipate bad news.

"Oh heck no. Xander was worried at first about King, but once the second rodent, Moby, arrived, he got over his shyness and both of them are getting along fine."

"Hold on a second. Fab," I yelled. Her head shot up, and I called, "Bostwick pay you?"

She shook her head with an angry glare.

I returned to the phone. "I'm back. You want an easy, well-paying gig?"

Liam laughed. "I've been warned to get details up front, but I'm doing it anyway."

"I'm thinking that's the same admonition Mother gave Spoon." I laughed. "I'll be emailing you an invoice in a couple of hours that you'll need to print out and deliver to Toady. I'll give him a call so he'll know it's coming. He's a good bill-collector." I'd be sure to suggest that he not outright threaten the man, just imply mayhem if he didn't cough up the payment on the spot. "I'm going to hand you off to Fab, in case she's got questions." I walked over and handed the phone to her. "Liam. You'll need to update your invoice to include the two rodent-walkers and Liam's services." I repeated our conversation. "Toady can be the one to greet the Bostwicks when they arrive home. I don't want Xander involved."

Creole and Didier had walked over after a conversation with Monty, the security guy, and eavesdropped on my call and hand-off of the phone. Creole shook his head.

"What?" I flashed an innocent face. "I've been known to handle a non-payer or two."

"Toady's not going to shoot him, is he?" Didier asked.

"Let's hope it doesn't come to that," I said.

Fab finished the call, then had a short conversation with Monty before he roared off with a wave.

The four of us went inside, got cold drinks, and sat out on the deck.

"My turn." Fab gave an exaggerated wave designed to draw all eyes to her, and it worked.

"According to Help, several days ago, a young woman was seen walking on the side of the highway out where he lives. Security cameras at the restaurant picked her up, but after that, she went missing. Her family filed a report. The cops searched and came up with no clues and no witnesses. None that came forward, anyway."

"What a creepy place to live," I said.

The guys nodded in agreement.

"Anything new on the bodies?" Creole asked.

"Nothing. I thought Madison and I would hit up the funeral home and see if the guys know anything about the bodies that were found. They have a friend in the coroner's office and are always up on the latest."

"That sounds like so much fun," I said sarcastically. The guys laughed. "Why don't you take Didier?"

"Nice of you to think of me." Didier glared, a spark of amusement in his blue eyes. "But I don't have any free time in my schedule. For that excursion anyway. That place creeps me out, and to think my wife has this ghoulish fascination is also creepy."

"Any other plans?" I asked Fab.

"I'm waiting on a call from Gunz, who maybe has a job for us. Something about getting paperwork straightened out for a friend, thrice removed."

"Translation: someone he doesn't know. Why doesn't he do it?"

"His family would like him to sit this one out since he's short on patience and has impulse control issues."

"Another person who shoots to get what he wants." Creole banged his bottle on the table.

"How dangerous is the job going to be?" Didier asked.

"Not at all," Fab reassured him. "It just takes someone with negotiation skills." She pointed at me.

Chapter Twenty

The next morning, Fab laid on the horn—my cue to hustle. She'd called Tropical Slumber and found out that they didn't have any send-offs planned, so now was a good time for a visit.

I hustled out of the house, yelling, "Coffee."

Fab crossed her lips with her fingers.

"What? We don't want to disturb the neighbors?"

She laughed as I climbed in. "We could hit Jake's for coffee and fill your cup with tequila."

"That's an idea for a very unproductive day. It just begets more tequila and then a long, drunken snooze."

Fab swung through the drive-through for morning motivation, then over to the funeral home. She slowed in the driveway, eyeing the construction in progress on a small building on the opposite side of the driveway from the main building, where final festivities were held.

I wondered what the corporation that originally owned the hot dog stand would think of what one of their prime locations had morphed into, a one-stop shop for all your funeral needs.

"What do you suppose is going on?" Fab asked, clearly not happy at not already knowing.

A *why are you asking me?* look on my face, I said, "Free advice: don't ask. It will be something weird." It wasn't a crematorium. They'd had one built years ago. Or a pet cemetery.

Fab parked in front of the door. The red carpet was missing; I hoped it hadn't been stolen. I'd rather buy them a new one than track it down.

Dickie and Raul, the owners, stood in the doorway, waving. I did a double take at Dickie, who normally sported a pair of suit pants and dress shirt but had on a pair of jeans today. The waistline would have been under his breasts if the tall, stick-skinny man had had any. He was the artist, code for dead-person dresser. Raul, buffed and sporting a twelve-pack, handled the business end and was the one loathe to turn down any idea, even when it was clear the situation should be dialed back.

Fab pointed to the construction.

"It's a surprise," Dickie said.

Fab grabbed Raul's arm and pulled him off to the side.

Astro and Necco, twin Dobermans, skidded out the door and ran to me for a head scratch. I waved at Dickie, who waved and grumbled, "He's telling her, isn't he?"

"It's hard to keep secrets from Fab."

Dickie mulled that over. "We're building a showroom/museum. We'll be arranging vignettes so customers have more artistic choices."

"Well…that's a great idea." I hoped I sounded convincing.

"When we're not in a conference with a client, we'll open it to tourists. To start, we're only going to open it on weekends and gauge the interest."

"Won't you have to hire someone to sit out here?"

"We hired Joseph," Dickie said, sounding surprised that I didn't already know.

"My tenant?" My eyebrows shot up.

"I'm guessing he didn't tell you."

"Must have slipped his mind." I smiled lamely.

Fab and Raul joined us, and we went inside. I chose the plastic slip-covered getaway chair for its location next to the door. For once, Fab sat next to me instead of going on her usual prowl, poking her head into the viewing rooms. Maybe she had a heads up that they were empty.

"Drinks?" Raul asked.

"Bottled water?" He nodded, and I added, "And some dog treats to maintain my status as favorite."

He came back with sausage stick things that I eyed skeptically, but the dogs perked up and eagerly sat on their haunches. They grabbed them out of my hand and gobbled them down in a flash.

Raul settled back in a chair across the room, Dickie preferring to stand. "The three bodies that were found in Card Sound were all friends out of Homestead and disappeared at the same time," Raul said. "According to our friend at the coroner's office, the cops believe they were killed elsewhere and dumped out there. Someone most likely figured the area is remote enough that the bodies would never be found."

"Did you handle the send-offs?" I asked.

Raul shook his head. "We do get a lot of business referred our way, but not this time."

"They're not the first bodies that've been recovered out there." Dickie clenched his hands.

"Your friend know if they have any suspects?" Fab asked.

"If they do, they're not sharing," Raul said. "I can make a phone call, see if there's an update and ask to be notified if there is one."

"A bag of remains was also recently recovered," I said, recalling the gruesome find.

"Haven't heard about that one," Raul answered. "I'll find out what I can."

"Almost forgot our other good news," Dickie said. "Since you spilled about the construction to Fab, I told Madison. So I get to tell them about our latest venture. We're going to offer weddings."

I coughed.

Fab glared at me, then asked enthusiastically, "Where?"

"The couples will have a choice: here in the main room or out on the patio." Raul flourished his hand. "We're having a gazebo constructed. Also turning two of the viewing rooms into dressing rooms, one on each end so the bride and groom don't run into each other. We've never had all the rooms occupied at once, so I don't see it as a problem."

"Did one of you get your license to perform weddings?" Fab asked.

"We mulled that possibility over and agreed that neither of us has an outgoing enough personality that we think would make the events a success," Raul said. "I'm surprised you haven't heard. Crum got his license, and he's going to perform the ceremonies."

I had just taken a long swig of water and almost spit it back in the bottle. "Crum? Joseph? How did you hook up with those two? Did you get it in writing that Crum will wear clothes?"

"We got to talking when he sold us the stripper pole, and he signed onto the idea. He has a knack for knowing what sells. He sold out the poles."

"I hadn't heard." I glared at Fab. I didn't want to know why they'd bought one and hoped Fab wouldn't ask.

"We bought one in case we ever got a request," Raul volunteered. "Crum agreed to dress appropriately, and if the purchase of a costume for a theme wedding is necessary, I assured him that we'd cover the cost."

"If you know someone looking to tie the knot in an outside venue, it really is quite pretty out there," Dickie said.

"I'll pass it along," I said with forced enthusiasm.

"You two always come up with the best ideas," Fab said supportively, standing and heading to the door.

The dogs bounded to their feet, knowing their best chance at another escape to romp outside was coming up.

I waved to Dickie, who stayed behind, and followed Fab and Raul to the car.

"The best ideas," I sniffed after closing the car door.

Fab honked and roared out the back exit. "What was I supposed to say?"

"Be mean, like you are to me."

Chapter Twenty-One

For once, we weren't driving to Miami. Fab's latest client lived in the Keys in a small weathered house off the Overseas. Gunz had put a rush on the job, and the only detail I'd learned thus far was that it required restraint.

"Now that we're here, are you going to part with the details of the case?" I asked.

Fab slowly cruised the street, u-turned, and parked down the block. "You have your Glock on you?"

"Of course. But you told the guys this was a paperwork job."

Fab reached between the seats and handed me an envelope off the back seat.

"I could've been going through this on the way over," I snapped and pulled out a sheaf of papers that turned out to be legal documents, the cover sheet a list of instructions. "Deeds? So what's the backstory? And here's another pesky question: who's doing what?"

"Mira Hunter's husband died and left her in financial straits. She was on the verge of losing her house when she got approached by a husband-and-wife investor team saying that they had a buyer who'd pay cash for a quick close. All she had to do was sign a quit claim deed. In her defense, she did a cursory check on the internet and, finding only good reviews on their website, signed everything they put in front of her."

I groaned. "I know where this is going."

"The interesting thing is that the investor couple never did anything with the property. Possibly because the duo was up to their necks in legal trouble for fraud, theft, and a handful of other charges. With the law breathing down their necks, they skipped town. They were hauled back, sentenced to jail, and they just got out."

"The client wants…?"

"Mira Thompson is the sweet woman's name."

I didn't bother to hide my eyeroll. "Knowing something about this process, I imagine that this is now a big fat paperwork mess."

"Mira needs us to get felon couple to sign another deed, transferring the property back into her name. She tried, but they refused and didn't offer an explanation as to why. Interestingly, they didn't hold her up for cash either. She did hire a foot-dragging lawyer, but ran out of money before it got to court. Not seeing any bucks in it for him, he bailed."

"Who lives here?" I asked. "Because if this is the house in question, it doesn't appear to be worth more than the cost to have it demolished." The wood-frame house showed signs that a multi-generational family of termites had built their nests inside.

"Felon couple lives here."

I had a bad feeling about this as I thumbed through the paperwork. "Jessie and Berta Samson would be their names."

"Okay."

"I'm going to use my powers of premonition here. We're going to go to the door and ask politely for them to sign these documents?" I pointed to my lap.

"When you have a premonition, you're supposed to rub your forehead." Fab smiled cheekily.

"And when felon couple says hit the road, then what?"

"We threaten them."

"A bribe would be better. Is there cash available?"

"Mira is fresh out, and since Gunz doesn't even know her and it's a favor to a friend of a friend...somewhere along the family line—"

I sliced my hand across my throat. "A simple no would've been faster."

"I had to stall because I don't want you asking for an alternate plan."

"Hmm..." I tapped my chin until I got an eyeroll. "Let's run a con on them. Bribe them with a big pay-off and renege, then beat it out the door."

"That's why, being the best friend that I am,

I'll be right by your side while you work your magic."

I snorted. "I'll do the talking. You're the muscle. Don't pull your gun unless it's self-defense."

Fab started the engine, coasted down the block, and parked across from the white shack.

I got out, envelope in hand, and surveyed the property. "The termites have been well fed." I was happy to have on tennis shoes as we walked over the weed-riddled gravel path to the front door. I knocked and heard the hollow sound signifying a cheap door that could be easily kicked in.

Fab stood behind me and off to one side.

The door opened, and a middle-aged man with a grey handlebar mustache—the color matching his hair—stood in the entry checking us out from head to toe. "We're not buying whatever you're selling." He leered.

"Mr. Samson, I've got an offer for you. I'm sure you can spare a few minutes." I smiled, reminiscent of a used car salesman.

"What's this about?" He squinted. "Cut to the chase. I'm smelling a con in a pretty package."

"Mind if we come in?"

"As a matter fact, I do. Three seconds." He tapped his wrist where a watch would've been if he'd had one on.

I trotted out my professional voice. "I'm here on behalf of Mira Hunter to offer you cash and a notarized document that there won't be any further litigation on this matter in exchange for your signature on a quit claim deed."

"Why would I want to do that?" Samson huffed. "I got the rights to sell and pocket a load of cash."

"Not if we get an injunction to stop said sale. You'd end up in court and run the risk of going back to prison." The chances of that were slim, but I was betting on him being ignorant of that fact. "I'd think you'd be tired of the place."

"Who's at the door?" a woman screeched from behind him. A similarly grey-haired woman peered around his shoulder. "What do you want?"

"Your signature in exchange for cash."

"What's this one about?" she asked.

"Mira Hunter."

"Dumb bitch thought she knew it all and didn't know anything," Mrs. Samson crowed. "It was easy to get her signature on the docs, and we never looked back. And you know what? It was all legal." She preened.

"Why not sell it like you promised and be done with it?"

"The money we can make renting it will pay our legal bills."

I disliked this couple with their squinty, beady brown eyes. "Here's the deal: sign and we'll be gone. Or I'll file a claim against the title, and you won't be able to sell it until you deal with me."

"How much?" She rubbed her fingers together.

"One thousand."

She laughed. "Ten. Greenbacks and we'll sign. You think I'm stupid? Cash upfront." Mrs. Samson rubbed her hands together and held her hand out.

Mr. Samson's eyes glittered. "We'll sign in here on the table."

"I'm not stupid either." I ignored Fab poking me in the back. "Meet us at the Postal Center. We'll have your signatures notarized, which you must know is required, then head over to the bank that's right there in the same shopping center where I'll make the withdrawal. We can take care of everything in one stop." I smiled, hiding my revulsion.

"We'll meet you there." Mrs. Samson grinned.

"Don't forget your ID," I reminded her.

Fab and I turned and walked back to the car.

"Don't say anything," Fab whispered. "They haven't closed the door."

"Let them stare. They're going to get our tag number, which I don't like."

"Neither had a weapon on them. Where the heck are you getting the cash?" Fab demanded once we got in the car. "If your plan is to actually pay them, withdrawing that amount will require filling out forms. And keep in mind, I highly doubt we'll be reimbursed."

"They're not getting a cent," I said adamantly.

"We're going to play this cool. Get the docs signed, go into the bank, and then it's your turn to shine. You get hot on the phone and make sure that when I come walking out, the Samsons are blocked in. We'll skate and get gone."

"You think we can pull that off?" Fab appeared suitably impressed.

"We can with a distraction."

Fab slowed, leaving the residential area and only sped up once the Samsons backed out of the driveway in their older model sedan, keeping them in her rearview mirror as she headed to the shopping center.

* * *

"You're on," I said to Fab, getting out of the car. "You have about fifteen minutes, tops, to get our distraction in place."

I went into the Postal Center and checked to make sure a notary was on staff, then waited outside for felon couple. My stomach was a bundle of nerves, and I hoped that this didn't end in some serious butt-kicking…or worse.

The Samsons rumbled up and parked in front of the bank, opting to walk down the sidewalk to meet me. "We'd like to check over the paperwork before we go inside." Mr. Samson held out his hand.

"Don't trust me?"

Samson jerked the envelope out of my hands

and slapped it into his wife's. She withdrew the deeds and scanned the documents.

I'd made sure that the documents were filled out properly, with no cross-outs, and, more importantly, that they hadn't been signed erroneously, thereby rendering them invalid before we even got started. Only an unscrupulous notary would put their seal on fraudulent-looking documents. If I didn't keep an eye on these two and refuse to let the documents out of my sight, it wouldn't surprise me if they had their dog sign them.

It was hot, and I was about to complain about sweat when she shoved the paperwork halfway back in the envelope. We went inside and up to the counter. I stood back and watched the process carefully, then stepped up to pay.

Mrs. Samson shoved the papers back into the envelope, sticking them under her arm. "I'll be accompanying you to the bank."

I watched Mrs. Samson like a hawk as we walked in silence to the bank, Mr. Samson going back to the car. I opened the outer door of the bank. "I'll take the paperwork now." To my surprise, Mrs. Samson handed it over without a word.

She looked around in a nervous fidget. "I'll be waiting right here." She motioned to a seating area that overlooked the parking lot.

I was happy to see that there were several people in line—the longer this took, the more time Fab had to act. When it was my turn, I smiled at the teller and asked for a hundred dollars in fives. I'd thought about asking for ones, but that would be obnoxious. Besides, it would be counted by a machine, so it wouldn't delay things enough to give Fab more time. At the same moment, the teller handed me an envelope of cash, my phone dinged. I felt like my sigh of relief could be heard throughout the bank. I thanked her and turned as two cop cars pulled in and parked next to the Samsons' sedan. Mrs. Samson barely covered a shriek. She ran outside and cut across to the street, jaywalking to the honking of oncoming traffic.

"Cops?" I said, surprised, as I hopped into the car.

Fab already had the car in reverse and started moving the second I got the door closed. "I didn't tell Gunz how to get the job done; I left it up to his discretion." She had the GPS programmed for our next stop.

"Let's hit the courthouse and file this document before one of the Samsons gets a wild hair to derail us. They'll never sign a second time, especially if they suspect we had anything to do with their current trouble."

At the courthouse, I got out and went into the County Clerk's office, leaving Fab on the phone, giving her client another update. There was no line, and I breezed through, coming back with a copy of the filed paperwork and sliding into the passenger seat. The final deed would be mailed.

Fab roared out of the parking lot and headed back out on the Overseas towards home. "Gunz wants us to pay a visit to Mira and let her know that everything was taken care of. I wanted to tell him that he could just call her, but didn't." She flicked down her visor. "Behind us." At the same moment, the car jolted forward as something hit us.

I looked in the side mirror and spotted a sedan behind us. "What's going on?" I expected her to pull over, but instead, she hit the gas and flew down the highway, weaving in and out of traffic.

"It's one or both of the Samsons; it's hard to tell. My guess is they're not happy with us."

"Now what?"

"We're going to lose them." Fab hit the gas as though she expected the traffic signal to stay green, but it conspired against her and turned red. She hit the brakes and squealed to a halt.

The Samsons had managed to hold their own and were now a couple of cars back. Mr. Samson lumbered out of the passenger side and ran down the highway. The man was in lousy shape and not very fast. He'd just gotten parallel with the rear bumper when the light turned green. He reached for the door handle and tugged, apparently not registering that it was locked.

Fab once again hit the gas. He stumbled back and shook his fists. The sedan, Mrs. Samson behind the wheel, slowed to pick him up, and the chase was back on, except they couldn't keep up now that Fab had taken the curve north and hit open highway headed out of town.

"If they lie in wait, they'll catch us coming back into town," I said. There was no place to park along the highway and remain unseen. They could pull off to the side, but we'd see them as they'd stick out, and there were signs posted making it illegal.

"That's why I'm turning back now." Fab turned left at the next light and hung a u-turn.

I kept my eyes peeled and didn't see them. "The problem is we have two people on our tail that feel cheated out of money they're not owed. You need to fix the problem."

Fab got on the phone and told someone what had just gone down. The call—which Fab did not put on speaker, much to my irritation—was short and terminated after she relayed the facts.

Without a word, Fab drove straight to Jake's and parked in front of the lighthouse she owned. I also claimed ownership, since it sat on my property. Its origins? Fab had been vague on the details. A moment later, a black Navigator pulled in alongside her. I didn't recognize the car or the driver.

"Grab your stuff," Fab ordered, getting out and meeting the driver of the other car, who had gotten out. After a short conversation and the exchange of keys, she grabbed her bag out of the back and beckoned me to get in the SUV.

I smiled lamely at the nondescript man dressed in tropical attire. His bold stare made it clear he wasn't a man to mess with. He nodded, got behind the wheel of the Escalade, and left the parking lot in a sedate fashion, not drawing any attention.

"Gunz apologizes for not exchanging the vehicles before there was a problem," Fab said.

"I'm surprised he didn't show for the exchange."

"He's keeping a low profile. As in out of sight. He's rehabilitating his image, leaving any whiff of criminality behind him."

"One thing for certain, he has spectacular rides." I turned and checked out the back, running my hand over the leather seat. "I want my Hummer back, but I'm happy those two cretins can't track me down using my tag number." I blew out a long sigh. "I'm not sure how we explain our latest acquisition. If you've got a good story lined up, now would be a good time to share."

"You're going to need two car explanations, since you let your family believe that you got rid of the Hummer. How are you going to explain its reappearance?"

"I'll think of something inane. I'm more worried about explaining this new ride to Creole, since when we left, it was on a paperwork job and I haven't placed a frantic call."

Fab laughed wickedly. "I've got advice for that."

"No thanks." I turned and looked out the window.

Chapter Twenty-Two

Fab dropped me off at my house and drove the short distance to her house.

"Honey, I'm home," I yelled, banging the door behind me. I spotted Creole sitting on the couch, appearing faintly amused as I twirled toward him, curtseying and flinging myself into his arms.

He kissed me and set me back on my feet. "We don't have time."

"Are you sure?" I scowled at him.

"Harder came to town for some reason I'm not privy to and stopped by the office. He suggested that we go to dinner, and instead, Didier invited him over. Harder then asked that Help be included." Creole slapped me on the butt. "You need to change."

"It must be important for the big gun to come to town."

I showered and changed into a black dress that I'd gotten while out shopping with Fab, pairing it with slide heels. When he saw me, Creole whistled and put his arm around me, walking me out the door and helping me into his truck.

It surprised me that he didn't comment on the absence of the Escalade, but he probably figured that Fab had absconded with it, as she was known to do just that. It was rare that Fab's driveway was full of vehicles, but when we pulled in, Help's truck was parked there, along with a Mercedes sedan and the SUV that was the Escalade's replacement.

Fab stood in the doorway and waved. "Did you know anything about this?" she asked as I walked into the entry.

"Last-minute invite. Let's hope the food is good," I teased.

Creole greeted Didier and Harder, while Help, who was tending bar, held up a couple of bottles.

The doorbell rang. I turned to Fab, who shrugged, then walked over and opened the door.

Mila charged into the room, flowers in hand, which she presented to Fab. Brad came in immediately behind her.

"They're gorgeous," Fab gushed, picking her up and swinging her around.

"My brother?" I said to Creole, who shook his head; he hadn't known Brad had been invited either.

"Where's my baby girl?" a deep male voice boomed from behind Brad.

"Caspian." Fab rushed toward her father, and

he enveloped her and Mila in a three-way hug, which the little girl loved. She held out her arms to the man.

"Caspian's the party crasher; I'm along for the fun." Brad laughed. To the questioning stares, he said, "Caspian stopped by the office — looking for anybody but me, I'd guess — and when I informed him of Didier's furtive dealings and the dinner I'd overheard plans for, he said, 'they're always saying *stop by anytime*.' So here we are."

"Everyone is welcome anytime," Fab assured us, backing it up with a look that defied anyone to challenge her, and when no one contradicted her, she headed to the kitchen, Mila skipping next to her.

"You're getting worse than Mother," I said to Brad.

He hugged me and kissed my cheek. "Speaking of…if you don't want Mother to know about this, you better be tight-lipped; she won't be hearing it from me."

Didier made the introductions, leading us into the living room/dining room that was the focal point of the u-shaped house. It had a breathtaking view of the pool area and the water beyond. Creole took drink orders.

"If this dinner has anything to do with the goings on in Card Sound, I should've been invited." Brad huffed in annoyance, his eyes full of amusement. "I played an instrumental role on the day the security system went in."

"How so, dude?" Help questioned, handing him a beer.

"I did my best to stay out of the way. When called on to check out the nearby mangroves for dead bodies, I didn't say 'hell no,' which was my first thought."

"You're a team player," Help said, the corners of his lips quirked.

"That'd be me. Helpful dude." Brad grinned.

"Thank you for hosting this impromptu get-together." Harder tipped his glass to Fab and Didier.

After dinner, we stayed seated at the dining room table. Dark clouds had rolled in late in the afternoon and loomed on the horizon, threatening a downpour. The sliding pocket doors had been pushed back, and a breeze wafted in across the water.

Fab had filled an oversized chair with pillows, making it comfortable for Mila to stretch out in. Headphones on, she watched a cartoon on the television that hung on the wall.

Harder stood and excused himself, coming back to the table with his briefcase.

"That reminds me," Didier said, eyeing the paperwork the chief was shuffling through. He left and came back with a manila envelope that he placed in front of Fab. "Special delivery from Toady. I'm to hand it to you directly. Not sure what else he thought I'd do with it. But now I have witnesses."

"Oh good." I clapped. "Let's hope it's full of cash."

"Is that why Toady said to tell you, 'I didn't threaten the man, but he knew I meant business'?" Didier asked.

Fab opened the envelope, peered inside, and smiled. "I thought I was going to have to put Bostwick in the freebie column. Thank you for dealing with this for me." She nodded at me.

"Cheap bastard thought he was going to trick you and stiff you. I don't think so," I said fiercely.

Harder's eyebrow shot up. "Make sure it's not counterfeit; it's on the rise again. We had a lull, but now twenties are showing up around town."

Didier related the rodent-on-a-leash story, which had everyone laughing. "Toady told me that he'd made acquaintances in the neighborhood and booked a pony-sitting gig that he and the kid are going to take care of while the owners take a short trip to Europe."

"Ponies? Star Island?" I said to Harder.

"Really rich people." Harder shrugged. "You can bet that if there's an ordinance against it, and there probably is, one of the neighbors will get hot on the phone to report them and then, hopefully, said pony will be moved to more appropriate surroundings."

"Hopefully, it's house-trained." I laughed, trying to picture that.

"You've had too much to drink." Creole

covered the top of my wine glass.

"I'd like to meet this Toady person," Caspian said.

"He's quite enamored with your daughter, and I believe he'd do anything for her," I said, winking at Fab.

Fab's cheeks turned pink.

"I'm working on rehabbing Toady's appearance so he's not an ad for thug-wear," Fab said. "I convinced him it was better to come as a surprise to unsuspecting people, so he could lay them out on the concrete in a split second."

"That's a good idea. It's exactly what Mother did for Spoon," I said.

"I've met Toady a couple of times," Harder said. "He's got friends in the department that speak highly of him, and no rap sheet, which is a good thing." He opened his briefcase and took out five photos, setting them on the table. "Recognize any of these fine criminals?"

The pictures were passed around.

Help recognized three of the four young men. "I've seen them around Card Sound, but not lately."

"This one—" I tapped the photo of the only woman. "—is Addy Clegg, creepy woman who got rid of the Hummer in record time. Since it ended up with that criminal Deuce, they must have had a business relationship, and considering the speed of the disappearance, it wasn't the first time."

"If Addy had her way, we wouldn't have gotten out of there alive," Fab said. "She didn't think twice before pulling the trigger."

Brad fingered the photo of the last man. "He's the driver who cut me off where the road merges with Highway One, then slowed, rolling down his window to flip me off. I turned in the opposite direction, not wanting any trouble."

"If these are cretins from the mangroves," I said, "you should hit up Cootie for a rundown on the neighborhood." I went on to tell those that didn't know how we'd met.

"You make interesting friends," Harder said with a hint of humor.

"I rather like the old guy, and he did help us when we needed it without expecting anything in return. I can make the introductions, but I'd appreciate it if you didn't arrest him for cooking moonshine."

"Distilling," Creole corrected.

Harder laughed and made a choking noise. "I'd be honored to meet Mr. Cootie."

"It's Cootie Shine. It's one of those deals where we'd need to show up at his trailer and knock, see if he's around. He probably would be, since his truck is waiting on a part. I should check on that," I said, more to myself than them.

"What's the story on the guys in the pictures?" Help asked Harder.

"They're members of a tight little club, The Bangers." Harder's eyes narrowed. "The initiation requires one to bring a victim and murder the unsuspecting person in front of the group."

Most of us sucked in a shocked breath. That kind of activity happened in other parts of the country, not in laid-back South Florida.

"How did you catch this break?" Creole asked. "I'm assuming they're not in custody."

"Got lucky with the arrest of this young man in Homestead." Harder pointed to one of the pictures. "He drove the getaway car in a failed robbery, and low and behold, blood was discovered in the trunk. There were rumors about his affiliations, but he was a tough cookie. His so-called associates must have been worried he'd talk because he was attacked in jail, beaten up, and left for dead… He survived, and at the behest of his mother and a lawyer from the old neighborhood, a deal was brokered for him to turn state's evidence. He's currently in protective custody. With his help, we're going to put this group in prison."

"Did he murder someone?" I asked.

"He did not. Driving the getaway car was a test, one of many, which would've escalated to murder if he hadn't gotten arrested. There were two other guys involved in the robbery, neither pictured here." He flicked at the pile. "One's body was dumped in a bay at a car wash. The other disappeared, and time will tell if he's dead, but if he isn't now, then he probably will be when one of the group catches up with him."

"I know the department has made deals with the devil for the greater good," Creole said. "This guy isn't so hard to take. Hope he takes his second chance and doesn't waste it."

"Another thing." Harder zeroed in on me, Fab, and included Help. "You need to stay away from Card Sound until we have everyone in custody."

"You don't have to tell me twice," I said. "That place gives me the creeps."

Fab agreed without having to be strong-armed. "About Addy, is she part of this club?"

"She's the mother of these three." The chief pushed three pictures forward. "It's hard to believe that she doesn't know about her murdering spawn. But maybe not. There's a lot of stupid people wandering around unattended. We'd like to have a long chat with her and ascertain for ourselves her involvement, or lack thereof."

"Addy didn't come off as the picture of stability," I said. "I have enough experience to know. She did fire that shotgun of hers a few times—the first two at us, but the last couple were, I think, a signal. Just my guess. Living out in the wilderness like that, there's no one to complain about noise, and if someone did hear, they'd mind their own business."

"Do you have a place to stay?" Creole asked Help.

"I've got vacation time coming and my plan is

to sign on to a fishing boat that's getting ready to pull out for a few days. Giving it a test run for a future second career. I know if I show up last-minute, I have a good chance of replacing a no-show," Help told him.

"If you run into any problems, give me a call; I can make it happen," Brad said. He still owned the majority interest in his fishing boat, though it had been a long time since he'd captained it, leaving that to his partner. "If my boat's getting ready to pull out, we'll take you on; we can always use an extra hand. If not, I've got plenty of connections."

"Much appreciated," Help said. "I've been meaning to talk to you about the fishing business, and there hasn't been a good time."

"I don't like finding out how dangerous this situation is," Caspian glared at his daughter. "You've had plenty of opportunity to tell me, and you haven't."

"After the initial confrontation, my only involvement has been setting up the cameras," Fab said. "Like Madison, I have no desire to go back out there."

"Anything else to share?" Caspian's brown eyes intensified on his daughter.

Fab and I exchanged a *who's going to tell them?* look.

"This ought to be good," Brad said.

I rolled my eyes at Brad and kicked him under the table. I held out my hand to Fab, thumb poised as if to flip a non-existent coin.

Fab waved my hand away. "I always lose these coin tosses of yours. I'll tell them. We were rear-ended."

Nothing like jumping into the middle. "You might want to start at the beginning. Once upon a time…" Fab and I laughed.

The men stared, unamused.

"And I thought I was kidding," Brad said.

"It started out as a good deed." Fab chuckled and went on to give them the detailed version of the day, not skimping, even though we were in the company of law enforcement.

"So, your friend got real cops to show up and…" Harder said.

"I didn't ask. I did say that we needed the two detained long enough to make our getaway," Fab said.

"It was a good idea to swap out cars," Creole said. "Felon couple, as you called them, will be on the lookout for the wrong vehicle. In addition, the window tint, which is *illegal* by the way, gives you some anonymity."

"You have interesting friends," Harder said.

"This particular connection is a friend of hers." I pointed to Fab. "He's been slow to warm up to me and tolerates me at best. No matter how much charm I unleash." That got a laugh from Creole.

"Anytime you need a car, I can have one here in an hour," Caspian said. "Better yet, it will come with a driver that has a license to carry and the ability to kick ass."

Didier hugged Fab to his side. "It's a full-time job keeping an eye on her."

Chapter Twenty-Three

Fab talked me out of the house with a bribe of coffee. It took the promise of extra whipped cream. She whisked me off to the Bakery Café, where I claimed our favorite seats. She went inside and ordered, coming back with a tray and, for once, her own danish and not just an extra fork to pick at mine.

"I need to go to the office today, and if you're a really good friend, you'll come along without any grumbling." Fab pulled out a chair, appearing ready to blurt out what was really on her agenda.

"You're in luck. I want to check on our assistant and make sure he's none the worse for wear after hanging out with Toady all that time. I didn't expect Toady to stay, but it seems to have worked out."

"Toady reported that they had a good time. Who'd have thought, when we first met him, that we'd end up working together?"

"I think he fell in love with you when he pointed his gun at the windshield and you got out of the SUV and got in his face. From there, a yarn for the diehard romance reader could be spun, except no happy ending. At least, not for the two of you."

"Too much coffee already," Fab tsked.

"Thief," someone yelled.

We both looked up as a young guy barreled down the sidewalk, familiar pink box in hand. Just as he passed our table, he tripped, face-planted in the box, and didn't move.

Fab shook her foot and stuck it back under the table.

"He's dead," a woman two tables down shrieked.

Fab extended her leg and kicked him in the butt…hard. "He twitched," she yelled back as she straightened in her chair.

The bakery owner, who I recognized, ran down the walk. Keeping her distance, she pulled out her phone.

"I'd never have thought of sticking out my foot," I said. "He'd be long gone. Maybe you'll get your picture on the Internet. Hot, sexy woman stops pastry thief. Let's hope he doesn't die," I whispered theatrically and got a glare, which amused me.

"I don't know what happened to the poor fellow, do you?" Fab asked with fake sincerity.

I shrugged. "I was minding my own business when he fell…not on my feet, thankfully. Close enough."

"We should leave."

"We're eyewitnesses."

"That don't know anything," Fab reminded me.

"Wouldn't be the first time."

A siren could be heard in the distance, getting closer.

Fab's phone rang, and she flipped me the screen before answering.

Gunz. Again. I frowned, but knew this wasn't the place for speakerphone. And besides, she wouldn't do that for one of his calls anyway.

A cop car double-parked in front of the café and Kevin got out. I waved.

"It's been a while," he said as he got closer and checked out the not-so-dead guy, who was beginning to stir. An ambulance rolled up. Kevin left the thief to the EMTs and went to talk to the owner.

Fab finished her call. "We have a job." She sighed. "Another favor that Gunz has delegated to me."

"I'm afraid to ask."

"Welfare check."

"The last time, or maybe the time before…" I made a face. "Anyway…the kid—who wasn't so young; grown adult, as I recall—turned out to be a mental patient and his girlfriend had outstanding warrants."

Fab gave me an *are you finished?* look. "In this particular case, it's a woman in her nineties. Her daughter, a cousin of his sister's cousin, had dinner with her mother last night, and when she called this morning, as she always does, the line was busy and has stayed busy. The daughter thinks her mother left the phone off the hook, as it's happened before."

"A landline? That's a rarity. Why doesn't the daughter get off her duff? While we're at it, why would she send Gunz?"

"Gunz's family is close-knit, and if there's a problem, everything is referred to him and he delegates." Fab shrugged.

I stopped short of snorting. I'd met two of the family members, who were certifiable and loved a good fight.

Fab's phone pinged with a message, which she opened and read. "Ms. Leona is a nurse, and she can't run out on her patients."

"If it was my mother, I'd be worried too. Did you inquire if the woman would be gunned up?"

"Just when I thought you were being very sweet. I take it back." Fab smiled sneakily. "I told Gunz that you were coming with me and perfect for the job. We're the perfect pair."

"I'm not certain if you meant that as a compliment." I laughed at her glare.

Kevin marched over and peered down at us. "What do you two know?"

"I'm sure you'd agree—nothing." I sucked down the last of my coffee, sorry to see my cup empty.

His lips quirked. "About this incident." He flicked his finger at the stretcher being loaded in the back of the ambulance.

I shrugged and looked at Fab.

"Nothing," Fab said.

"Is this a case of stolen bakery goods?" I asked.

"That, and stupid tried to rob the register. He wasn't successful at either," Kevin informed us.

"I need to go and check on my friend's grandmother." Fab smiled sweetly. "It's not like you don't know where to find us if you have more questions."

Kevin looked ready to snap cuffs on her. Lucky her that being annoying wasn't an arrestable offense.

"Here's what we know," I interrupted the stare-down. "Someone yelled. He tripped and was out. You arrived."

"Was that so difficult?" Kevin asked Fab and walked off.

"I think he likes us," Fab said.

I laughed.

Chapter Twenty-Four

It was a beautiful day for a drive up Highway One, sunny with white fluffy clouds dotting the sky. It was mild by the usual standards, and a light breeze blew off the water from both sides of the road.

Fab took the cut-off to Palmetto Bay, a small town on the eastern coast of the state. She turned onto a quiet street in a well-kept neighborhood of older homes and green, manicured lawns.

Eloise Leona's home was in the middle of the block opposite where another street intersected, and the streets were narrow, leaving no room for on-street parking. The driveway was a weed patch of broken concrete. Green and black fungus grew up the side of the crumbling cream stucco two-story house, which showed signs of neglect and disrepair.

"It's creepy-looking," I whispered.

Fab hit the brakes and swerved to avoid a Golden Retriever that had run off the property and into the street. She turned onto a side street and looped back around. The dog hadn't disappeared, but had gotten out of the road and now sat on the sagging curb. Having decided there was no way to park in front of the house and run up to the door without taking up half the road, she backed down the intersecting street and parked facing Leona's house.

I reached behind the seat and took my tennis shoes out of my bag. "What?" I said to Fab's questioning look, throwing my sandals on the back seat. "I'm not going to trudge up the broken path and through ankle-length weeds to the front door in sandals. My good deed doesn't deserve to be repaid with bug bites on my feet."

Fab also swapped out her shoes. "What's up with the dog?"

"Maybe he's lost. You ask him."

We got out and headed in the direction of the house, and the dog ran toward us, got within arm's length, stopped, and began to bark.

"Stomp your foot like the badass you are and maybe it will run home." I laughed at her scowl. "Hey, pooch." I held out the back of my hand for the obligatory sniff, but the dog continued to bark, then ran in circles, only to start barking again. He hadn't run away and wasn't aggressive, and I suspected he was trying to tell us something. "Unless you can decipher dog-speak, I'm thinking he wants us to follow him."

"He's not our client." Fab jerked on my arm. "This way. We'll cut around him and he can run home."

That great idea only lasted a second. The dog continued to bark, now running alongside us.

"It's probably Eloise's dog, who got out for a romp and she hasn't noticed and let him back inside," I reasoned.

Within feet of the door, the dog stopped barking and started whimpering. He head-butted my leg, and I reached down to scratch him. "It's been a while since we needed a dog treat. Hopefully, Eloise will have one, and if the dog's not hers, she'll know who owns it."

The greying and faded drapes were drawn across the windows. Fab rang the bell, but neither of us heard any sound. She opened what was left of the screen door—the bottom half had been chewed away—and raised her hand to knock on the weathered door, then dropped it suddenly and pushed the door open into the mildew-musty living room.

"Mrs. Leona," Fab called. "Eloise."

The dog, who'd hung back, bounded inside and skittered across the darkened living room, skidding to a stop next to a body that lay face down, a knife protruding from its back.

I pinched Fab's arm to stop her from taking another step. She grunted, and I pointed to the carpet, where the body lay in a pool of blood that had seeped through the fibers. An overturned side table, a broken lamp, books strewn about...judging by the disarray, they'd put up a fight. From this distance, and with the victim's head turned away, it was hard to tell if they were male or female. The bathrobe suggested that it was a woman, one with short grey hair. I wasn't going to volunteer to make the sad phone call to Mrs. Leona's daughter. Unless this was her handiwork or—I drew my Glock and looked around the room—the killer was still here.

Fab had come to the same conclusion and drew her weapon.

"We need to get the heck out of here and take the dog with us; his bloody paw prints everywhere aren't going to be helpful."

"Careful where you step," Fab admonished.

"Poochy," I called and slapped my thigh, and to my relief, the dog responded. I backed up towards the door, double-checking with each step I took, and clucked at the dog. I didn't stop until I'd crossed the street and was leaning against the bumper of the SUV. "Sit," I told the dog and scratched his head.

Fab wasn't hot on my heels, but that didn't surprise me. I had no plans to move from my post unless I heard a scream.

It didn't take long before Fab reappeared, phone to her ear. After a few words, she hung up. "Gunz wants us to handle whatever this turns out to be." She hit the speaker button and made a call.

"911, what's your emergency?" the call-taker asked.

"I'm calling to report a…" Fab looked at me.

"Murder. You can't knife yourself in the back," I said for her.

"Are you certain the person is dead?"

"I'm certain. Her skin is a bluish color." Fab squeezed her eyes shut for a moment.

The woman on the other end of the phone asked the address and then a series of other questions. "Did you look around inside? Are there any other victims?"

"There's no one else on the first floor. I didn't go upstairs."

"Go to a safe place and stay there. I'll stay on the line with you until officers arrive." As I walked away, I could hear the call-taker asking more questions: "How do you know the victim? Why did you go there and when did you arrive?"

I whistled to Poochy, who I swear looked back at me with a *That's a whistle?* Expression, but stuck to my side. I opened the liftgate and motioned for the dog to hop up.

Fab rounded the side of the SUV, thrusting her phone at me.

I crossed my arms. "Aren't you supposed to be talking to the 911 woman?"

"We got disconnected." Fab jabbed her phone at my chest. "You need to call the daughter and break the news."

"On the phone." I squirmed and took it from her. "The cops generally perform this unpleasant job, and they have experience."

"Carrie is expecting a call from her mother, and we've got to tell her something. It's not a situation to lie about, and let's face it, there's no good way to hear this news."

She'd ignored my suggestion to let the cops handle the call. I'd ask, "why me?" but I already know the answer. I stared at the screen.

"Find out what we're supposed to do with the dog," Fab said.

I hesitated to push dial for the number Fab had pulled up on the screen. "We don't even know that the person inside is Eloise Leone."

"Yes, we do. I did a visual ID. She matches the picture Gunz sent me."

"You're so gruesome." I shuddered and took a deep breath, backing up against the bumper and sliding into the back next to the dog, feet hanging out the opening. Fab leaned against the side. I pushed the button and was a little surprised when the nurse's desk at the hospital answered, since I was expecting it to be a personal number.

When Carrie Leone came on the line, I took another deep breath. "This is Madison Westin. I'm here at your mother's house at the request of Mr. Gunz, and I'm sorry to tell you that your mother is deceased."

After a long silence, she asked breathlessly, "Are you certain?"

"I'm very sorry to break the news to you this way," I said sadly. "The paramedics are on the way, as well as the police, and they'll be able to answer your questions better than me. I can have them call you at this number or however you'd like."

"The two of us had dinner together last night and enjoyed ourselves," Carrie said, sounding stunned. "We laughed; we shared stories. At least we had that."

"I'm so sorry." I sighed and hung my head, not sure what to say next. I let the silence drag on until Carrie was ready to speak. If I were in her shoes, I'd want someone to listen to both the said and the unsaid. I ended up breaking the silence. "I hear sirens."

"I'll need to make arrangements to get away from work," Carrie said.

"About the dog?" I asked.

"Max?" Carrie heaved a sigh. "You'll need to take him to the pound. They can find him a home. I'm not able to take him. I work long hours and don't care for animals."

"They'll euthanize him." I wanted to yell, "I'm not doing that," but bit back the words.

"Please don't make me feel worse than I already do," Carrie scolded, the grieving daughter replaced by a professional who'd seen it all. "I have my mother to deal with, and that's my first priority."

"The police just pulled up, and I'm sure they'll have questions. I'll give them your number so they can contact you directly."

"Please do that. I'll text you my cell number. I'm on my way." Carrie hung up.

Fab met the cops as one parked behind the other and both got out and approached her.

"Max, huh?" The dog eyed me expectantly as I scratched his head. "I promise you, I'm not taking you to the freaking pound. My dog skills aren't up to par, but I do have treat-sneaking skills. I'm certain Eloise would want you to have another happy home."

One of the officers broke off and came over with a determined stride. "You okay?" he asked.

"I…uh…" I stuttered through what I'd seen and told him that I'd immediately backed up. "The daughter isn't taking the dog, so I will," I said. "You wouldn't happen to have a leash?"

"I've got some rope I'll get you. Stay right here; I'll have more questions for you."

He left and joined his partner, who'd opened his trunk. The two put on booties and stayed off the concrete as they made their way to the door. They went inside and, judging by the time lapse, gave the scene a cursory check and came back out.

I shifted my position to sit with my back against one side, knees drawn up. From my vantage point, I had a view of the front of the property. Max crawled over and rested his head on my thigh.

The neighbors had begun to gather in small groups in the middle of the street.

One man walked over and asked me, "What's going on?"

"Mrs. Leone has passed on," I said, not about to add to the drama with salacious details. Those would get out soon enough.

The cops stood in the street at the end of the sidewalk and questioned Fab. One went back to his patrol car before heading in my direction, notepad in hand. His presence got rid of the nosey neighbor.

He gave me a reassuring smile, asking my name, address, and contact number. Then he fired one question after another at me: how did I know the victim, why had I come to the house, what time did I arrive? Did I see anyone leaving or anyone in the area when we pulled up? Did I know anyone who would want to harm the victim? Where was I before coming to the house?

I answered his questions in a straightforward fashion, knowing that I was zero help. He thanked me and walked over to meet the detectives who'd just arrived. Two crime scene technicians in a van parked right behind them and got out, grabbing oversize briefcases and cameras. The converging streets were now blocked with law enforcement vehicles.

I pulled my phone out of my pocket and called Creole.

"Hey, babe," he answered.

Tears stung at my eyelids. I gulped in air.

"What happened?" he demanded.

"The welfare check, Eloise Leona, she's dead."

"Didier," he yelled, then said to me, "Okay to put you on speaker?"

I mumbled my agreement. "Mrs. Leone was

murdered," I said, whispering the last word.

"Just breathe," Creole said. "Where's Fab?"

"She's with the cops and so professional; you'd be proud of her. I'm the one who feels like I'm coming apart at the seams. I'm trying to hang in there and be helpful where I can." I relayed the details from when we arrived at the property to the gruesome discovery.

"We can be there in an hour," Creole offered.

"No need. Neither of us got hurt. I'm certain that after a hundred more questions, they'll let us go. Fab and I need to be here when the daughter arrives, in case she needs someone to lean on. Then we're headed home."

"Call when you leave," Creole said.

"Tell Fab to call," Didier said.

"Will do." I hung up and leaned my head against the back window, closing my eyes and petting Max absently.

"You awake?" Fab poked her head inside.

"Tell me we can go now?" I asked, opening my eyes.

"We haven't been released yet. What about the dog?"

"I'm going to find Max a temporary home and, with any luck, a permanent one. You're going to deal with Carrie Leone when she shows up. Deal?" I stuck out my hand, which Fab ignored.

"I overheard the cops talking," Fab said, annoyed that I shook my head accusingly. Of course, she did. "What? I was standing within a foot; they had to know I could hear, and they didn't tell me to get lost."

"Tell me already."

"There are drops of blood from the front door and along the concrete that fade out just past the curb." Fab pointed directly across the street. "That's why you see more cars rolling up."

I looked out the window and noticed that two unmarked cars and three more cop cars had pulled up.

"One of the neighbors told the cops that Eloise is friends with a fiftyish woman who lives nearby; he's seen her come and go from the house a number of times lately."

"That's a wide disparity in age; more like mother and daughter than friends."

Max started panting.

"This dog is thirsty and probably hungry. Can't we use that as an excuse to leave?" I asked. "If not, then wiggle your way over to one of the lookie-loo neighbors—your best bet would a man—and shake him down for a bowl that we'll return before we leave."

A tall, middle-aged woman with a blond bob decked out in scrubs approached on foot from the opposite end of the block. I'd bet on it being Carrie Leone. I wasn't going to be the one to have the sad conversation with the woman. It should have been Gunz, but he hated drama of any kind, and his first option would be to foist it off on someone else. I nudged Fab with my foot and looked over her shoulder.

Fab turned and caught sight of the woman and, to my surprise, didn't tell me to get moving and go talk to her. She closed the distance and, after a short conversation, walked her over to the officer in charge. Max raised his head as the two walked by, but showed no interest and laid back down, closing his eyes.

A detective approached and introduced himself. "You doing okay?"

"I don't know how you do this every day." I grimaced.

"Thankfully, it's not every day. We have a low crime rate here in Palmetto Bay." He asked all the same questions as the previous officer, which I answered in the same straightforward fashion. "If you remember anything else, no matter how small, call me." He handed me his business card. "You're free to go."

I slid out and went around, lowering the back seat so Max could sit right behind us. I grabbed a bottle of water, rinsed out my coffee cup, and filled it, holding it out for the dog, who lapped it up.

Fab didn't waste time getting back in the car once she was cleared to go by the cops. I'd already gotten into the front.

"I'm going to ask Creole to put the word out to his friends who're still on the force that we'd like to know the who, how, and why of this case.

I'd suggest asking Gunz, but I doubt he'll even inquire about the details." Once we were back on the highway headed south, I texted Creole, as promised.

"And doggie?" Fab smiled at the big head hanging between the seats.

I punched in the number for Xander and hit the speaker button. "Get your feet off the desk," I barked when he answered.

"I'm lying on the couch with my laptop, feet hanging over the side. I wasn't brought up in a barn, although that might've been fun," Xander joked back.

"That is until you wanted to work your electronic genius and, oh…no power."

"That's a downside." Xander chuckled. "You never call unless you want something."

"You know how I told you this job would be a little of this and that? Well, I'm calling because I need you to find someone to foster a Golden Retriever named Max until we can find him a home. Someone who has attention to spare, since he's shook up and needs love."

"How am I supposed to do that?"

"Just think of it as one of those ridiculous A minus B equals something math problems. You have about an hour."

"Drive slow," Xander huffed and hung up.

"If Xander comes through, I may have to reassess my thinking and admit that having him as an assistant is a good thing," Fab said.

"His title is VP, and he's already proved himself by not squawking over rodent-sitting," I reminded her.

"Bostwick called." Fab scowled. "Left a message that he didn't like being ripped off by my exorbitant fees and wouldn't be calling me in the future. I responded by blocking his number."

"You may want to rethink that. There could be big money in exotic pet-sitting."

Her response was to grip the steering wheel tighter and glare at the road, hitting the gas.

My phone rang again as the city limit sign came into view. "Xander," I answered. "Good news?"

"Maybe. I called Billy, since he knows everyone and I don't know anybody. Like, five people, if that counts. He's got a friend, Aqua, whose trout just died of old age, and he's willing to take Max as a try-out and see if they bond."

Billy was Xander's roommate, and it didn't surprise me that the man would be helpful. All Fab or I had to do was ask and he'd make it happen. It was true that he knew everyone in the Keys, or so it seemed.

"A trout? That's not experience for owning a dog."

"Trout was actually a dog—a Newfoundland." Xander laughed. "Clever name, I think. Trout lived to be ten, so Aqua did something right."

"You tell Mr. Dog Owner that we'll be

checking on Max. If they aren't simpatico, then he should give us a call. We'll find another home. He's not to do anything funky, like drop him on the side of the road, because I'll track him down and put bullets in his a— backside."

"Bring Max to the office. Billy's picking us up."

Chapter Twenty-Five

Three days later, when I showed no signs of snapping out of my funk, Creole had had enough and dragged me out of bed and into the shower. After thrusting coffee in my hand, he disappeared into the closet and came out with a sleeveless hot-pink dress with a flared skirt, nude low-heeled pumps hooked over his fingers. "I think these go together." He eyed them suspiciously and tossed them on the bed. "Get dressed."

"Where are we going?" I whined, slowly sipping my coffee.

"You're going to lunch. I've got a meeting."

Fab flew up the Overseas, heading back north after we ate at a new restaurant in Marathon that Didier had picked out for the two of us to try. It was a perfect sunny day and not too sweltering, so we'd been able to sit outside and enjoy the view of the water, neither of us tired of watching the waves crash onto the small beach.

"I can't believe the guys ganged up on us and insisted we go out to lunch. Stay out of trouble is what they meant." Fab, who had fumed on the drive down, was now only pretending to be annoyed.

"Creole suggested shopping. He's so mean." I turned and smirked out the window. "I don't want to disappoint him, so let's stop somewhere."

Once back in the Cove, Fab headed straight for an outdoor shopping center we frequented that had a couple of our favorite stores.

I tugged on Fab's arm before she could pull into a parking space. "That woman up there is harassing that girl." I pointed through the windshield at the two, who stood off to one side, up against the bumper of a sedan.

Fab slowed and crept forward. The girl was twentyish, maybe, with stringy long brown hair and eyes bugged out from fear. She swung her fist, but the older woman had a vice grip on her other arm and jerked her off balance.

As we rolled up almost on them, I said in shock, "That's Addy."

Fab blew the horn, lowered the window, and yelled, "Are you okay?"

"Woman's crazy," the girl screeched. Addy loosened her hold, and the girl wrenched free, snatched up her backpack and bicycle, and jumped on, pedaling towards the street.

Addy moved with surprising agility, cutting between the rows of cars and dipping out of sight. A brown sedan—a make I couldn't identify, the back panel grey from body work that hadn't been painted — squealed out of a space and sped for the exit.

In hot pursuit, Fab had to brake for a car backing out. "I just want to make sure Addy's going to leave the girl alone."

"What do you suppose that was all about?" I scooted forward in my seat. "Addy must have scared the girl pretty badly, because she just cut across the highway, barely watching out for traffic. Good thing that driver was paying attention and swerved."

The bicyclist disappeared into a strip center and around the back. Addy turned north.

"Wonder where Addy's going?" Fab hit the gas and sped up the highway. "Isn't she wanted for questioning?"

"The guys aren't going to like that we're chasing Addy." I gripped the armrest. "Can't we just have an uneventful day out?"

"Too late for that."

"Not if you turn around and we go shopping."

Intent on the road, if Fab heard, she wasn't acknowledging me. "I'm going to hang back and follow her a little ways," she said. "Maybe we'll get lucky and get a location on her that we can pass along."

"Listen to me," I snapped. "Don't do anything heroic. If she gets away, oh well. From what little I know about her, if she got a second chance to shoot one or both of us, she'd take it."

"We're ready for her this time."

228

I was torn between not wanting Addy to ride off into the sunny day and get away and not wanting to follow her to who knew where. "I'm calling 911." I waited for Fab's reaction and, not getting one, figured that was her way of agreeing.

"911, what's your emergency?"

I reported the attempted kidnapping and told them I knew Addy Clegg to be wanted for questioning in a murder case while Fab hung back like she'd said and followed the nondescript sedan up the Overseas.

When asked, I attempted to read the tag and realized it had been shaded out. If a cop noticed, she'd be pulled over. My guess was she'd have some plausible excuse. I was at least able to give a good description of the car and where it was headed. It didn't surprise me when Addy drove past the Highway One cut-off and headed towards Card Sound. My stomach churned at the thought of driving through mangrove row, as I'd dubbed it in my mind. Miles of nothing.

"The call dropped." I stared at my screen with a sinking heart. "Addy has to have noticed by this time that she's picked up a tail," I said. "We've been following her for miles, and only two cars have passed us."

"I've hung back far enough that she can't make a clear ID and know we're the same car that's been following her since the Cove."

"We both know that if something happens out

here, we're screwed. There isn't a single person to come to our aid," I said, trying to keep the fear out of my voice. "I'm hoping the cops get out here pronto and arrest her."

The miles ticked by, and neither of us said anything as we followed the woman.

Addy suddenly turned off the highway.

"Keep a watch out," Fab directed. "I'm going to slow down while we look for where she turned in. Once we've located the exact spot, I'll turn around and get a closer look on the way back."

"Some kind of road marker would come in handy." I got out my phone, hit the video button, and held it up to the windshield. I wasn't about to roll down the window on the off chance that Addy had doubled back to the road and would recognize us.

"I think she turned in here. Maybe." Fab pointed over the steering wheel.

"Seriously? There's nothing to indicate a turn-in. Nothing but a solid wall of trees." I craned my neck to watch the side of the road and stared intently as we drove past.

Fab u-turned and drove back down the road even more slowly this time. "Oh damn," she said, one eye on the rearview mirror. "Addy just pulled back onto the road and is gaining on us."

"At least, we're headed back toward civilization." I drew my Glock, not about to be caught off guard a second time. "If anyone can outrun her, it's you. Don't do anything crazy, like initiating a middle-of-the-road showdown. There's nothing in it for us."

"If I were riding shotgun, I'd be tempted to shoot her tires out." Fab hit the gas and flew down the two-lane highway far above the posted speed limit.

"Just get us home in one piece." I kept my eyes glued on the outside mirror and breathed a sigh of relief as Addy's car, which had almost closed the distance, began disappearing behind us.

But Addy didn't give up and continued to follow us.

Thankfully, Fab didn't push it, losing Addy at the first intersection. Down another block, she rocketed into a liquor store parking lot, around the building, and pulled up next to the side.

"I can't continue to speed along this section of highway; it's a speed trap heaven. We'll give Addy a few minutes to see if she continues this way or gave up. If she's a no-show, I'll get back on the road. Hopefully, she's turned around and headed back to the weeds."

A few minutes later, the little sedan passed us. Addy never turned her head, intent on the road ahead.

I jerked on Fab's arm. "Don't go after her. The last thing we need is her on our tail again; we might not shake her again. Or she might be clever enough to stay out of sight and follow us home."

"There are so many SUVs on the road, she's not going to pick ours out, and besides, she's not expecting us to come up behind her, which I'm going to make sure doesn't happen." Fab pulled back into traffic.

"Just let her go. This could end very badly and involve innocent parties." I leaned back against the seat. "Where are the cops?"

"Maybe the 911 operator thought you were a crank call."

"Much to their annoyance, I'm certain. They respond to plenty of those." I made a face. "They'll have a record of my number, and I'm sure I'll hear back sooner or later."

A half-mile later, we passed Addy sitting in a left turn lane. I twisted in my seat and was relieved to see her continue back the way she came.

"I'm no longer in the mood for shopping," I said.

"Since you're the one with the video, you can explain what happened to Creole. He can decide if it will be any help to law enforcement and whether to forward it or not."

"I'm not sure how helpful it will be, but there's a clear shot of the vehicle and the video will make it easy to locate where she's living or close to it. How is Didier going to learn about this afternoon's events?"

"I'm going to tell him much, much later." She smiled devilishly.

Chapter Twenty-Six

Creole invited Harder to dinner when he called with an update on the Leona murder case, and Harder suggested the Crab Shack.

"Harder is getting a bad rep for only showing up for murder talk," I said, following Fab and Didier into the restaurant while Creole cut around and headed to the reservation desk.

Decorated with fake palm trees and fish mounted on walls strung with ropes of lights, the restaurant had a low-key atmosphere. The patrons dressed casually in tropical chic.

"He's been coming down here a lot lately," Creole said as we followed the hostess out to the deck. "He's joined the poker group, and he and Caspian have talked about going fishing, which is code for picking up women."

We'd arrived early and the restaurant was only half full, the outside seating empty, even though it afforded a view of the cool waters of the Atlantic Ocean. The four of us took seats, placed a drink order with the server, and ordered an appetizer platter.

Harder sauntered out after our drinks arrived, whiskey in hand. Not his usual formally dressed self, he blended in in silk shorts and a tropical shirt. He tipped his glass and took a seat. "So what's new?" He laughed.

Creole nudged my shoulder.

"Why me?" I grouched. "Fab was driving."

Fab used her finger as a stirrer, then flicked vodka at me.

"Now what?" Harder demanded.

Fab told him how we'd run into Addy and followed her.

Harder snapped back. "You couldn't call 911 and report it to the cops?"

Didier grinned down at his wife. He wholeheartedly agreed.

"We did, or Madison did. But they were a no-show." Fab said, *see, we did do the right thing* in her tone.

"There was a four-car accident in that area around that time. That must have kept all the nearby cops busy," Harder said.

"Are you interested in a copy of the video Madison shot?" Fab asked Harder.

"How long were you going to sit on that?" Harder shook his head in annoyance.

Fab pulled her phone out of her purse and forwarded him the video that I'd sent her. "Done."

"Any pictures?" Harder asked. Fab shook her head.

The appetizers were delivered and drinks refilled.

"These look good," Harder appreciatively eyed the stuffed shrimp he'd picked up.

"They're a family favorite," I said.

"What do you suppose Addy was doing with that girl?" Creole asked.

"Nothing good, you can bet," Harder said. "It's hard to believe there's an innocent explanation, since the young woman appeared to be in distress."

"What's happening with the Leona case?" I asked.

"Sorry you had to walk in on that scene," Harder said. "It's difficult even for the most hardened of us."

"We went there thinking the woman had left her phone off the hook and we'd tell her to call her daughter and reassure her all was well and leave," I said.

"It's a sad way for a ninety-year-old woman to end her life," Fab said. "It looked like she put up a struggle." There was no way Harder would get out of offering up a few details if she had anything to say about it.

"Mrs. Leone did put up a fight but was ultimately overpowered," Harder said. "I have some good news, or as good as it can be. There's been an arrest in the case and a confession, which makes our job easier, though even without the confession, there was a mountain of fingerprint evidence and a blood trail."

The server interrupted, dropping off menus

and asking about refills.

"I'll signal you when we're ready to order," Creole told him and, after he left, turned to Harder. "I like it when there's no doubt as to the guilt of the perpetrator."

"It's worse when a case goes unsolved," Harder said. Creole nodded in agreement. "You ladies left before the arrest. That surprises me."

"Sorry we missed that," I said.

Creole nudged me.

"Are you going to cough up any details, or do we need to look it up online?"

"Fabiana," Didier grouched, followed by something in French that didn't faze her at all.

"It surprised me when the detective reported how helpful you were. He used the word 'professional' and no mention of the snarky tone you take with me." Harder smirked.

"I have my moments." Fab's blue eyes sparkled with amusement.

"Mrs. Leone had formed a friendship with the woman across the street—Rowena Blakely, a divorcee in her mid-fifties. Unbeknownst to Mrs. Leone, the Blakely woman was jealous of the relationship she had with her daughter. The attention she gave her and their outings grated on Blakely. The evening before, the two women had had plans to get together, and Mrs. Leone had cancelled to go to dinner with her daughter."

"That pushed Blakely over the edge?" Fab asked in disgust.

"The Blakely woman already had anger control issues and a rap sheet going back ten years, which included two charges of battery," Harder said.

"If she got therapy, it clearly wasn't effective. More likely, she got better at hiding her erratic behavior," Creole said.

"After her mother's murder, Carrie Leona went over to break the news to Blakely, since she'd been friends with Carrie's mother. Upon opening the door, Blakely told her, 'Your mother started a fight and I had to defend myself.' Then went on to tell her that they got into a fistfight, and shoving, hair pulling, and screaming ensued."

"A ninety-year-old woman in a fistfight?" Creole said. "That's a stretch. And I assume she didn't have a rap sheet."

"You'd be correct," Harder said. "It was at this point that the Blakely woman told Carrie that she'd left her knife behind and wanted it back."

"It was convenient that she brought her own knife," I said in disgust.

"Thankfully, Carrie had the presence of mind not to react and to get away from the woman," Harder said. "She immediately reported the conversation to the detective in charge, and he confronted Blakely, who told him the same story, adding that she was hit in the head and blacked out."

"Yeah, sure," Fab sniffed.

"Lucky for us, Blakely hadn't changed her clothing, and her pants were covered in dried blood. She also had cuts on her hand. She told the paramedic that was called to check her out that she'd said she had an 'altercation with the woman in the house last night.' The medical examiner reported that in addition to the knife wound, Eloise Leona had suffered cuts and blunt force trauma to her head. Blakely was arrested and charged with murder, battery on a law enforcement officer, and resisting arrest."

"So she beat up a cop?" Fab asked with a smirk.

"I'm fairly certain the officer had her subdued quickly, in case you were worried." Harder smirked back at her. "Sound like something you'd do, Ms. Merceau?"

"Even I know that would be a stupid move," Fab said. "Since it wasn't her first time in cuffs, she should've known that."

"Hi everyone," Mother said, having approached the table unnoticed. "You don't mind if we join you, do you?"

There were several sets of deer-in-the-headlights looks. Who would dare say no?

Spoon stood next to her, appearing chagrined. He attempted to stop her from sitting but was outmaneuvered. True to form, Mother stopped at the bar and ordered drinks on the way in, and they appeared as the couple sat down.

"Hi Mother," I said, and introduced Harder to Jimmy Spoon.

Harder nodded, amused. "We've met."

"It's been a while," Spoon said, and met his stare directly.

"I'd like to be reassured that this get-together isn't official police business involving my daughter," Mother said.

I looked at my mother and rolled my eyes, which I knew she hated. But it didn't faze her. She ignored me.

"I'm not here to haul her off in cuffs. This time." Harder winked at me.

"Harder has friends in the Cove, and we're in that group and go out to dinner on occasion." Creole shot Spoon a look that said, *Control your woman.*

The big man shrugged, telegraphing, *You're on your own.*

"What brings you two out on a weeknight?" Fab asked.

I bit my lip to keep from laughing.

Mother ignored her too. "I'm happy that we ran into you; I don't see you as much I'd like," she said to me and ran her eyes around the table. "I planned to call tomorrow and get the story on how it was that you were involved in rescuing a dog. Did you hear about this?" she directed at Harder.

"As a matter of fact, I did. Madison was extremely helpful in rehoming the dog for a woman who was no longer able to care for it herself," Harder said smoothly.

"Does Billy report every phone call he has to you?" I sniped at Spoon.

"It wasn't like that."

"I'll bet," I mumbled, calming slightly. "It turned out that Billy had a friend who was eager to give the dog a home, since he'd just lost his own. But I'm certain you're aware of all the details."

"It was Xander who was singing Billy's praises, happy not to disappoint you," Mother said. "Billy was vague on the details, which led me to believe there was more to the story."

"Your daughter has a soft spot for animals." Didier smiled at me. "It's not the first one she's rescued."

I wanted to jump up and kiss his cheek.

"You have anything to add?" Mother stared at Fab, one of those Mom looks that make the timid squirm. Never one to be intimidated, Fab stared back until Mother looked away.

"We were just getting ready to order dinner," Creole said.

"Thanks for inviting me," Harder said. "As always, I'm enjoying myself."

Chapter Twenty-Seven

My phone rang early the next morning. Never a good sign. Doodad's picture popped up on the screen. "Anyone die?" I asked when I answered. Lying next to me, Creole groaned and tugged a pillow over his head.

"I wouldn't be calling if—"

"Just tell me."

"My tooth broke, and I'm hoping to get in to the dentist first thing. No one is answering their phone, and I need someone to open."

"That would be me. As long as no one wants a fancy mixed drink."

"No worries there. It'll be the 'morning beer for late breakfast' crowd. I'll relieve you as soon as I'm done."

"I'm ordering you to take the day off. You're not to worry. I'll get someone to fill in." I rolled over to get out of bed and was pulled back to lie staring at the ceiling.

"I think I'm indispensable." Doodad half-laughed. "I'll be by after my appointment to check on you."

We hung up.

Creole pulled a corner of the pillow up. "You're going to bartend?" he asked in disbelief.

"I am." I glowered at him. "I've filled in a few times, and the place is still standing."

"No flirting for tips."

I laughed.

* * *

Dressed in my work uniform, a jean skirt and t-shirt, I carried my tennis shoes into the kitchen and sat at the island, finishing the cup of coffee that Creole had waiting. The phone rang again; this time, it was Fab. "I was getting ready to call you," I told her and shared that I'd be working at Jake's.

Creole leaned against the doorjamb and listened in, to my side of the conversation anyway.

"Ick," Fab said. "I'd be terrible at that."

"I guess this means you won't be coming along for moral support."

"Sorry." Her tone conveyed that she was relieved. "Didier and I are going to lunch. That's what I called to tell you."

"I'm surprised you're not in trouble with your husband for chasing Addy all over town."

Creole grinned.

"I had to promise on the life of my firstborn, Didier Jr., that I wouldn't do it again and would, after reporting it to 911, stay out of it."

Maybe. Probably not. "Fab Jr. is now your second child?"

"Something tells me she's going to need a big brother to keep her out of trouble," Creole said.

"I won't worry about you, since you're going to be with Didier and I'm certain he can keep you out of trouble. If not, then no one can," I said. "When I told Creole, I blamed it all on you, since you were driving."

"I would've done the same thing." Fab laughed.

We hung up.

Creole closed the space between us and wrapped his arms around me. "You have a good day at the office."

* * *

I blew into the driveway at Jake's and slowed, checking out each business that shared the block. It didn't surprise me that none of them showed signs of life, since not a one of them kept regular business hours. I parked behind Jake's and entered through the open kitchen door.

Cook waved and came out of his office. "The nephew that bartends for the gamblers is going to relieve you. He's on his way back from Lauderdale, so it'll be a couple of hours." Doodad, who saw to every detail, had obviously called ahead.

"Thank you. I'm thinking it won't kill Doodad

to take the day off. He works too much as it is. I've been telling him to hire a couple of extra people, but he ignores me."

"He tells me competent weirdos are hard to find."

I laughed and continued down the hall to the bar, storing my bag under the counter. I crossed the room and opened the doors to the deck, letting in the fresh air, and turned on the ceiling fans, inside and out. It was easy to open, since the bar had been re-stocked the night before. Checking my watch, I unlocked the front door five minutes early, poking my head out to see if anyone was waiting. The parking lot was still empty. I propped open the door and, going back inside, turned on the jukebox.

It wasn't long before the first customer lumbered in — pure white hair and a beard to match, wrinkles lining his face to mark his age — and headed straight to the bar, sliding onto a stool. He did a double take, seeing me behind the bar. "Where's Kelpie?" He looked around.

I'd seen him in here before, but his name escaped me. "Day off." I pasted on a smile.

He was visibly disappointed with my answer. "I'll take whatever you've got on tap."

We had several brands, but rather than asking, since it seemed like I was supposed to know, I guessed. The worst that could happen was he'd spit it out and I'd graciously offer a refill, as long as no liquid landed on me.

I filled a glass and set it down in front of him, forgoing my first choice of slinging it down the bartop. I bit back a laugh at how that would be the talk of the bar when it hit the floor and glass and beer flew everywhere.

"How's your day going?" I asked.

He grunted, clearly not over the fact that I wasn't Kelpie.

The regulars filed through the door, and it wasn't long before all the seats at the bar had been claimed. A few did double takes, and the first guy spread the word that it was Kelpie's day off. I'd have to talk to Doodad about cloning her, since she was clearly a hit. I did a good job not spilling anything all over anyone. The men thought they were funny, trading outrageous stories of their prowess, most of which were difficult to believe. A couple of women took the last two seats at the end and played the two bartop poker machines that were good for points only.

Suddenly, the front door crashed open and a chicken bounded through, bunching the crotch of the costume in its hand. "Where's the bathroom?" The male voice came out a bit garbled. "I'm about to go on the floor."

I almost told him to hit the road, but thought better of that, not wanting a big mess to contend with or to have to clear out the bar.

"That way." I pointed down the hall.

The men at the bar, who had gone silent, now

laughed, making chicken noises and watching as he loped away.

The bathroom door had barely closed when it reopened and another man rushed out and ran back to his stool. "The chicken is puking," he announced, clearly happy to be the first with the news.

It took me a minute to comprehend what he'd said. I stared at the man who broke the news and then at the bathroom door. I took a deep breath. If my past had taught me anything, it was that I could handle anything. Hopefully.

"Would one of you men check on…him and see if he needs help?" I asked, just stopping myself from calling him the puker. Not getting a response, I took another deep breath and walked down the hall, pausing in front of the men's room door. Hearing moans, I pushed the door open a crack. "Do you need me to call 911?"

The response I got was a gunshot. Followed by a scream.

I backed up until I hit the wall.

The white-haired man jumped up from the bar. "What the devil?" He beelined down the hall. "Call 911." He rushed inside the bathroom and came back out after a moment. "The bullet wasn't fatal, but he's bleeding and needs medical attention."

I already had my phone out and had begun to back up towards the bar. I noticed that half the stools were empty and a few customers were rushing for the exit, knowing the cops were about to show. The ones that were left had their phones out.

Sirens could be heard in the distance, and I ran to the front door and propped it open. Two cop cars rolled into the driveway. Kevin got out of the first car. I told him what happened as we rushed back inside.

"Did you say chicken suit?" Kevin demanded.

I nodded.

"You just made my job easier. I was looking for him; he tried to rob the liquor store. Except the clerk wasn't having it and pulled a shotgun. The clerk reported that the robber fished around in his costume and then ran."

The white-haired man standing outside the bathroom door called, "The chicken needs medical help — he shot himself in the groin. By accident, I believe."

The cop behind Kevin snickered.

I slipped around him and went back to the bar for cover. The paramedics were the next to show up and rolled a stretcher by me.

Cook came rumbling down the hall, scanning the bar. "If you'd kept the cops out of it, we could've done a brisk lunch."

"There's two left." I pointed to the deck, at the men who'd taken their beer outside to finish it. "You tell the chicken, next time don't shoot his man-goods off. Then I won't need to involve law enforcement."

Cook did a double take, flinched, and mumbled to himself, going back to his domain.

"Big tip for anyone you can get to clean the bathroom," I yelled at his back, then shuddered and successfully prevented myself from conjuring up the scene.

It took a while, but the paramedics eventually rolled the man out of the bathroom and out of the building.

Kevin reappeared; his partner had gone out the back. I handed him his usual soda, and he tipped his can to me. "Thanks for the help in catching the fugitive. Some guys just don't have a head for crime."

"Too bad they can't figure that out before they get arrested. I imagine it'll be a while before he's out of jail and looking for more excitement."

Kevin ignored that. "Anything else I should know about?"

"I'm always asking that same question at my businesses, and it usually comes with an answer I don't like."

He grunted and handed me his empty can. I threw it out and handed him another, and he waved and went out the front.

The relief bartender had finally showed. "It seems quiet today," he said, trading places with me.

"I'm sure it'll pick up." I grabbed my purse, happy to get out of there. I stopped at the office and pulled a cone with an "out of order sign" over in front of the men's room.

I didn't make it out the door before my phone rang.

"My truck won't start," Mac said in a frantic tone. "Desperately need a ride. You can't let me down."

Having forgotten I parked in the back, I circled around and got in my SUV. "I'm on my way," I reassured her. I'd already hung up when I realized that I should have asked a few questions. I crossed my fingers, hoping that the oversight wouldn't come back to haunt me, as if that it would do any good.

Thanks to green lights and light traffic, I made it to The Cottages quicker than usual. I turned the corner, slowed, and did a triple-take. Mac, Crum, and Joseph stood at the end of the driveway like a scene out of an old gothic movie; Crum and Joseph dressed in ill-fitting suits and Mac in a dress of layered lace.

Mac ran to the driver's side, and I rolled down the window. "We need a ride to Tropical Slumber. They're having the first wedding, and Crum is officiating," she said in an excited tone.

Who gets married at a funeral home? Instead of asking, I motioned for them to get in and hit the button to unlock the doors. "How are you getting back?" I asked when they'd piled in, Mac in the front.

"We're getting a ride in the hearse," Mac said, enthusiastic about the idea. "I called Dickie and

Raul and told them we were on our way, and they offered to bring us back. I was the one who requested the hearse. I've wanted to ride in one for a while but wasn't sure how to ask. So I just blurted it out."

"Hmm." I nodded, unsure of what to say that wouldn't dampen her spirits.

"Listen up, everyone," Crum boomed from the back seat. "I need to go over the service one more time."

To my relief, Joseph and Mac groaned.

"You've got it down pat," Mac assured him. "Surely, as many times as you've gone over it, you must have it memorized."

"Did you forget that Dickie said you could put notes on the podium and sneak a peek?" Joseph reminded him.

I turned to Mac. "What's your role?"

"Joseph is an usher, and when he's done, we're going to pretend to be a couple," Mac said with a smile.

"You getting paid to be a guest?" Like when the guys needed to hire mourners, but I didn't mention that.

"This is a freebie," Mac said. "It's a young couple, and they couldn't afford a lot of frills. I'd suggest that you come along, but it's a formal wedding." She eyed my jean skirt.

I smiled lamely, happy that I didn't have to come up with an excuse.

"Dearly beloved, we are gathered here

today…" Crum said in a loud voice.

"Isn't that the way a funeral service starts?" I asked, and stepped on the gas.

Crum snorted. "I know what I'm doing."

I careened around the corner.

"I've heard several people joke that you drive like an old woman; you go to driving school?" Joseph asked.

"I'm trying to be considerate and make sure you're not late." I turned into Tropical Slumber and squealed to a stop at the front door. They piled out.

Before Mac closed the door, I said, "If your ride home in the hearse gets cancelled—because they have to pick up a dead person—call a taxi and pay for it out of petty cash."

"Wouldn't it be exciting if they had a pick-up?" Mac said with a big grin. "I wonder if there'd be room for all of us to ride along."

"I'm sure they'd love the company." I waved and was happy she didn't notice that I hit the locks as soon as she closed the door. To my credit, I exited the property with no drama.

I drove home, thinking about drinking for dinner and starting early.

Chapter Twenty-Eight

Fab texted, "On my way," and minutes later, laid on the horn in front of my house. She had to have been outside the whole time, parking her Porsche and hopping into the SUV. The woman's attempts at humor fell flat unless I'd had more than one cup of coffee, which wasn't the case that morning. She'd called last night and said she had a meeting with a new client and to dress nice, offering no other details, which was nothing new. One of these days, I should refuse to budge. I grabbed my tote and slammed out the gate.

"How did your day go yesterday?" Fab asked when I got in the car.

"Totally uneventful," I lied, and made a drinking sign with my fingers.

"You're going to withhold the details of the shoot-out and that there was almost a fatality?"

"You found out on your own, which saves me from repeating events you already know about. Turns out almost is just as good for business as a dead body; Jake's was packed yesterday once word spread. Here's something you might not know, and we can't have that: I called the hospital this morning, and the chicken was booked into the jail ward."

"You're mean."

I ignored her. "Happy ending for me. I went home with the intention of getting sauced and was limited to one drink as Creole had other ideas for the evening."

"Don't want to hear the details." Fab pulled through the coffee drive-thru, placing an order for our favorites.

She then took the highway north, hooking up with the Interstate and taking the exit for Miami Beach. She pulled up in front of an upscale, ocean-front restaurant, relinquishing the SUV to the valet.

"The client chose the restaurant," Fab said, as though I was about to challenge the choice.

To my annoyance, we were led to a table tucked away not only inside but in the corner. The client apparently had no appreciation for fresh air and a great view.

Fab made the introductions.

Betsy Ridgely wore her net worth on her fingers and around her wrists, and judging from the size of the stones, it was considerable. The fortyish blonde gave me a once-over, and from the judgement on her face, I fell short of her standards. She flicked her hand, and the server appeared and poured us each a glass of wine.

"I don't think this job requires an extra person,

and it's a matter of the utmost secrecy," Betsy said. "Unless you think it absolutely necessary," she added with a note of reluctance.

"You were vague about the details of this job on the phone. I'll need more information so I can plan an overall strategy," Fab said in the same irritating tone the woman had used. It didn't faze her; instead, it identified the two as kindred spirits.

No details, and yet you're meeting with her anyway.

"I want you to coach me on how to retrieve some personal items that were stolen from me and be backup during the retrieval process."

I squinted at the woman over my wine glass, not liking the direction of this conversation.

"What are the items?" Fab asked.

"There are several pieces of jewelry and two paintings; all of them heirlooms that have been in my family for years, handed down to me by my mother."

Another flick of Betsy's hand and the waiter was back, offering more wine. Fab and I shook our heads.

"Where are the items now?" Fab asked.

"A condo just down the street." She waved dismissively toward the beach.

"Why don't you start at the beginning?" I snapped, trying to control my annoyance and coming up short.

Betsy turned to me and gave me another once-over, frowning, as though to say, *How dare you speak?*

I gritted my teeth and flashed a benign smile.

"That's a good idea," Fab said. "It will give me a better idea of the big picture."

"My husband, the bastard." Betsy sighed and drained half her wine. "You'd think I could get a little peace now that he's dead. But no. While I was married to the man, he was rarely discreet, in the last year of his life, he took a mistress and gave her my personal items. I want them back." She slammed her glass back down.

"Did you file a police report?" Fab asked.

"What a waste of time. They investigated, and she fed them lies about the items being gifts. They told me my only option was civil court; a judge would have to make a determination of who the rightful owner was." Betsy's face filled with anger. "Another slap in the face, my husband also bought the condo down the street with my money and put her name on the deed, and there's nothing I can do about that, either."

"Are you ready to order?" the server asked. Wine bottle in hand, he refilled Betsy's glass.

I pushed aside my wine glass in favor of water; this conversation needed a clear head. I noticed that Fab hadn't touched hers either after the first couple of sips.

"I'll let you know when we're ready." Betsy waved him away.

"You want me to do what exactly?"

"Get me inside," Betsy said with a sneaky smile. "While I'm retrieving the items—since I know what I'm looking for—you stand guard. We'll set up a contact system, in case I'm about to be interrupted. Wouldn't want that." She laughed nervously.

"Have you lost your mind?" I ground out the words.

"I knew that *she* was going to be a problem." Betsy shook her head, disgust on her face.

"I've got a couple of questions of my own," I said. The woman turned her attention to Fab with a dismissive sniff. "You do realize that what you're suggesting could get you prison time, and a lot of it, depending on the value of the items? Is that a risk you're willing to take? You'd be putting your freedom on the line."

"You're so dramatic." Betsy let out a big sigh, keeping her face turned away.

"In case you're unaware, rich people are put in jail all the time," I said, matching her affected tone. "This stupid scheme of yours is guaranteed to get you a prison sentence. Since you're not up on your burglary skills, that's almost certainly where you'll end up. And even if you get away with it, you couldn't ever wear the jewelry in public. The other woman would have you arrested, and based on the police report you filed, it wouldn't be hard for to her to prove her case."

"That bitch took enough from me. No more," Betsy fumed.

"Guess what? That bitch is going to get the last laugh: you decked out in prison garb," I said, conveying my opinion that she was a dimwit.

"If they're as valuable as you say, surely the items were insured," Fab said. "Did you file an insurance claim?"

"I contacted them first, certain they would investigate rather than pay a claim they didn't have to. That was another surprise from the bastard. He cancelled the coverage."

"Let's say you're successful and retrieve your items. Are you prepared to have the cops breathing down your neck?" Fab asked. "You'll be their first suspect. Plus, if this woman has insured them, the insurance company will investigate relentlessly."

"No one cares that my husband steals my possessions and gives them to his lover," Betsy said angrily. "Nothing would happen to you," she said to Fab. "The risk is on me."

"You're misinformed," I hissed. "Fab would be up to her neck in felonies. The two of you would probably be tried and sentenced together. Being a lookout doesn't get you a lesser sentence."

Betsy continued as though I hadn't spoken. "This job will be in and out," she said to Fab. "I've got it all planned; even bought a key from the housekeeper."

"There's another person who's set herself up to be charged with a crime," I said in a huff.

"Will you at least think about it?" Betsy asked Fab. "I happen to know that the bitch was invited to a pool party out on Fisher Island this weekend. I also received an invitation but can't bear to show up and have my jewelry flaunted in my face."

"We shouldn't even be listening to this," I said to Fab. "Knowing about a crime and not reporting it could get us in trouble."

"Why don't you go sit in the car while the two of us discuss this case?" Betsy ordered with a flick of her finger.

"You can—"

Fab nudged me under the table.

"This is not a job for the inexperienced," Fab said in a placating tone. "It seems exciting on the surface, but it can go wrong in any number of ways in a hot second. Madison is right about the potential charges that could be levied against us all."

"You came highly recommended as someone who could get the job done. Have you gone squeamish?"

Calm-and-cool Fab had gotten on my nerves. I wanted her to yell, *Hell no!* in the woman's face and get as far away as possible.

"You need to rethink this," I said, trying for reasonable and not sure how I sounded. "The consequences are steep, more so if your quick in and out goes horribly wrong. Worst case scenario, you could end up dead, or this other woman could, and then you'd never see daylight except from an exercise yard."

"She's a nuisance." Betsy quirked her head in my direction.

I slammed my hand on the table, hiding my flinch. My water glass wobbled, the silverware rattled, and the commotion got the attention of the other table. "I may be the only clear thinker here. Fab is not doing this job. And if you have any intelligence, you'll drop this hare-brained scheme."

"I've had enough of you," Betsy said.

"I feel the same way about you," I shot back.

"Would you wait for me at the front?" Fab asked me.

"I'm not going anywhere without you." I pushed back my chair. To Betsy, I said, "Fab. Is. Not. Doing. This. Job. If I hear that you've even contacted her again, I've got police contacts and I'll turn you in."

Betsy hissed and spit flew.

I stood, bent slightly, and in a venom-laced tone, said, "I better never hear your name again."

The woman smirked, and it was all I could do to keep from cold-cocking her, give the onlookers from the nearby tables a show as she tumbled backward out of her chair.

Fab grabbed my arm. "I'll be in touch," she said to Betsy and shoved me forward.

I yelled over my shoulder, "No, she won't."

A dozen pairs of eyes watched Fab drag me out.

We stood on the sidewalk and didn't say a word until the valet brought the car and we were inside, driving down Ocean Boulevard.

"Are you pregnant?" I asked in an angry tone.

"No." Fab appeared confused.

"That's good. At least, your first child won't be born in prison, which is what would happen if you were stupid to take this job. What the hell?" My anger and frustration roared out. "You don't need the money."

"I'll admit that I love the rush of adrenaline coursing through me on one of these jobs. The fear of what might happen is exciting."

"If Didier could hear you, he'd be devastated." I turned away and pretended that I was walking on the beach, which was hard to do sitting next to the sulky French woman.

Chapter Twenty-Nine

We didn't say a word to one another on the drive back home. I knew that Fab wouldn't give a second thought to all the trouble the meeting with Betsy Ridgely could put us in. She'd gotten out of so many bad situations that there was a part of her that thought she was invincible. I also knew that she'd calmed down a lot since meeting Didier, but she needed to do more.

Fab pulled off the highway in Florida City to get gas, and we both got out. She went to pump the gas while I walked around the car, stretching my legs. I thought about going inside the convenience store for something junky to snack on and talked myself out of it.

"Get in the car," Fab ordered.

"But—"

"Now."

I got back in, slammed the door, and glared at her. "Okay, Mother. This better be good. We didn't even get gas."

"The guy in the next lane over..." Fab tapped the side of the steering wheel. "...the one pulling out, I recognize him from the photos Harder showed us. He's one of the brothers the cops

262

would like to speak to." She pulled out right behind him and followed him back to the highway.

"We're not following him," I said.

"We might as well. We're going in the same direction." *Duh* in her tone.

"I'm warning you now, so you better be listening: if you turn off this road to veer towards Card Sound, I'm getting out. Do you hear me?"

"The guy in the car ahead of us can hear you."

I pulled my phone out of my pocket and snapped a couple of pictures, uncertain of the quality, then hit the speed dial.

"Who are you calling?" Fab slapped at my arm.

"Do I dare ask how your day's going?" Creole asked when he answered.

"Maybe later." His loud groan didn't go unnoticed. "Fab stopped for gas and recognized one of the brothers from the photos Harder showed us, and we're… hmm… following him."

"Where are you?" Creole snapped.

"We just left Florida City and are on Highway One, headed south back to the Cove. We don't have a lot of time before we have to decide which way to turn, and depending on… I might be getting out."

Fab shook her head in frustration.

"You got a tag number?"

"I snapped pictures a little ways back and just forwarded them to you."

"Good job. Call 911 and answer all their questions. Remember: they'll have to verify he's wanted before they'll do anything. Prevents them from being used to pull over an innocent man as part of someone's feud."

"I'm calling now."

"Should I stay on the line?" Creole asked.

"We'll see you at home." I hung up and repeated what Creole had said. Fab nodded, showing she heard, but continued to stare intently at the highway, slowing to stay a couple of car lengths behind the other car.

"Why am I the one calling in the emergency…again?" I said.

"At least no one's dead this time."

When the woman at the dispatch center answered, I told her about spotting the man at the gas station and where it was located, and that I knew him to be wanted for questioning re: murders in Card Sound. I gave a description of the car and said it was headed south on Highway One. She asked for my name and number, and I gave them to her. She promised to look into it and hung up.

I called Creole back and updated him.

"Are you coming home?" he asked.

"Let's hope so." I sighed and hung up. "Creole didn't say it in so many words, but it's probably his hope that we don't get caught up in the middle of anything." I stared at the road, noticing that Fab had slowed. "What are you doing?"

"I'm going to hang back, wait for the cops to show up, and watch how they handle the arrest. If I stay right on his bumper, we'll miss all the action."

"And that would be bad why?" I asked in frustration. "We both know how this is going to end: one more of those brothers in custody."

"Get ready to shoot some video," Fab ordered.

It didn't take long for two cop cars to fly by us. Fab slowed even more.

They pulled in between us and the car in question and put on their flashing lights. I was about to tell her we would need to get over to stay out of the way when the chase was on.

"This isn't going to end well," I said. "I'd really like it if we could get home unscathed. I don't want to be one of those bystanders you read about that ends up dead."

"This is going to shock you, but I agree," Fab said.

I clutched my chest. Fab ignored my antics.

Two more police cars arrived. The dispatcher had done her job and verified I wasn't a crank caller.

"This is going to get ugly if it goes much farther." I scooted forward in my seat, trying to visualize the layout of the road ahead. "He's going to run up on a traffic signal and possibly crash into other drivers that aren't paying attention and aren't aware of the police pursuit."

The two latest cop cars got in between us and the ongoing pursuit and slowed us all down, bringing us to a complete stop. At least we had a front-row seat.

"Something's happening." Fab jabbed her finger at the windshield.

I powered down the window and held up my phone.

The driver had pulled to the side of the road and bounded out of his car. He jumped over a short retaining wall and into the water not far below.

I'd estimate it to be a three- to four-foot drop. Not well thought out, since there was nowhere to swim to except a marshy area that would loop around and take him over to a side road. He'd be lucky to get that far.

"I wonder if runner dude knows he just jumped into Crocodile Lake?" I shuddered.

"If not, he might figure it out in an unpleasant way." Fab snapped her jaws together. "It's going to take a while to fish him out, dead or alive."

One of the cops was directing traffic, and we crept by at a slow crawl.

"May as well go home. Creole can get us an update." Fab had her eyes pinned to the water. "Do you think he can get pictures?"

"Don't ask. He's not going to find that amusing."

Fab hit the gas and, to my surprise, stayed right at the speed limit. "Wonder where my husband is?"

"Probably waiting on you to get home, since I'm certain Creole got hot on the phone with an update. You know that they have a dude pact to keep each other informed of our antics. If you have any complaints about their reporting system, take it up with them."

Chapter Thirty

It wasn't until Fab drove through the security gates and onto the private street where we lived that I broke the silence. It had given me time to plot. Being a best friend is serious business.

"I've got a surprise," I said.

Fab looked sideways at me as she cruised up to my door and came to a stop.

"I'm going to need the car for later." I knew from past experience that she planned to take my car home and leave me with her Porsche, which she knew I hated to drive. "I'm taking Creole to dinner." To my surprise, she parked and got out without a word of complaint.

"A surprise, huh?" She attempted her mind-reading trick, but I blocked her.

"Wait right there." I jumped out and, before closing the door, said, "Don't get in your car yet." I unlocked the gate and ran inside, holding up a finger to Creole, who stared from the couch. I reached in the kitchen drawer, hooking a pair of handcuffs on my finger and attaching one end to my left wrist, then dashed back outside with my arm hidden behind my back.

Catching Fab off guard, I launched myself at her, hugging her, and managed to slap the other cuff on her before she realized what I was doing.

Fab shrieked and yanked on the cuff. "Get this off." Her arm shot in the air, dragging mine straight up.

"Ouch," I yelped. "You break my wrist, and I'll be moving in with you while you nurse me back to health. Be warned: I'll be the whiniest patient ever."

"Explain yourself," Fab fumed. "Before I give you a one-arm beat-down."

Creole, who'd followed me out of the house, leaned against the fence and chuckled.

"This is for your own good," I said.

Fab jerked her lockpick out of her back pocket.

Ready for her, I smacked it to the ground.

Fab leaned in and roared in my face.

Impressive.

"*Ladies,*" Creole said with a grin. "As much fun as it might be to watch the two of you roll around on the ground, I'm taking the high road and offering my mediation skills."

"You want to help?" Fab roared. "Get these off." She jerked our arms out in front of us.

"The only way these are coming off is if someone responsible shows up to sign for you." I tugged our arms down, which elicited an exasperated breath from Fab. "Since I know all the same people you do, I know there's only one person that has the intestinal fortitude to deal with you."

"This friendship is over."

"Like you're not going to miss my charming personality." I stepped away, putting as much distance between us as the cuffs would allow. "Soon you'll be back, suggesting we get drunk together."

Her lips twitched.

Gotcha.

"Listen," Fab said, managing to get her anger under control. "We can work this out."

"What can I do to facilitate a truce?" Creole asked, enjoying every moment.

"Call Fab's other half and tell him to hustle his backside." I grinned cheekily.

"You need to stop whatever this is," Fab said. "I thought we were best friends. Now I'm not so sure."

I tried to clap, and Fab jerked my arm back. "The sad face is a good one. Needs a bit of work, which I can help you with."

"At least tell me what's going on," Fab ordered.

"I'm waiting for Didier to get here so I don't have to repeat myself." I stepped forward and tugged on the cuffs. "Would you like to go inside? Or do you want to stand out here and continue to sweat?"

Creole had pulled out his phone and was talking and laughing, explaining the situation. "You need to hurry. Just in case there's a fight.

You wouldn't want to miss it."

"That's so ungentlemanly," I said when he hung up.

"Like you, I can't behave all the time."

Fab gagged. "If you two are going to start with the cooing sounds, please," she yelled, "*spare me*." She glared at me, yanked on the cuffs, then stepped backward and leaned against her car.

Minutes later, Didier roared down the street and parked. He climbed out of his Mercedes and assessed the situation. "Can't wait to hear what's going on here." He grinned.

"We should go inside for a couple of reasons, and that it's cooking out here isn't one of them." I wiped non-existent sweat from my forehead and flung it at her. Fab jumped back, and I stumbled into her. "I could use a cold drink, and that's also where the keys are, if you want to get sprung from my side."

"I've got them right here." Creole held up the keys.

"You've had them this whole time?" Fab seethed and whipped our arms out in front of us.

"Not so fast." I held up my right hand. "Didier, do I have your solemn oath that you're going to keep an eagle eye on this woman? Your word is good; signing in blood seems over the top."

"I swear." Didier crossed his heart, then took the keys from Creole and unlocked the cuffs.

Fab made a show of shaking her wrist. "We're

going home." She turned away, grabbing Didier's shirtsleeve.

I jumped forward and fisted the back of her top. "You're not going anywhere. Not yet anyway. No, go inside." I gave her a shove. "I'm out of patience with you and the humidity."

Didier put his arm around Fab. "I'm thinking I need to hang onto these." He shook the cuffs.

"I'm going." Fab stalked past Creole and into the house.

"Make yourself comfortable." I pointed to the living room. "Beer?" The guys nodded, and I got two bottles of their favorites from the refrigerator and water for Fab and me. I sat next to Creole, across from Fab and Didier, immune to her glare. "Fab and I had a meeting today with her latest client, the insufferable Betsy Ridgely."

"Name-calling is beneath you," Fab said.

"Actually, it's not. It's my way of saying I'm hoping to never hear the woman's name again."

"If that's all, we'll be leaving." Fab started to stand, and Didier pulled her back down.

"I'd like to hear the rest of what Madison has to say."

"I went to great lengths today to make sure that Fab doesn't end up in jail." That was an exaggeration, but it wouldn't be the first time. "Making sure that prison orange isn't in Fab's future requires Didier's good influence. Do you want to tell them what this client wants or should I?"

"I'm not taking the case," Fab said militantly.

"First I've heard you say the words." I handed her my phone. "Call Snobby Betsy and tell her to take a hike. Also suggest she lose your number."

"I'll do it when I get home." Fab pushed my phone away.

Sure. I told the guys about the lunch and how Betsy wanted to execute her plan, since Fab was sitting there with her lips glued together.

"Bad idea," Creole said. "Snobby Betsy gets caught, and it's highly likely that you'll both end up in jail."

Didier turned Fab's face to his. "You're not invincible."

"I really wasn't going to take the case," Fab whined. "Granted, I didn't come to the decision right away, but I got there on the drive home."

Didier brushed her lips with his. "While I've got you in confession mode, did you leave the car chase to the cops?"

"Sort of," Fab hedged. "I slowed and stayed well back as the chase unfolded. The cops slowed traffic, and we had a ringside seat as the driver jumped into the water. I'm guessing he didn't see another way out. End of excitement." She was clearly disappointed.

"He took a dive into Croc Lake," I said.

Creole grimaced. "If he's not found, they'll know what happened."

"Anyone know when the last croc attack was?" I asked and got no response. "Haven't heard about one since I've lived here."

"Can we count on you for an update on the case?" Fab asked Creole.

"I can do that," Creole said. "Once they get this guy in custody or a body bag, they'll have two more brothers to go. And the crazy mother needs to be brought in for questioning."

"It's hard to believe that Addy's ignorant of what her offspring are doing and doesn't know they're murderers. If she does, not saying anything is as good as being complicit," I said. "I suppose it's possible to have your head parked that far up your backside."

Didier tsked.

Fab stood. "Well, this has been fun," she said, her tone saying *clearly not*. "We have to go." She tugged on Didier's arm. "I'm leaving my car here and riding with my husband. It's the least you can do."

"Just know I'm not responsible for any dust that gets on it from being out overnight." I stood. The woman had to have her cars spotless or they wouldn't run properly. I didn't complain because, as a result, mine stayed clean as well.

Didier leaned in and kissed my cheek. "Don't worry about Fab. Now that I have my prisoner in custody, she won't be going anywhere."

Creole laughed. "Good luck, buddy."

Fab glared at Creole, then crossed the kitchen and went out the door.

"Are we still friends?" I called as she flounced

out the gate.

"No, but I'll see you tomorrow."

Creole pulled me into his arms, and we waved as Didier shot down the street. "Fab's annoyed, but she knows that you did her a big favor. She just needed a push to tell that client of hers to take a hike."

Chapter Thirty-One

Creole scooped me up and, my feet resting on his, walked me into the living room and sat me beside him on the couch.

"I have one more step in the plan I cooked up to keep us out of trouble." I leaned forward and grabbed my phone off the table. "Do you mind if I call before I lose my nerve?" I scrolled through my phone and showed Creole the screen with Chief Harder's name. His eyebrows went up. I pushed the number.

"I'm going to pull a Fab and listen in," Creole said, and reached over to hit the speaker button.

I crossed my lips with my finger.

"Miss Madison," Harder answered. "Are you needing bail?"

"Worse. I need a favor." My stomach was a jumble of nerves, and I took a couple of small breaths to calm myself.

"I'm amassing a significant pile of IOUs with your name on them. I'm going to have to come up with something spectacular to whittle them down."

"Does that mean you're saying yes?"

"That means, young lady, that I'll listen and

let you know," Harder said sternly.

"I'm going to need client confidentiality," I said softly. "This involves a felony. But it hasn't happened yet."

"I suppose you want me to clean up whatever mess you're about to confess to and wrap it up with a pretty bow so no one goes to jail?"

"You're so smart." I breathed a sigh at his laugh. "It involves an attractive woman—a blonde with a bad attitude—but maybe you can help with that too."

Creole nudged my shoulder.

I told him about Fab's meeting and that I didn't want any of the three of us to end up in trouble with the law. More so me and my friend.

"Too bad Mrs. Ridgely's husband isn't alive to arrest," Harder grouched. "I can't make any promises. Give me the woman's number, and I'll call and invite her to my office for a sit-down. If she's smart, she'll allow herself to be talked out of her bad idea. I've done this once before, only it was a young man and he re-thought his felonious intentions and moved on with his life."

"You're the best." I smiled at Creole.

"You and your friend were helpful in the apprehension of Mr. Clegg today. We would've got him eventually, but maybe not before he killed someone else."

"I take it he didn't get eaten by a croc?"

"Not today, thankfully. The officers were already unhappy about having to fish his wet behind out of the lake, but half-eaten would have made it really messy. Or worse, having to shoot the reptile to save that piece of… Happy to have him in custody."

"Fab gets the credit for recognizing him from the pics you showed us. She may not remember names, but she's good with faces."

"I'll let you know if I have any success with this client of Fab's."

We hung up.

"If I'd called, he would've laughed and hung up," Creole said.

"He's a good friend."

Chapter Thirty-Two

It had been a quiet couple of days. Fab had called to tell me that she and Didier were going out on her father's yacht. Having honeymooned on the luxurious *Caspian*—named after its owner—I was a bit envious, knowing the fun that was to be had.

Getting a call from Gunz surprised me, since he was one of Fab's nefarious friends, until he grouched that he hadn't been able to get ahold of the woman.

"Your coach is ready." He laughed, finding himself amusing. "I'm at my office and we can swap out."

Gunz's office was the lighthouse, which he rented from Fab. He hadn't hung out his shingle, and his car parked in front on rare occasions was the only sign he used the space.

I hung up and turned to Creole, who sat at the island, a pile of paperwork in front of him. "The Hummer's ready for pickup."

"I should go with you," Creole offered. "This might be my only opportunity to meet the elusive Gunz."

"Hmm…" I tapped my cheek. "I'm certain Gunz wouldn't appreciate me bringing a cop with me, even if you're no longer with the force."

"What do you know about this guy?"

"That he's been a friend of Fab's forever and if you need something done, he can make it happen. Hence, the Hummer getting fixed. Gunz decided a while back to clean up his gangster act, and now he's a private moneylender."

"That's all fun and games until someone borrows over their head and can't pay it back."

"If it makes you feel better, I haven't heard of any recent deaths associated with him."

"It doesn't," Creole grumbled.

"I've met the family, and he's the normal one." I laughed, walking away. I changed into the t-shirt dress draped over the end of the bed, pairing it with wedge flip-flops and wrestling my red mane into a hair clip. I twirled in front of Creole, and he gave me a thumbs up.

"What's Fab going to say when she finds out that you're driving *your* car without her permission?" he asked.

"Changes are coming." I stomped my foot, which amused Creole. "I'm going to start driving once in a while, before I forget how."

Creole had the keys to the loaner in his hand. He quirked his finger for me to lean in for a kiss, which I did eagerly. At the knock on the door, he burst out laughing.

There was only one person it could be.

"You knew, didn't you?" I accused Creole as I opened the door to Fab and Didier.

"At least she knocked." Didier shrugged. "I'd suggest that you change the security code to keep her from getting the gate open. Though I suppose she could climb over." He peered down at her.

"Welcome back, you two." I beckoned them inside.

"Were you planning on calling and letting me know that the Hummer is ready?" Fab asked.

I raised my brow, telegraphing *How did you know?*

"I called to find out when it was going to be finished. I didn't ask what took so long because I know they do a first-rate job."

"Since I thought you two were still out cruising around, no, I wasn't." I smiled at Fab. "Besides, you'd interfere with my plans for a long joyride— stopping at a greasy food stand, eating in the car, and dumping the trash in the back. Love that old-pickle scent."

The guys laughed.

Fab had taken to ignoring me when she didn't like what I had to say. "Good thing we stopped by or you wouldn't know that the funeral boys called. They have an update on that last bag of remains found in Card Sound."

I grimaced. "Yay. Since you appear excited, there must be pictures of, or heaven forbid, a close-up look at whatever was left." I'd bet that neither of our husbands were going to volunteer to ride along.

"We'll soon find out."

"You two have fun." Creole held out the keys, which I took and put in my pocket. "Are you going to tell Fab the new rules?" he asked, amusement in his eyes.

Fab stared at me. "What?"

"It's a surprise."

Fab groaned. "I hated the last one. You sure know how to make a girl squirm at the word surprise."

Creole and Didier laughed again.

"It would be nice if you two stayed out of trouble." Didier kissed his wife before she crossed the threshold.

"That's the upside to hanging with dead bodies; their trouble-making days are over," I said. Creole hung my bag over my shoulder. "I'm going to need coffee first," I said, and followed Fab out to the car.

Gunz had left by the time we got to the lighthouse. Fab went in and swapped out keys while I walked around the Hummer, inspecting every inch. "The body guy is a master," I said to Fab when she joined me. "This car has had the you-know-what smooshed out of it several times over, and you can't tell." I admired my reflection in the paint job.

Fab barely batted an eyelash when I slid behind the wheel and held my hand out for the keys. This was a day that called for an IV drip of caffeine, and since that wasn't to be had, I swung through the coffee drive-thru, feeding our need, then drove the short distance to Tropical Slumber.

Fab's phone rang as we pulled into the driveway. She looked at the screen and groaned. I parked under a tree across from the entrance and prepared to listen.

"Fabiana Merceau," she answered in her snootiest tone, hitting the speaker button.

"This is Betsy Ridgely. I want to thank you for having Chief Harder talk me out of following through on my worst instincts." She let out a little laugh. "You can't imagine my surprise when he called and demanded that I come to his office. That caught me off guard, and my knees knocked so hard I was certain he could hear it over the phone. He was vague as to the reason but informed me, in that authoritative tone of his, that it would be in my best interest to show up."

Fab arched a brow at me. I smiled back at her.

"I'm happy that the chief was able to convince you of all the ways your plan could've ended with you in jail," Fab told her in a sympathetic tone.

"Richard was quite nice and took me to dinner. I made a friend, and he assured me that I could call if I started thinking about making another unwise choice."

I shook my head.

"I do have a complaint about the woman you

brought with you," Betsy said in a superior tone. "She acted totally inappropriately and didn't know her place, which, in my opinion, was to keep her mouth shut and let you handle the meeting."

Fab sighed dramatically. "It became quite clear to me that day that the relationship wasn't going to work out, so I fired her."

"You really can find a better helper," Betsy said. "Again, I want to thank you. You'll be my first call if I have another job. Legal, of course." She giggled.

"About that. I'm no longer taking clients, as I'm closing my business to devote more time to my family," Fab said.

"Oh… That's great. I wish you all the best."

I waved at the phone as Fab disconnected. "You should give that *helper* of yours a good reference."

"Probably not." Fab sniffed. "Harder? Really?"

"Betsy chick's stupidity not only put you at risk for incarceration, but me as well. I'm not risking my freedom for stinkin' jewelry, and I don't care how much it's worth for a woman that insufferable…and that's being nice." I imitated Betsy's snotty tone: "Harder was a perfect choice. He has a soft spot for a woman in distress, as long as said woman hasn't already committed a felony."

"Come on, helper," Fab said, shoving her phone in her pocket and getting out. "Before the guys wonder what's taking us so long."

"We have a new code—I tap my foot three times, you get us out of here. Pronto."

We cut over to the red carpet, which had been replaced, and danced to the front door, laughing.

Raul, who already had the door open and was leaning against the frame, clapped at our performance. Dickie stuck his head out over Raul's shoulder. The dogs bolted around the two men and romped over to the grass to chase one another.

"Come see our new addition." Raul directed us over to one side. "I thought we'd sit out here under the new pergola. We recently had our first wedding out here, and we have hopes that it will become a favorite venue choice." We rounded the corner and saw that they'd also added a complete outdoor kitchen, bar, and seating area.

"How did that go?" I asked.

"The whole day went off without a hitch. The bride was beautiful." Raul smiled at Dickie. "We had a worry or two about how Crum would work out, but he came through with a great performance. The couple was very happy."

"I did the bride's makeup." Dickie appeared flushed. "It's a different technique than on a dead person, but I thought it came out good and not overdone."

I smiled lamely and let Fab do the talking.

We slid onto bar stools while Raul went behind the bar and served cold drinks—our usual waters and soda for the two of them.

"We knew you were interested in the bodies found in Card Sound," Dickie started. "So when we went to dinner with our coroner friend, we asked a couple of questions. Raul did. I would never." He looked flustered at the thought.

"The latest remains are that of a woman, but she's yet to be identified," Raul said. "Another body was found a few days ago, floating under the bridge. It will be interesting to see what the cause of death is determined to be in both cases."

"Murder in at least one case," I said. "Since you can't dispose of your own remains."

"Lot of crime going on out there, according to our friend," Dickie said.

"They've got one suspect in jail," Raul said. "No way he didn't have help."

"Any local gossip?" I asked. "I know you make friends in interesting places."

"It hasn't been a big story," Raul said. "Not a lot of details coming out of our law enforcement friends. It also hasn't been covered by the media in any kind of eye-catching way. A casual mention here and there and no follow-up."

"Probably a good thing." Dickie fidgeted. "It might affect tourist business to our area, since we're only a few miles away, but I don't suppose it's a destination spot for anyone."

"That's because there's nothing out there except a restaurant," Fab pointed out. "I will say that every time we've driven by the parking lot, it's been full. Nothing against the place, but I don't recommend you go sample the food. At least, not until this case gets solved."

"I've heard that the majority of folks that live out there are off the grid," Raul said. "The few that do live there know everything that goes on but keep their mouths shut. They'd probably also like the case solved, but if they have information, they're too afraid to come forward for fear it would get back to the wrong ears."

"The last tidbit our friend shared," Dickie said, "is that a team of officers are being brought in to clean out the area. Everything's on the hush-hush. Be interesting to see what they uncover, if anything. It was his guess they'd find nothing more than poachers."

Fab, who'd been scoping out the property and staring across the driveway, asked, "When's the museum going to be finished?"

I looked down, in case I couldn't control my eyeroll.

"We're trying to hire a decorator, but we haven't come across anyone that's interested in the job yet," Raul said, not happy.

"Look no further," I said enthusiastically. "The answer to your decorating dilemma sits right here in front of you." I pointed at Fab. "Her house, her office…she's done an amazing job." If looks could kill, I'd be an incinerated mess. "I'm certain her husband would want to lend his talents as well. He's also got a great eye for what works."

Two pairs of expectant eyes turned on Fab. Her cheeks turned pink with embarrassment at the sudden attention…or anger; it was a difficult call. I smiled at her.

"I've got a full calendar of clients," Fab said, then noticed the smiles disappearing off their faces. "But I'm certain I can find someone more qualified than myself. I'm thinking someone with a theatrical background to give it the right flair."

I wanted to clap. *Nice save. And no, my friend, this isn't a job you'll be foisting off on me.*

"You'd do that for us?" Dickie sat forward with a look of expectancy that was foreign on his pale features.

"You leave it to us." Fab wagged her finger between me and her.

"I knew she'd be the perfect choice," I cooed, upping my excitement level and getting an *I hate you* glare from Fab in return.

Raul patted Fab's hand. "Who knew we'd become such good friends?"

Who knew indeed?

Fab checked her phone. "I've got another appointment. I picked up a lawyer client, and he's got his first job for me, which he wants taken care of right away."

We stood, and Fab and Raul hugged. I waved stupidly at Dickie, who grinned ever so slightly and waved back, then patted Fab on the shoulder.

"We hear anything else, we'll let you know," Raul assured Fab.

The dog's heads snapped up from where they lay taking a nap, and they jumped up and stood by the two men as we made our way back to the Hummer.

"Catch," I called to Fab and tossed her the keys. "You can take me home."

Once the doors were closed, she snapped, "You're lucky I don't make you walk," and flew out of the driveway.

"Do you really have an appointment, or was that a ruse to get us out of there?" I asked.

"I must've forgotten to tell you." She sighed dramatically. "Tank called this morning and has divorce papers he wants served."

Chapter Thirty-Three

Fab took one of her many shortcuts to her office, pulling up alongside the black Mercedes sedan that was parked in front. Fab and the other driver rolled down their windows. Tank handed her a manila envelope, which she stuffed between the seat and console.

I couldn't hear the conversation because Fab had hung her head out the window, and it was frustrating. I clipped her in the back. "Any problems we should know about?"

Fab ignored me, and before I could scream across the car, she waved at Tank, rolled up the window, and sped off.

"What's the gist of this job? Because if I'm going, you'd better give some details. Or I'll get out here, walk to Brad's, and get a ride home from him." I hit the unlock button.

"What's gotten into you?" Fab asked, mimicking Mother's *don't make me* tone, which was usually followed by a threat. "Couple getting a divorce, and legally, the papers need to be served so the unhappy twosome can go their separate ways. Satisfied?" She hit the locks.

"Is it local? Because I'm feeling too fragile to

leave town today."

Fab snorted.

"So unladylike. You'll get extended nostrils from doing that," I admonished in a patronizing tone.

Fab laughed. "That's such drivel. But I'm going to write it down, along with a few of your mother's other doom and gloom references, to use on my kids for behavior modification."

"You sound like a shrink. You should hope that when you have kids, the only thing you have to worry about is bodily function noises."

Fab flicked her hair and trotted out snooty girl. "Back to business. We're headed to Marathon."

"If Tank is going to have *you* serving papers, you might want to check to see if it requires a special license, since I'm almost certain that it does. Lest you get hauled into court and a judge asks you, 'What the heck, young lady?'"

"If that's necessary, then you get the license."

"You see a pig flying by?" At her confused glare, I said, "Because that's how soon I'll be doing that."

"As my partner—"

I let out a loud sob. Her head jerked around. "It's so sad…" I continued to make fake sounds. "…when your helper, sidekick, and whatever other titles I've been assigned, goes off the rails and cops an attitude."

"Stop with the noise."

I took a deep breath and shook my head. "Okay, I'm back to normal. I saw you roll your eyes. What's the plan for today's next round of fun in the sun?"

"Tank represents the husband, who assured him that his wife would be at home. We knock, hand off the papers, and leave."

"I'll wait in the car."

"No, you will not. If you're good, I'll buy you a lemonade afterwards."

"Yum." I licked my lips.

Traffic was really moving. Fab chose a lane and stuck to it, driving down the Overseas. It didn't take long to get to the address, a newly constructed two-story waterfront mansion. The gates stood open. She rolled through and turned around to park facing back towards the street.

Together, we walked up a short flight of steps to the front door. About to ring the bell, Fab paused, turned, and doubled back to the SUV. Retrieving the envelope, she came back and rang the doorbell, which could be heard all the way out on the porch. I hung back, looking for the fast getaway out of habit. The only one was back out the front gates. I didn't like our chances of climbing over if they closed for some reason.

A middle-aged man with his hair slicked back and coke-bottle glasses stuck his head out the door, gave Fab a once-over, and licked his lips. "You from Mr. Cannon's office?"

"Is Lorna Hill at home?" Fab asked.

The man pushed the door open wide. "Come in."

I grabbed the back of Fab's top as she stepped forward. "That's swell of you. But it's against the law for us to come inside." Unless he was familiar with the law, he wouldn't know I'd just made that up, and we'd be long gone by the time he bothered to check.

Fab shot me a sideways glance but stayed put.

The man appeared unsure of what to say and finally sputtered, "I'll get her." He closed the door.

Fab and I stood there in silence as the minutes ticked by. Frustrated, Fab started tapping her foot.

"I'm nervy enough to ring the bell again," I said, having had enough of staring at the paver design of the driveway.

Fab cupped her hands against the side window and peered inside just as the door opened.

"I hope you're not getting fingerprints on the glass," the blond-haired woman said stridently. She looked like she'd stepped from a 50s ad with her bouffant, full skirt, and cashmere sweater. I wanted to ask her if she itched when it was hot outside.

"Lorna Hill?" Fab asked. When she nodded, Fab thrust the envelope at her.

"What's this?" She jerked her hand back, and it fell to the ground.

"You've been served," I said solemnly, trying to imitate what I'd once seen on television.

"I don't understand," Mrs. Hill shrieked. She kicked the envelope with her pointy high heel, and it clipped Fab in the shin. "What do you know about this, Myles?"

Mr. Hill—he had to be the husband, not the butler like I'd assumed–stuttered in the face of her anger. I couldn't imagine why he was stupid enough to be there when the divorce papers were served…unless he wanted to see her reaction.

Since this wasn't one of those situations where we needed to say our good-byes and express what fun we'd had, I tugged on Fab's arm and nodded in the direction of the SUV.

"Don't take one more step," Mrs. Hill ordered. "You're taking those with you." She kicked out her expensively clad foot.

"You're apparently unaware of how this works. Once contact has been made, you've been served and the case will proceed," I said. It was clear that Mrs. Hill hadn't known that fact, and it ratcheted up her anger.

"You need to work this out with your husband," Fab said, and turned away.

The woman launched herself across the porch and toppled Fab to the ground, trying to wrestle her around. Fab elbowed her in the gut, which elicited a grunt, and the woman started to pummel her.

Mr. Hill slammed the door shut.

I jumped forward, unsure what to do since my fighting skills were non-existent, and fisted my hand in Mrs. Hill's hair in an attempt to yank her back. What I got was a handful of wig. The woman shrieked again, running her hand over the short dark strands of her real hair, her red-painted lips forming an O. Capitalizing on the element of surprise, I jerked her sideways, and Fab scrambled to her feet.

The door opened again, followed by a gunshot that sent several pieces of concrete flying. Mr. Hill appeared proud of himself, but was clearly not in control of his firearm—it shook in his hand.

"I could shoot you, and it would be self-defense," he bellowed at his wife.

Fab whirled around, kicking one leg out, and sent the gun flying into the bushes.

"You stupid ass," the wife yelled at him. She bent down, picked up the envelope, and slapped it at Fab. "Take these and get off my property."

Fab shrugged it off. "Both of you sit," she ordered. The woman sputtered in outrage. She was in a half-kneel when Fab gave her a shove, and she landed on her butt.

"That means you too," I said to the husband, but he shrugged away and ran into the house. He reappeared a minute later, rolling his suitcase down the steps and across the driveway. The door of the garage had gone up, and he popped the trunk on a Lexus and threw the suitcase in.

He jerked open the door and turned. "See you in divorce court," he yelled, then cut around the Hummer and squealed the tires out of the driveway.

"Stop him," Mrs. Hill screamed.

"He's on the main highway by this time." I was tempted to jump down the steps, but opted to walk down instead of running the risk of falling.

"This is you bitches' fault," Mrs. Hill screamed.

I half-expected her to lose her voice.

Fab leaned down in her face. "You better hope your husband doesn't need a witness to go before a judge and testify to what went on here today. Because as much as I'm loathe to make a court appearance, I'll show up and make today's events sound like Armageddon." She lifted her top, showing her weapon. "You should damn well thank me for not shooting you. And I will if you move from this spot before we get off the property."

Fab bolted down the steps and grabbed my arm. We jumped into the car, and she sped off in much the same fashion as the husband.

"I'm thinking Mrs. Hill didn't know her husband wanted a divorce...or did know but didn't think he had the balls to file," I said.

"Language, Madison." Fab burst out laughing. When she recovered, she said, "It's time to sign up for self-defense classes; we both could use a refresher."

"There's something we agree on."

Fab handed me her phone. "Call Tank and report the job completed."

I scrolled through the contacts, found the number, and was annoyed when I got voicemail. "Mr. Tank, this is Madison, and the job is complete. Another thing: if I find out you knew in advance that the Hill couple had lunatic tendencies, I'll personally kick your big butt." I put the phone in the cup holder.

"I bet when he hears your message, his three-hundred-pound frame will be shaking in his sandals."

"I'll have tequila in my lemonade."

Chapter Thirty-Four

The next day, Fab wanted to do some serious shopping and dragged me along, informing me that it was my job to make sure she didn't buy out the stores. When it came to spending money, the woman never listened to me, but I didn't point that out, knowing she wouldn't listen now. It turned out to be one of those days where whatever she found wasn't just right. After lunch at our favorite taco truck, which I got to choose, I had her stop at the grocery store. That morning, I'd threatened to cook dinner, and Creole had laughed, knowing that I used to be the cook extraordinaire in the family, but moving to South Florida had quelled that interest. Both Fab and I had lucked out, in that we had husbands who loved to cook, and tonight, I was making the choices.

Didier would be proud of me—I stuck to the outer aisles and bought all fresh foods, which included vegetables and a piece of fresh fish that, if I had my way, would be grilled. I turned around at the register to go back to the bakery and choose a fruit tart. Fab also added a few items to the basket after calling Didier.

We left the store and unloaded the cart into the back of the Hummer. Then Fab turned the cart around and rode it back to the cart stand with one foot resting on the bar, the other pushing. I laughed at the grown woman having fun, laughing as she went.

"Well, if it isn't the pretty little redhead." A woman appeared from between the cars, a floppy, wide-brimmed hat hiding her face from full view. "I've thought about you a lot. Did you miss me?" The voice, which seemed familiar, sent shivers up my spine.

"Not really." I stepped back, subtly attempting to move my arm behind my back.

"None of that," the woman spat. Her arm shot up, and her hat landed on the ground.

Addy was the last person I'd expected to come face-to-face with, and she caught me off guard, smashing something against the side of my head.

I stumbled backward. My head felt wet, and when I touched it, my fingers came away red. I blinked and shook my head to regain my wits.

Addy managed to keep me upright, hooking her arm around my torso and attempting to get me to move forward.

I screamed. It sounded pitiful to my ears. The last thing I heard was a shout as I slipped to the ground and everything went black.

* * *

I slowly opened my eyes and found myself reclined in the passenger seat, the pain registering before the events came back to me.

Fab, who was driving with a crazed expression, glanced over. "Thank goodness your eyes are open. We'll be at the hospital in a few."

"Home," I stuttered.

"Not until a doctor checks you over."

"Addy?" I croaked, gently touching my head and wincing.

"Bitch got away," Fab seethed. "I'd have gone after her, but she shoved you in my arms and took off and I wasn't leaving you. I'm so sorry. I stopped to help an old dude with his groceries, flirted a bit, and when I looked up, I saw you slumped in her arms."

"I never saw her coming. She hit me with a stick or something."

Fab raced into the lot of the emergency room, found a space, and parked. She threw the door open and jumped out. "Don't you dare move. I'm going to get a wheelchair." She slammed the door before I could respond.

I watched through the windshield as she flew through the automatic doors and came barreling back out, pushing the chair about the same way as she drove. She skidded to a stop and opened the door.

"I don't want to hear any whining out of you; you have blood on the side of your head."

"I hope she didn't rearrange my brains. I need

them." I managed a smile at her snort. "What do I tell the doctor?"

"The truth. You were attacked by a crazy woman." Fab helped me out and into the chair.

"Does this have a seatbelt?" I felt at the sides.

"You have my promise I'll get you inside in one piece."

It must have been a slow day for emergencies. There were two people in the waiting area, and they didn't appear to be at death's door.

Fab pushed me up to the counter and did all the talking, answering all the woman's questions and telling her I'd been attacked in a grocery store parking lot.

My head hurt and burned like the dickens. I slumped to one side and closed my eyes. I tugged on Fab's skirt and she leaned down. "Call Creole," I croaked.

"The second we get you checked in," Fab assured me.

I could hear someone's voice approaching, and then a nurse took control of the wheelchair and pushed me down the hall for a CAT scan. I lay in the loud machine and hoped they'd get done soon and give me something for my throbbing head. It wasn't long before I was taken to one of the private cubicles.

Fab, who'd been on the phone, speaking in a low tone, shoved it in her pocket and moved to a chair in the cubicle as the nurse helped me onto the bed. "The husbands are en route."

"How many do you have?" the nurse joked.

I liked her and relaxed at her humor. "One. Seriously, he's all I can handle, and I know he feels the same about me."

Another woman came and introduced herself as Dr. Gwen. She came to the side of the bed where I sat propped up and removed the temporary bandage to examine the side of my head. "You're lucky. A stitch or two and you'll be fine."

The doctor — who was in her forties and curvy, with a friendly smile — told me that she specialized in emergency medicine and had worked at the hospital for a number of years. Her authoritative demeanor put me at ease. She injected a local anesthetic, cleaned the wound, and sewed up the small gash in the side of my head, covering it with a small gauze pad.

Kevin poked his head in the door. Our eyes met. He gave me a once-over and grimaced, but ever so quickly — you had to be looking at him to notice.

"It'll be another few minutes, Deputy Cory," Dr. Gwen said. "I'll let you know when you can question the patient."

Kevin nodded and motioned to Fab, who followed him into the hall. They stood in front of the window, where I could see them talking.

"We'll keep you a short time for observation, and if you don't have any issues, you'll be released to go home and rest. The scan didn't show any internal hemorrhaging or skull fractures, and lucky you, you lost a minimal amount of blood. A little glue, some stitching, and it will heal without scarring."

"No Frankenstein stitching?"

Dr. Gwen laughed.

Creole ran up, Didier at his side, and skidded to a stop in the hall, grilling Fab and Kevin simultaneously. Didier stayed behind to fire a few questions of his own as Creole opened the door to the room.

I waved.

Creole closed the space between us in a few steps and introduced himself to the doctor.

"Madison will be ready to go home in a little while. We'll try not to keep her any longer than we have to, and we'll have her paperwork in order by the time she's ready to go." Dr. Gwen told him. "Just make sure she gets plenty of rest and doesn't overdo it."

"Who are you again?" I blinked at Creole.

"You're not funny," he groused.

The doctor laughed. "I'll be back to sign you out."

"Tell me what happened." Creole leaned down, brushed my hair back, and kissed me. "Fab confessed to hitting on an old guy and didn't see what happened until you were being dragged away."

I told him in as much detail as I could.

Kevin knocked and walked in. "I've got a few

questions." He fired them one after another and got the same answers as Creole. "I'm not up on the investigation in Card Sound, but I'll get up to speed on it. I'll get a photo of this Addy Clegg character and get it circulated so local law enforcement can keep an eye out."

"I'm rooting for you to arrest her," I said. "The sooner the better."

"We like our reputation for having a low crime rate and being a safe place to live and want to keep it that way. I'd rather be called out on one of your bar fights," Kevin said with amusement.

"Ssh." I crossed my lips. "We haven't had one in a while and want to keep it that way."

"I know where to find you if I have any more questions." Kevin waved and left.

Creole pulled up a chair. "I'm not letting you out of my sight."

"If you think I'm going to complain about that, you're wrong. I just want you to take me home and ply your nursing skills." I gave him an exaggerated once-over. "Do you have an outfit?"

Creole laughed, reaching over and pulling me into his arms. "Your friend is beating herself up because she wasn't paying attention."

"That's nonsense. If Fab hadn't been there to rush to the rescue and stop Addy when she did, who knows what her plans were for me. This could've had a different outcome, and no one would have known where to look." I shuddered at the thought of another trek through the mangroves.

"We're going to get her." Creole hugged me hard.

* * *

Back at home, Creole settled me on the couch with orders not to move without his assistance. Fab had argued with him in the parking lot of the hospital, wanting me to recuperate at her house, which Creole nixed with my full agreement. It was much more comforting to be in my own environment, even with the cats howling for attention.

Fab and Didier had arrived ahead of us, and with Creole's permission, she used the code and went inside to put away the groceries while Didier chopped the vegetables and fish and made skewers.

"I'll have a pitcher of margaritas," I said when Creole and I arrived at the house.

"They're not very good without the tequila," Fab said.

I made a face. "Ick!"

The guys went outside to fire up the barbeque.

Fab came over to where I was sitting on the couch and put her hand under my chin, turning my head and staring at the bandage. "You've got good color. No funeral pallor for you."

I moved my legs to the coffee table so she

could sit next to me.

"Didier and I were talking on the way home and decided that all of us need to stay on high alert."

"I'm not allowed to leave the house without my husband's permission, and I don't think he's going to give it anytime soon."

"You don't look very upset about his edict." Fab faux-frowned.

"A couple of days ignoring the craziness sounds good to me."

The guys had taken over dinner—cooking it and setting the table. To my surprise, I was actually quite hungry. We moved the party outside to the deck as the last of the white clouds drifted across the horizon. A light breeze blew in off the water.

Chapter Thirty-Five

Having had enough of recuperating under Creole's watchful eye, I called Mother to wrestle a day of fun with Mila, since neither Fab nor I had had her to ourselves in a while. I tried to impress upon Mother that sharing Mila's time wouldn't kill her, which landed on deaf ears. And she wondered why I was forced to choose the sneaky route. I called Fab and ran my plan by her.

Fab liked my idea, but thought it had zero chance of success. "The only thing saving you from certain death is the guards Caspian posted."

Caspian had called for an update from his charming daughter, as he liked to call her, and got a colorful rendition of Addy's attempted kidnapping. In response, he'd flipped and sent over two armed guards with instructions not to let either of us out of their sight. Fab threw a hissy fit, but Caspian was adamant that until "crazy broad" was in cuffs, they stayed. He'd gotten even more protective since becoming friends with Harder and getting updates from him too.

I put my foot down and decreed that the men were not going to sit or stand out in the scorching heat, dripping in sweat. Fab agreed, unlocking the side entrance to her backyard so they could sit inside or out and have access to the kitchen. We'd agreed not to sneak around and, in fact, to inform them of our comings and goings.

I texted my guard that I'd be leaving the house in ten minutes, and when I walked out the gate, he was parked in front, waiting on me in an SUV with tinted windows. I walked over, and he rolled down the window. "I'm stopping at the Bakery Café, then going to my brother's. I won't be there very long and will be returning home. Don't worry, you'll be able to keep up with me."

He grinned.

I drove into the underground garage at Brad's, my escort following me, and lucked out with available guest parking. I grabbed the pink box off the front seat and took the elevator to the top floor, where I knocked on the door and waited patiently.

The door opened, and Mila ran out, dressed for the day. "Auntie Mad," she squealed.

I picked her up and spun her around.

Behind her, Brad was looking harried and running behind as he still had on sweats and a t-shirt. His frown disappeared at the sight of the box, and he pulled me inside. He crossed to the kitchen and set the box down, then turned and enveloped me and Mila in a hug. "I don't know what you're up to, but seriously, today's not the day."

"There's never a good day," I grouched.

Brad took Mila from my arms and set her on the floor. "Go find your favorite book." She ran out of the room. "Slow down," he called after his daughter. He turned my face from side to side. "You look pretty good, all things considered. I got the update from Creole. Too bad Addy's not a man. If I caught up to her first, I'd beat the you-know-what out of her."

"I called Mother, and her schedule with Mila is booked to infinity. So… I'm here to appropriate your daughter."

"You're putting me in the middle? Making me choose?" He groaned. "What are your plans if you take her for the day?"

"Whisk her off to Fab's, where we'll turn my bedroom into a playroom. You've seen that bed?"

"It's kind of obscenely large."

"It's perfect for jumping, rolling around, and having a great time. There will be all kinds of healthy food, courtesy of Didier. There's a ton of security, thanks to Caspian. Even now, a guard's waiting downstairs to escort us back."

"You're making me choose between being a crappy son and a crappy brother." Brad was definitely torn.

"I'm making it so you can claim ignorance and everything can be blamed on underhanded

Madison." I smiled cheekily. "Mother is due here in a half-hour. In that time, you'll need to shower so you can leave for the office, right?" He nodded. "So you'll tell Mother in an offended tone that you can't believe your own sister would be so sneaky as to stop by with treats—" I pointed to the box. "—and offer to watch Mila while you get dressed, only to nap your daughter, leaving behind a note." I pulled a piece of paper out of my pocket.

"Maybe I can pull that off if I don't get too wordy."

"Stick to the script."

Mila bolted back into the room, favorite book in hand. Brad hoisted her in the air and kissed her cheeks. "You have a fun day." He peered over her head. "Shall I tell her to enjoy her last day with you? I'll have to come up with a good explanation for your sudden disappearance and why she now has to visit Gammi in j-a-i-l." He set Mila on the island to look at her book.

"And people say I'm the dramatic one." I pointed to myself in faux shock.

"Warning: Mother is going to storm your house and, when you don't answer, head straight to Fab's. So don't be surprised." He pointed to my bruised face. "You're already in trouble. I'm willing to bet you didn't tell her about your latest adventure. She's also going to notice that the Hummer's back and know that you lied about getting a new car. Your sins are multiplying. I'm going to miss you."

"I'm a grown adult." I waved him off. "I know it's not an excuse she'll accept. My plan on that front is it to tough it out and hope I can skate past her radar." I ignored his shaking head and tapped my nonexistent watch. "Time's a-wasting. You don't want to be late to the office."

Brad kissed my cheek and Mila's, then picked her up and set her on the floor.

"Ready for an adventure?" I asked Mila, and held out my hand, which she clasped. At the door, I grabbed her backpack and flung it over my shoulder. Brad leaned against the wall and watched with amusement as we left.

I picked Mila up so she could press the elevator button, we got in, and she told me all about her book as we rode down. The guard, who stood waiting at the fender of his vehicle, met us and took the bag while I buckled Mila into her car seat. The ride home was uneventful, and I drove straight to Fab's. As expected, she met us at the door.

"I can't believe you pulled this off," Fab said in awe. "Does Brad know?"

"Of course he knows. I feel bad that he's going to have to break the news to Mother, but if he follows the script we went over, he should survive unscathed."

"What do I tell the guard when he calls and asks if he can admit her?"

"I didn't get that far in my plan," I said.

"That's not like you."

"Do you think when we have children we'll get to raise them? Or will we be relegated to visiting once in a while?"

Fab made the decision to have the guard tell Mother that we were gone and would be back in the afternoon. It gave us the morning to roughhouse and act like hooligans. Fab taught Mila an abbreviated version of the cartwheel. I passed and instead took pictures. Lunch rolled around and we picnicked on the floor, and afterwards, the three of us were ready for a nap. Maybe not Fab, but she lay down with us anyway.

Mother was back in late afternoon, her muscle in tow. She flounced through the front door, irritation etched on her face. Spoon wasn't able to maintain his straight face; his lips continued to quirk.

Mila charged Mother and hugged her legs. She picked her up and laid a loud kiss on her cheek, then checked her over. "None the worse for wear, I see." She handed her to Spoon, who Mila had held her arms out to as soon as she saw him. Mother flicked her hand at me, cutting off a response. "I should be shocked, but I'm not. I realize that I have a hard time sharing, and when you called, I should've been more accommodating. I'd like more grandchildren; having a crowd of kids at my house every day would suit me just fine."

I turned and rolled my eyes at Fab. *Told you so.* I turned back. "I've given you two. You can't even be bothered to give them a head rub."

"Really, Madison. Those cats?" Mother shook her head.

Spoon smirked.

Fab laughed and, when she recovered, glared at me as though I'd tricked the laughter out of her. "Cold drinks all around?" she asked and led us out to the patio. She pointed Spoon, who wasn't the least bit disgruntled, to the bar and settled in a chair, picking Mila up and putting her on her lap, opening her book.

Without asking, Spoon served us what he knew we liked and joined us.

Mother, who didn't drink around Mila, sipped on iced tea. "I thought you traded the Hummer for another SUV."

"Actually, I had it repaired," I said, trying to pass it off casually.

"I walked around it and inspected it. Whoever did the work did a great job," Spoon said. "Equal to my shop. Maybe it's someone I can use in the future."

"Like you, he's appointment-only, and I can't pass along his name without asking first," I said.

"What about the other car you bought?" Mother asked.

"It was actually a loaner while the Hummer was being fixed."

Mother sighed in annoyance. "It's not that I

don't want you to use Spoon's shop. I just don't want him ending up dead."

"Your mother and I have had a long discussion. In the future, call me, and I'll decide for myself whether I want to lend assistance."

Mother blushed and covered her husband's hand with her own.

"I get Mother's point, and frankly, I don't want anything happening to any of us."

"The hot gossip at the beauty salon was that my daughter was attacked in the parking lot of a grocery store."

I struggled not to squirm under Mother's stare. Sadly, I was out of practice.

"I laughed it off, since I hadn't heard a word about it," Mother continued. "Then I read about it in the local paper. Would it be a good guess that the stitches on the side of your head are where you got clocked?"

"I didn't see it coming." I did my best to sound casual, as though being accosted in a parking lot was a regular occurrence. "The woman stepped out from between two cars and landed a powerful whack."

Spoon glared at the side of my face. "Cops catch the person?"

"They've identified her, and now it's a matter of picking her up." I made it sound imminent. "Fab was the star of the day. She came to my rescue." I smiled at her.

"If I'd been a bit faster, the old hag would be

in custody." Fab grinned at Mother's head shake. "Mila's not listening; she's reading." She ran her hand over the little girl's head where she was lying against Fab's chest, staring intently at the pages of the book, talking out loud.

"Next time, call your mother," Spoon said. "She shouldn't have to hear second-hand or be the last to know. You know she's good in a crisis."

"Honey." Mother made a cooing noise.

Fab arched her brow.

"You'll be happy to know that I've been maintaining a low profile." And now to change the subject. "I know it's shifty, snatching Mila for a playdate, but we had a fun time."

"I'm afraid to ask where you took her," Mother said.

The arrival of the guys saved me from having to answer. It couldn't have been timed better. I didn't want to lie or confess that we'd been home the whole time.

Creole bent down and kissed my cheek. "I can't believe what you did to your poor brother," he whispered.

What? I squinted at him. "Yeah, poor Brad."

Creole nudged me over and sat down beside me in the over-sized chair.

Didier kissed Fab, then picked Mila up and swung her around. "Brad's on his way over with a mountain of pizza boxes. He promised everyone's favorites."

Chapter Thirty-Six

The next afternoon, Fab and I were sitting at the island in her massive kitchen, drinking iced tea, when my phone rang. Fab grabbed it out from under my hand and frowned, handing it to me.

I smiled at Creole's face on the screen and answered. It didn't go on speaker, since neither of our husbands would agree to that.

"Harder's in town and has invited us to dinner," Creole said when I answered. "He suggested Jake's, saying that he'd already asked Henry if he'd make something special."

"The only people I know who're on a first-name basis with Cook are Mila—who's four years old—and now Harder."

Creole laughed. "Is that a yes?"

"Wonder what's up? This is a first, Harder inviting us anywhere."

"I'm on my way home."

"Dinner with Harder?" Fab said when I set down the phone. "Where's my and Didier's invitation? He must want something. You better hope he's not cashing in all the favors you owe at once, because it would be a doozy."

Harder would never ask me do anything illegal, so that wasn't a worry. "Have you forgotten that you don't like the man? Besides, you don't have to get invited to everything."

"Yes, I do," Fab huffed. "You know how I hate second-hand information."

"I'll secretly record the dinner conversation. Happy now?"

"You'll end up in jail, and me too after you say it was my idea."

"Refresher: the rule is one of us has stay out of lockup to arrange bail. I won't be able to count on Creole, since he'll be mad that I did such a thing."

"At least you won't have to dress up." She eyed my jean skirt and t-shirt top. Her changing the subject should have had me wondering what she was planning.

I stood up and twirled. "I'm going home and changing into tropical cute." I reached for my keys. "Mom, do I have permission to drive *my* car?"

"Don't be out late."

* * *

Creole picked me up, and on the way to Jake's, I called and instructed Kelpie to clear the deck.

"No worries, Bossaroo; no one likes to sit out there anyway." I had a vision of her dancing around as she talked, entertaining the customers. "You can't hear squat, meaning the music, and if any fun breaks out, ya miss all the action."

"Our guest is the Chief of Police. Do you think you can lasso your regulars into some good behavior?" It was a simple request that I shouldn't have had to make, but nothing was ever a sure thing where the bar was concerned.

"Yeehaw."

I jerked the phone away from my ear. When she was done with the sound effects, I said, "Remind Cook we're on our way; he's making something special."

"Today's special is goat burgers. Will that be okay?"

Dead silence. "You're fired. Since I'm certain it was your idea."

"You're so easy to prank." Kelpie laughed. "No worries, I've got it all under control."

We hung up.

Creole grinned. "It's hard not to like her; nothing ever gets to her." He pulled into the parking lot and honked at Harder, who'd just gotten out of his car.

"That was good timing. I hope he doesn't keep us in suspense about the reason for the invite."

We got out and met halfway to the door.

"You look good, considering all the drama." Harder kissed my cheek.

We walked inside and stopped at the bar, placing our drink order, then headed out to the deck. Harder smirked at the "Keep Out" sign on the knob.

I was happy to see that the area had been spit shined and the table set. The overhead fans whirled, and I flicked on the lights that ran around the railing.

"Thank you for meeting me," Harder said.

The door opened, and Kelpie came out, tray in hand. She served Harder, bending and giving him an unobstructed view to her navel. With a smirk, Creole nudged me under the table. Enjoying the view, Harder winked at Kelpie. Bold as brass, she winked back and added a kissy noise. She set Creole's and my drinks down with barely a glance and left.

"I bet good employees are hard to find," Harder said, smiling at the door.

"I could write a book."

The guys laughed.

Harder toasted: "To good friends."

The three of us looked up as the door opened again. Fab and Didier crossed the threshold, drinks in hand.

Fab slid into a seat next to me. "I hope we're not late."

Didier nodded and sat down.

"You weren't invited," Harder snapped.

"We weren't?" Didier turned to Fab.

"I'm certain our invitation was overlooked." Fab put on a good innocent act. I wanted to clap.

"It wasn't." Harder shook his head.

I bit my lip to keep from laughing.

"We're leaving." Didier stood.

"No, we're not." Fab tugged on his arm and, at the same time, glared at Harder. "You'd never be this rude to Madeline, and she does stuff like this all the time. You either don't know or have forgotten that Madison and I share everything—well, almost—and second-hand news is tiresome."

Wait until Mother hears about this. She's going to be impressed.

"Harder's requested something special from the kitchen," I said inanely to interrupt the glare-down. I smiled covertly at Didier, who responded with a slight shake of his head.

"Sounds good," Creole said. "How about another toast? To friends, wasn't it?" He tipped his beer bottle.

"I'm about to propose something. Just know that you can say no." Harder's gaze turned to me. "There's no obligation, and I want that understood up front."

Creole's hand covered mine. "What's up?"

"I'd like to use Madison as a decoy to flush out Addy."

"Absolutely not." Fab slapped her hand on the table. "You're an ass for suggesting such a thing. That woman's crazy."

I smiled weakly, agreeing…except about the ass part. I chugged down my margarita. Setting the glass down, I said, "Show of hands—who wants a refill?"

All hands shot up.

I took my phone out of my pocket and called inside, placing the order.

"I'm not comfortable with my wife being bait," Creole ground out. "I want this woman caught as much as you do, but I'm thinking you need to come up with Plan B."

Fab started to say something.

Didier cut her off. "Since I'm certain that my wife was about to volunteer, the answer is no to that also."

"I confess that what you're suggesting scares me to the tips of my toes." I played with the stem of my glass, wishing it were full.

"N. O." Fab barked. "Decoy? Really? Why the urgency?"

"We have it on good authority that she and her spawn are murderers. The family that murders together… We've got one of the sons in custody, but there are two more on the loose, plus Addy. We'd like to get them locked up before another body turns up."

The door opened and Kelpie danced in, setting down the drinks and giving an off-balance curtsy and a wink to Harder before backing into the main bar area.

"How would you keep me safe?" I downed half my glass.

"We would put a tracking device on you, mic you up, and there would be eyes on you at all times."

"Put a red wig on me, and I'll do it," Fab volunteered.

"No way," Didier said gruffly.

"Addy would notice in a second," I said. "Apparently, I'm the tastier of the two of us."

Fab and I grimaced.

"She said that?" Harder asked. "I don't want to think about what that might mean."

"Then what?" I asked. "Go out to Card Sound for another crawl through the mangroves?"

"You'd go shopping, hang out around town being very visible. We'd have undercover officers watching your every move in hopes of flushing Addy out."

"Since we don't know if her attempt to kidnap me was a fluke, who knows when or if she'll try it again. She did seem to be enjoying herself, which was unnerving."

"She was too prepared," Fab said. "Remember the girl from a week ago? Who knows where she'd have ended up if we hadn't intervened."

"Madison and I need to talk about this," Creole said. "I'm telling you now that if, and it's a big if, it happens, then I'll be part of the team."

"I also want to be on that team." Fab raised her hand.

Didier sighed. "I'll do whatever you ask of me."

"None of you are going to be on the team. The department has professionals that know how to do their job so no one gets hurt. The three of you will stay out of it," Harder admonished.

The door opened, and one of Cook's assistants rolled a cart through, set two enormous platters—an assortment of house favorites—in the middle of the table, and put plates in front of us.

"How about we table the discussion until after we eat?" I suggested. The last thing on my mind was food, and the thought of eating made me queasy. I attempted a smile.

Fab turned in her seat and cracked open the door. After a minute, she waved frantically and held up her fingers, then closed the door. She'd re-ordered our drinks in sign language that I'd yet to learn.

"It looks yum," Fab said. "You order this all on your own?" she asked Harder in a tone that suggested he wouldn't know how.

"You're annoying. But I'm certain you know that," Harder grumped.

Didier kissed the top of her head.

I picked at my food and ran it around the plate, recreating a car chase. The conversation went on around me, and I barely listened, hoping there wouldn't be a quiz later. How could I not say yes, even though it was just about the last thing I wanted to commit to? But the very last thing I wanted was for another dead body to turn up when I could've stopped it from happening.

"I'll do it," I blurted.

Creole rested his head against mine and sighed. "We should talk about this."

"Are we going to change our minds?" I whispered.

He kissed my cheek and pulled me closer. "We'll get back to you tomorrow," he told Harder.

"I knew that would be your answer." Fab sniffed. "I still vote for me donning a wig and borrowing some of your clothes."

"And a pair of flip-flops." I winked.

"You and Creole talk it over and, if you have any questions, call me and we can meet again to discuss the details," Harder offered.

It was a first that I had no interest in taking home leftovers. Fab took charge and had everything boxed. And was bold enough to bring an abrupt end to the evening. "We have a lot to think about."

I was grateful, having given up on the idea of sneaking out and down to the beach. At some point, I'd have had to cut back to the highway so Creole could find me and take me home.

Harder said he'd be in touch, then headed straight to the bar and took care of the check. Judging by Kelpie's grin, he'd left her a good tip. To my surprise, he then cut down the hall to the kitchen.

Kelpie flagged me over.

"Copper's cute," she gushed. "The nice thing is, he doesn't know it, or if he does, he's not all full of himself."

"You were outrageous tonight," I admonished.

"I told him I'd been really, really bad and he might want to arrest me." Kelpie crossed her wrists.

"You did not."

"He grinned, but seemed speechless. Before he cut out the back, he said he'd see me soon." Kelpie preened.

Creole came up, put his arms around me, and said to Kelpie, "If Harder starts coming in on a regular basis, you'll have to stop with the machinations you're always planning."

"You act like we'd ever consider doing anything illegal." Kelpie sniffed and turned away, but not before I saw her smirk.

"Kelpie girl," a customer yelled. "Shake it down here and bring a beer with you."

"Hold your water," Kelpie yelled back and sidled down the bar.

Creole walked me outside, where we joined the rest of the party in the driveway.

Harder joined us and wrapped me in a hug. "Just remember that 'hell no' is an acceptable answer."

"I don't see any way that it won't be a yes, considering that no one wants another murder," I said. "We'll call you tomorrow."

"Don't be surprised if you wake up cuffed to Creole and he's lost the key," Harder joked.

"I pulled that trick on Fab, and she wasn't happy, to say the least."

"Did someone happen to get video?" Harder asked.

"The person that shoots the videos and takes the pictures was otherwise occupied." Didier hugged Fab to his side.

Fab pulled me away and enveloped me in a hug. "We're going to talk tomorrow," she whispered in my ear. "No way are you doing this by yourself, no matter what anyone says."

"You're the best," I whispered back.

We said our good-byes, got in the SUV, and followed Fab's Porsche home.

Chapter Thirty-Seven

Stakeouts are boring, but then, I suppose anyone who's ever done one knows that, and grumbling to oneself doesn't help the time go by any faster. This was my third day hanging out around town, checking out all the businesses. Window shopping, checking over my shoulder in the glass, moving from one store to another. Today, I'd hit the grocery store. It was the lure of the coffee bar and outside tables, where I could sit and keep my eyes peeled from under my lashes for a familiar face. I spent my time playing solitaire on my phone, losing almost every hand.

The detective on the case had had his tech guy fit me with a small, round earpiece that picked up and transmitted sound and also doubled as a GPS.

"Testing," I mumbled, knowing that the two-way piece was meant to allow me to take direction from one of the officers, not to engage in small talk.

The guy on the other end chuckled. "Hang in there; you're doing great."

"Hmm…" I said, not wanting to attract

attention by talking to myself, although enough people did it these days.

When I'd met with Harder and a couple of the detectives on the Addy Clegg case, I'd been assured that I wouldn't be leaving the area. Once Addy was spotted, she'd be arrested. *That's if she doesn't get away*, I'd thought but didn't voice. Creole had suggested to Harder that they use a female undercover officer, but to our surprise, they already had. Harder hadn't mentioned it to avoid pressuring me. They'd chosen a woman similar in stature, who'd been certain that she'd spotted Addy and tipped off the investigators, but the woman in question had disappeared. It was the consensus that Addy had gotten a good look at the detective, known she wasn't her prey, and left.

Creole, who had a lot of patience for "hurry up and wait" from his days as a cop, had demanded to be part of the team, and Harder okayed it with several stipulations. Creole was sitting under a tree in an innocuous white van parked on the far side of the lot, a couple of branches blocking it from view unless you walked over to that area.

Never one to take no for an answer, Fab didn't in this case either, even after Harder told her to stay out of it. She'd been upfront with Creole and told him that she planned her own watch on me with the help of her backup, Didier. She had a few tricks up her sleeve that she hadn't shared until she sprang them on me.

She'd gone shopping and came to the house, upending the contents of a bag on the bed. Out tumbled a long-sleeve t-shirt, crop sweats, and tennis shoes. "You need to be comfortable. When this is all over, you can throw them in the trash."

My favorite comfort-wear. She knew me so well.

Gunz had come through with some high-tech devices from an unnamed friend. Fab was excited to try them out, but wished the circumstances were different. She'd outfitted me with an earpiece almost identical to the law enforcement one, which she put it in my other ear. She reminded me not to answer when she spoke to me, as the cops, and more importantly Harder, would then know she'd ignored his order. She also produced two small square GPS units and a sewing kit, and we sat on the couch and sewed one into my sports bra and the other into the pocket of my sweatpants.

"Just in case," Fab said. "We're a team, and we always have each other's back." She leveled a stare at me, and I nodded and hugged her. "I don't want to forget." She hung a medallion necklace around my neck, which I knew to be a camera. "A well-dressed woman needs her accessories."

That got a chuckle from both of us.

Fab swapped her Porsche for the white beater truck I kept parked at the office. For once, she hadn't parked out in the hinterlands. Unlike the cop van, she'd found a space in front, opposite me, where she and Didier were hunched down, watching my every move and at the same time keeping an eye on traffic entering and exiting the lot.

A young guy, baseball hat pulled down, rushed out of the store, not watching where he was going. He clipped my leg and grouched, "You need to stay out of the way."

His irritated tone caused me to look up in shock. "I'm sitting, dude." *You walked into me.*

"If it's not one excuse…"

I searched his face. There was something familiar about it that I couldn't quite put my finger on, a weird sense of having seen him before, but where? "Have a nice day," I said sarcastically.

Without saying a word, he turned and stalked to an older model Ford pickup, and when he backed out, I noticed it was minus the rear plate.

"He needs to lay off the coffee," the cop in my ear said.

I looked down and smiled.

I pushed my dark-tinted sunglasses down and checked out the parking lot over the rim of my coffee cup. Nothing exciting. People doing exactly what you'd expect them to do—buying groceries and leaving. I swiped at my neck hair, hating the sensation of it standing on end. It did no good. The uneasy feeling wasn't going away.

I checked my watch for the umpteenth time and sighed to see that the time allotted for the stakeout was about over for the day. I'd be happy to go home, as I'm sure would the others. I knew we all wanted it to be over. I switched back to my card game to see how badly I was losing.

Out of nowhere, Addy Clegg stood in front of me, a gun in her hand, finger on the trigger. "It's up to you how many people die." She gestured with the gun. "Get moving."

There was something hypnotizing about the barrel of a gun being pointed in one's face. No one seemed to have noticed...except, of course, me. "Gun," I whispered and rose in what felt like slow motion, trying to assess my options for escape. But I didn't see any that wouldn't put a lot of people at risk, not to mention a bullet in my back.

"Move it," Addy repeated and moved behind me, poking the muzzle in my back.

It felt like the order was coming from the gun itself rather than Addy, and there's no arguing with a gun. Ironically, she was parked right next to Fab, who stared out the window, unable to get her door open, as Addy had blocked it with her own. She shoved me inside, and I felt rather than saw the needle that jabbed into my shoulder. Cooperating had been a very big mistake, but it was too late now, I thought as I slumped down on the seat.

Addy jumped behind the wheel and raced away.

Realizing that I wasn't completely out of it, I struggled to move and sit up, which turned out to be a useless attempt. I continued to lie at an awkward angle, face smooshed against the seat. Whatever Addy had drugged me with, I hadn't passed out but was, instead, relaxed to the point of being useless. I peered up through the window and mumbled, "Blue skies, white clouds." I highly doubted that would be the least bit helpful for those I hoped were hot on her bumper. The silence that answered me scared me even more.

Addy drove for what seemed like hours but probably wasn't. Eventually, she jerked the steering wheel, sending the car careening onto loose gravel, losing traction and then finding it again. I felt the tires scramble to find a grip. We skidded sideways, and she parked.

I sighed in relief.

Addy jumped out, jerked open the back door, and pointed the gun at me again. "Get out."

I tried again to sit up and slumped.

Addy reached in and grabbed my arm. Grunting, she dragged me off the back seat and dumped me unceremoniously on the ground, shoving me with her foot. I looked around and was surprised to see that she'd found another piece of cleared land in the midst of the mangroves. This time, the clearing felt more remote in an already isolated area. This piece of land was smaller than the last, the house on wheels parked in the middle, this time still hooked to a trailer.

Addy cast a glance in my direction, then unloaded a box from the back of the car and into her house. She came back and hooked her arm around me, attempting to pull me to my feet, and ended up dropping me back down.

A sharp pain ripped through my palms, but it grounded me and cleared my brain somewhat. I breathed in a deep lungful of air as though I'd been deprived.

"I know you're capable of standing, and if you don't, I'm rubbing your face in the dirt. A few ant bites, and you'll be up on your feet." Addy gave me a sharp kick in the hip.

Where is everyone? I didn't see any way out of this on my own.

I managed to crawl into a sitting position and looked up at the woman. "Are you going to kill me?"

Addy's beady brown eyes sliced over me. "Not right away. I'm looking forward to having my friend back."

What friend? Her words frightened me. They made no sense, since we were never friends and, to my knowledge, had never met casually or even been introduced, for that matter.

A truck rumbled into the driveway, which gave me momentary hope. It was dashed when I looked up and didn't recognize the dark vehicle. The guy who got out was the same one from the parking lot.

He jerked me up one-armed and hauled me up the steps and into the house. "Where do you want her?" he asked Addy.

Addy pointed behind me.

The guy dumped me on the couch that ran along one side of the small oblong space. Two or three hundred square feet, if I had to guess. On the opposite wall was a strip kitchen, and a bed at the far end. One door, which I assumed was the bathroom. Even assuming I could shake the lethargy, the windows were too small to climb through.

"Really, Ma, you and your collection of friends are downright weird."

"Shut your mouth," Addy snapped.

"Whatever. You need anything else before I go to the warehouse?"

"I got it under control."

He kissed Addy's cheek. "Stay out of trouble." He laughed at his joke.

What had gone wrong? Addy! She'd somehow driven into the parking lot under the radar and taken me in broad daylight, and no one, not even me, was paying attention at the right time. This wasn't supposed to end with me facing down a crazy woman alone.

As though reading my mind, she said, "So stupid of you—sitting duck is what you were."

She took her gun of out of her pants and put it on the counter.

"I agree," I murmured under my breath. The stupid thing had been agreeing to this stakeout, thinking that nothing could go wrong. "What was in the shot you gave me?" I asked.

"Valium. It relaxes you without putting you out cold. I want you to be cooperative, not asleep. An old woman like me can't be hauling you around."

Cooperative? Seemed like another word for giving up. I'd become numb but could feel the fear settled in my spine reaching new heights. Would this be one of my last memories before I died? I was certain there was no get out of jail free card. Where were the others? They should have been there by now.

"Don't look so worried, sweet thing," Addy said, snapping open a folding chair and sitting across from me. "I'm not going to kill you. At least, not right away. Don't make the mistake the others did—" She waved her hand absently. "—and try to get away. There's nowhere to go." She cackled. "Although, somehow, you and your friend got away the first time. I'll want to hear the details of how you managed it. It brought a lot of cop attention out this way when there'd been almost none. It used to be a nice, quiet place to live how you want." She laughed again.

I turned toward where she'd waved and, for the first time, realized that I shared the room with three... A scream lodged in my throat. There were two women — my identification based solely on the clothing choice: dresses on each — their visible body parts wrapped in gauze, including what would have been their faces. Each had on a wig, one of them a red-head. In the only chair was what I guessed was a man due to the suit he wore, with netting down to his shoulders. I inched away, my butt slipping into the crack between the couch and a built-in cabinet.

Noticing that she no longer had my attention, she said, "A lot of people disappear, never to be seen again. You'll be one of them soon enough. Enjoy life while you can, I always say."

I looked into her face and saw pretty much what I was expecting, a vacantness, a slyness. She thought she was about to get away with another... I balked at putting it into words. My brain was on overload, processing this nightmare slowly.

"Let me go," I pleaded. "You want a friend; I'll come visit."

"You're lying. Saying what you think needs to be said to get out of here," Addy said bitterly. "If you're always here, you'll be at my beck and call. I'm thinking I might enjoy more than one-sided conversations. You play cards?" She brightened at the thought.

I nodded and drew in a deep breath. "I could introduce you to my friends who run the local funeral home. The three of you could share tips; they might even hire you. They're opening a funeral museum and are looking for ideas." I went on to tell her what they had planned, most of which I made up since I hadn't listened that closely. Anything to get me out of there.

"Now that's really weird."

Three people in various stages of decomposition wasn't weird? I cast a sideways glance at the threesome and wondered how they got caught in her web. Did she kidnap them all? *Keep her talking*, I told myself, *buy time for reinforcements to show up.*

Addy's hand began to shake. She stood and opened the cupboard to one side of the sink, taking down a bottle of scotch and filling a glass halfway. She downed it in a gulp. Tossed her head back and belched. Screwing the cap back on, she put the bottle back in the cabinet.

I was trying to fight the effects of being drugged, but was overcome by moments of vagueness, having to remind myself where I was and how I got there. Being drugged did crazy things to the brain. I didn't see any avenue of escape and had to admit that I wasn't in any shape to make a run for it. My only hope was talking her into letting me go, as remote as that seemed. Time to use my eccentric-people skills. Homicidal added a new layer to Addy's personality that I didn't deal with on a day-to-day basis.

Addy opened a drawer and pulled out a hypodermic needle, laying it on the counter. "A treat for later. Don't want to give you too much. I'm looking forward to the card game." She tossed a deck down. "Just know, you cease to amuse me and…" She drew a line across her neck, complete with sound effects.

The door crashed open and hit the wall.

"Hands up," an officer shouted, gun pointed at Addy. He moved out of the doorway, and another officer joined him, weapons all trained on the woman.

Outside, sirens split the air and cars rumbled across the gravel, squealing to a stop.

Addy made a lunge for her gun.

"Don't do it," the first cop shouted.

Addy hesitated. The second officer knocked the gun out of her reach.

Not one to give up, Addy picked up the chair and tossed it at the officers. When she bought the place, she obviously hadn't thought about the extra space she'd need to make a successful getaway. It took both officers to bring down the screaming, cursing woman. They held her down and cuffed her, then hauled her up and outside, reading her her rights.

Creole rushed inside and grabbed me, holding me to his chest. "Are you all right?" he murmured in my ear.

He meant physically, I guessed, and nodded. "Get me out of here," I whispered softly.

"I've got you." Creole squeezed harder. "And I'm not letting go. Let's get you home."

Chapter Thirty-Eight

"I'm sorry things didn't go as planned." Creole carried me into the house, setting me on the couch.

I'd refused a trip to the hospital since Addy hadn't physically hurt me and the effects of the valium were wearing off.

"You need to call Harder," I said. "One of the sons the cops are looking for is hanging out in a warehouse somewhere close to where Addy lived. My guess is that it's Deuce's old criminal headquarters."

"Too bad I don't have your phone; he'd answer faster," Creole joked as he called Harder. When he answered, Creole relayed my message and hung up. "Harder said to tell you he'll call tomorrow and he's happy you're safe."

Fab bounced down next to me. "You better be okay."

"What took you so long?"

Fab's face filled with frustration. "I was ordered to stand down and wait for law enforcement. You don't know how hard it was, sitting by the side of the freakin' road grinding my teeth. If Didier hadn't physically restrained me a couple of times, I would've busted in and shot her ass."

I laughed and smiled at Didier. "It's quite a job being her partner."

Didier leaned down, hugging me hard, and sat down next to Fab. "Happy to see you."

"Fab's the reason we found you as quickly as we did." Creole smiled at her. "Thanks to the GPS units she outfitted you with. The equipment went down, you disappeared, and I about went out of my mind before Fab called and told me she was in hot pursuit. About halfway there, our electronics went back up."

"I hate it when you go off on your own," Fab grouched.

"We agreed long ago that we can't both get arrested at the same time, and now I'm adding kidnapped. It was comforting knowing that you were out there and would be tracking us," I said.

"What did she do to you?" Fab asked.

Didier tugged on her arm. "We should go and let Madison rest. We can get updated another time."

"Nooo…" Fab wailed.

"Stay." I held up my hand. "It's easier to tell you all at the same time. Once you hear some of the details, you'll understand why I won't want to be repeating them."

They took a seat. I wasn't sure where to start and just dove in.

"I don't know what happened to the necklace." I patted my neck. "No pictures." I frowned.

"It came off when Addy was manhandling you into the back of the car," Fab said. "I'm sorry it got that far. I was afraid she'd shoot you if I pulled a gun."

"She probably would have," I said. "The upside is that, if not now then soon, the cops will have the whole Clegg family in custody. There must be murder in their DNA, if there is such a thing." I told them everything that'd happened.

"Addy killed so she could have friends?" Fab asked in shock.

"And the sons as initiation into a club." Didier shook his head.

"In all my years in law enforcement, I never had a case where the whole family was homicidal," Creole said. "Sounds like a few cold cases are going to get solved."

I leaned back into his arms. "Which one of you is cooking dinner?" I looked up at Creole, then over at Didier.

Chapter Thirty-Nine

Two mornings later, Fab and Didier showed up with a pink bakery box filled with danishes. Creole and Didier had a meeting, and Creole didn't want me to be alone.

"I'm fine."

"Humor me." He kissed me. "If Fab's got some new client, you tell her, 'Have fun without me.'"

I laughed.

It was like the old days; the four of us sitting around the island drinking coffee, and Fab and I being grilled about our plans for the day. Since I didn't have any, I let her weave some nonexistent agenda that the guys laughed at.

Creole's phone rang, and after looking at the screen, he took it outside to answer. He wasn't gone long. "That was Harder," he said, coming through the door. "Your tip on the warehouse panned out. Both Clegg brothers and several others were arrested. They had two stolen sports cars in the place."

"Happy to hear that the whole lot of them are behind bars," I said.

"If anyone suggests looking at land out in

Card Sound again, I'm going to pass."

Didier laughed. "Agreed there."

"Enough of the Cleggs," Fab said. "Didier and I are going to invite the two of you to dinner." She sported the secret smile that made sensible people do a double take.

"Why not just do it and stop hinting around?" I said.

"Didier and I are trying to agree on the perfect restaurant."

"We are?" Didier teased her.

"Hmm… that means that the two of you are up to something, probably unsavory…"

"Not if Didier is involved," Creole cut in.

"The answer is no," I said.

"We're busy." Creole tried not to laugh but failed.

"You don't even know the date," Fab fumed.

"You want a guaranteed yes?" I asked the pouting woman. "Have Didier cook, and we'll eat out on your end of the beach. You've got all that fancy furniture that no one ever sits in. Time to break it in."

"Hamburgers?" Didier offered, ignoring Fab's snort.

"Dinner is the surprise?" I asked. "That seems understated for you. I bet you've got something else up your sleeve."

"I wish I hadn't been sworn to secrecy." Fab zipped her lips and turned her eyes to Didier, apparently hoping to change his mind. Instead, he glared a warning.

"Since when do you do what you're told?" I asked Fab.

Didier crossed his arms, amusement in his eyes. "I'm interested in the answer."

"I do my best."

The three of us laughed at the outrageousness of that statement.

* * *

The guys had barely cleared the threshold when Fab announced, "Field trip."

"What does that mean?" I asked suspiciously.

"It means it's local, so we're not going far."

I looked at her jeans and my jean skirt. "Should I put on tennis shoes?"

"You look fine." Fab eyed my sandals and looped her arm around mine, leading me out the door and hitting the locks for the Hummer. "You know, that pickup of yours looks junky but runs like a charm."

"It's a great backup."

Fab cruised down the highway, and true to her word, she'd only gone a couple of miles when she turned into the driveway of the faded, run-down pink-and-green adult motel that Creole had been in negotiations to purchase.

"I've been wanting to see this place ever since Creole announced he had a contract on it." Fab parked in front.

"Except the deal fell through, and last I heard, it's back to pending approval," I said in frustration. "When you've got a live one on the line, cash in hand and willing to meet code requirements, you'd think the lender could cobble the paperwork together in an efficient fashion."

"According to Didier, the hang-up was the city. They wanted the property so they could work a deal with a contractor to build condos. That's the reason the deal fell through the first time. But said builder wants a high-rise and the area isn't zoned for that, so that deal fell through. Hence the reason your offer is getting a second look."

"You give good updates. I'm happy the city's deal went south. We have enough condos around here."

Instead of jumping out, Fab put her arms on the steering wheel and stared at the building. "Why do you want this place? You couldn't set your sights on something five-star on the beach?"

"That's totally unaffordable," I sniffed. "The occasional motel that does come up for sale goes to a big investor who can outbid everyone else and knows they can recoup their money by slapping on the name of a well-known chain. Even a view of the road garners a hefty price tag."

"When you took over The Cottages, they were barely breaking even," Fab mused. "You want to do it again?"

"Some months, not even that. Now they're a cash cow. This place could be doing the same thing."

"Hmm..." Translation: she wasn't so sure of that. "This used to be pay-by-the-hour accommodations."

"It didn't start out that way. It's got an interesting history. The original owner built it as a medium-price motel. After his death, an unscrupulous partner with dollar signs in his eyes installed the jiggly beds and mirrors on the ceilings."

Fab got out and opened the back door, taking out her camera and snapping photos as we walked past the broken-down fence that kept out no one, since the security fencing had a hole cut in the center.

We started on the office side and peeked in all the windows, room after room, empty and dirty. We circled the pool — which was badly in need of re-plastering, if it could be saved at all — to the other side. I headed to the corner room in the front. "This is the room that's said to be haunted." I turned the knob and was disappointed to find that it was locked, although it didn't surprise me.

"That's nonsense."

"I hope not. It's rumored that Isabella Sloan's unsettled — sometimes a gracious hostess and other times tossing things around the room." I cupped my hands to the window and peered inside. "First, her husband died suddenly; then, the partner swindled her out of her half of the property and, to make matters worse, left her penniless. She arrived one night in the rain, checked in, and refused to leave. Not long afterwards, her body washed up on the beach. It was ruled a homicide, but no one was ever charged. The story is her antics made it impossible for them to get guests to stay the night in the room."

Fab had taken out her lockpick and opened the door.

"We could charge extra to be scared during the night instead of getting a good night's sleep." I followed her into the large, dusty, cobweb-filled room.

"This place needs a lot of work. Must be the reason the asking price is low." Fab walked across the room, poking her head in the bathroom. "Let me guess, you're going to befriend ghost woman?" She eyed the king-sized bed, which dipped precariously to one side.

"Since her antics appear to be confined to this one room, I'm thinking of renting it to hardy souls only, ones who've signed a release."

"So if they keel over from a heart attack, they can't sue."

"No suing," I agreed. "All this speculation is a moot point, since the deal's already fallen through once and who knows if it'll go through this time."

"If you want it, I hope you get it," Fab said as we walked outside and she locked the door.

"Now that you've seen the property, what do you think?" I asked as Fab took pictures of the exterior and stared across the street at the small strip of beach that could be seen.

Fab shot me a thumbs up.

Chapter Forty

"Surprise number two!" Fab yelled, driving back down the Overseas.

"One is enough. Maybe next week." I tried not to laugh at her frown and turned to look out the window, grinning at my reflection. "Can you take me home? I need a nap. I'm feeling fragile." I added a touch of poutiness to my tone.

"Okay."

Now that surprised me.

We were only a few blocks from our turn-off and rode in silence the rest of the way. She drove through the security gate, but instead of turning right, towards my house, she went left, down to the other end of the street, turning into her driveway and parking in the front.

"Get out," Fab ordered. "You try and make a run for it, I'll drag you back." She got out and waited for me, not taking her eyes off me until we were inside.

"If this is your second surprise, it better include food." I looked around, waiting for something to jump out at me.

"Tequila." Fab unhooked my purse off my shoulder and tossed it on a table in the entry.

I followed her into the kitchen, where she had a tray, glasses, and liquor set up on the counter. "You should've started with the best part first." I slid onto a stool. "I'll take a pitcher." I licked my lips.

"Before I can unveil the whole surprise, you need to go into the bedroom you've yet to move into." She sighed.

"Can you stay on point?"

"Change into the outfit that's laid out on the bed. No, I didn't go shopping," she responded to my questioning look. "It's something of yours that you left the last time you were here." She waved her hand towards the hall and turned towards her room. Over her shoulder, she said, "Ten minutes."

It didn't take long for me to change into the hot-pink tankini and sheer white cover-up dress. I smiled down at the flip-flops—new and designer and, of course, matching my bathing suit. I cut the time limit close, making my way back to the kitchen, no longer worried about a surprise now that I knew it included a bathing suit and tequila.

Fab reached into the refrigerator and brought out a chilled pitcher of margaritas, one of vodka martinis, and a bowl of olives.

"The next part is the best," Fab said. "It's fitting that we should be the first to christen it. It will make up for... You weren't supposed to leave the parking lot."

"Stop it right now," I grumbled. "Where would I be if not for you and the GPS units? If you hadn't been there to lead the parade? I could list all the what-ifs of how it could have gone wrong and left me at the mercy of a certifiable woman. Crazy isn't strong enough." I scrunched up my nose.

Fab loaded up the tray and handed it to me, then pulled out a bucket, filling it with ice. "Follow me." She led me out the back, past the pool, and down to the beach.

"When did you get that?" I gasped.

Floating on the water was a blue-and-white portable dock, and on the shore, four oversized inflatable chairs.

"After seeing the one at your wedding, I told Didier that I wanted one, and he made it happen. It's not as big, but still has plenty of room, and this one's inflatable, so it can be stored easily."

"You have the funnest house on the block."

We both laughed.

She set the bucket on the dock and took the tray from me, putting the pitchers in the bucket to keep them cold and raising an umbrella I hadn't noticed before to shade the drinks.

I untied two of the chairs from a stake driven into the sand and pushed them into the water. She opened the door to a small cabinet that held towels and tossed me a sunhat.

"The dinner invitation is for tonight, and we're doing it here," Fab said. "Your beach idea was a good one. I called Cook and asked him to prepare us something yummy, then called Didier and told him he needed to pick it up." She filled our glasses and handed me one. "Best friends," she toasted.

"Is this going to be like a dinner at Mother's, where everything erupts into bedlam?" I looked at Fab over the rim of my glass. "I could start it after I find out what all of you are keeping from me. I know that there's at least one more surprise to pop."

"I've been sworn to secrecy." Fab zipped her lips.

"Who knows you better than me? Besides Didier," I answered for her. "I think I know, but don't want to get you in trouble; then you'll have two irate husbands coming down on you."

Fab grimaced.

We'd finished half our pitchers when someone played with the doorbell, the chimes audible all the way out on the beach.

"Those are loud." I made a face.

"Who would do something so juvenile?" Fab craned her head towards the house. "We're both accounted for. I suspect the door is going to answer itself." She grabbed another olive.

"Honey, I'm home," Didier bellowed from the doorway.

"Me too." Creole waved.

It wasn't long before the two men, dressed in bathing trunks, walked down to the beach. Didier had a bucket in his arms that matched the one Fab had brought down earlier.

"Nice." Creole whistled, untying the remaining chairs and wading out into the water with them in tow.

I leaned toward him for a kiss. "I'd say we need one, but why? We'll just use theirs. With all the fun toys, Fab's getting more like her father every day."

"I'm thinking we need to have a beach barbeque and invite the family," Didier said.

"We're in." I pointed at Creole and myself.

Didier passed Creole a beer, and they each claimed a chair.

"Let me guess," Didier said, eyeing Fab, "you didn't let all the details slip, but enough to leave Madison wondering what the heck? I'm disclosing upfront that I have money on your answer."

"Reluctantly." Creole downed half his beer. "We both wanted to bet the same, but he called it first. Five bucks on a losing bet was the highest I'd go."

Fab shook her head. "I didn't say anything."

Creole and Didier turned to me.

"Not in so many words, but I got the gist, or so I think."

Fab flourished her hand at Didier.

"I'd stand for the presentation, but then I'd

have to float." Didier cleared his throat. "Creole has subjected me to several conversations concerning the motel you're interested in."

"You eavesdropped," Creole corrected.

"Didier learned that from Fab." I laughed.

Fab shot me a dirty look without heat.

"Creole spoke so loud, I couldn't help but overhear," Didier defended himself. "He also availed himself of my invaluable advice, which required sharing more details."

"Yeah, that's because he couldn't hear the other side of the conversation. I don't put my calls on speaker."

I shook my finger at him.

"Can I finish?" Didier waited for Creole's nod. "Since it's about to close for real this time, my lovely wife and I would like to insinuate ourselves into the motel deal and partner with the two of you."

"Won't that ruin your image? The hot, sexy, French couple partnering on an adult motel?" I asked.

"Upscale porn," Didier countered.

I looked at Creole, and he was laughing. I tugged his chair next to mine and whispered, "Yay or nay?"

"I can't hear," Fab grouched.

"The big guy says it's my call. Hmm…" I tapped my cheek and laughed when Fab flung water on me. "Why the heck not? But we have to make a pact that this venture won't end our friendship."

Creole stuck his hand out, and the rest of us piled on.

"After checking out the property again today…" I said. Didier shook his head. "That was my clue that Fab had an interest. Anyway…what about a theme motel? One room can be tropical porn and the rest in a beach theme of some sort. Fab's got a connection with that designer dude she found for the funeral guys, and he could come up with a few ideas that would make us shine."

"You did what?" Didier asked Fab with undisguised interest.

"Don't skimp on the details," I said.

Fab told them all about the latest offerings at the funeral home and finished up with details about the museum that even I hadn't heard, including that it would soon be open to the public.

Both guys made choking noises.

I covered my face and laughed.

"He's that set designer from South Beach," Fab reminded Didier. "The funeral guys are ecstatic and can't say enough nice things about his ideas."

"Don't you mean Digger Dudes?" I asked.

Creole tapped me on the leg and grinned.

"Stop," Fab admonished. "It will slip out in front of them, and don't think I won't blame you."

Didier lifted his glass. "To our partnership."

~*~

PARADISE SERIES NOVELS

Deborah's books are available on Amazon
amazon.com/Deborah-Brown/e/B0059MAIKQ

About the Author

Deborah Brown is an Amazon bestselling author of the Paradise series. She lives on the Gulf of Mexico, with her ungrateful animals, where Mother Nature takes out her bad attitude in the form of hurricanes.

Sign up for my newsletter and get the latest on new book releases. Contests and special promotion information. And special offers that are only available to subscribers.
www.deborahbrownbooks.com

Follow on FaceBook:
facebook.com/DeborahBrownAuthor

You can contact her at Wildcurls@hotmail.com

Deborah's books are available on Amazon
amazon.com/Deborah-Brown/e/B0059MAIKQ